Haven House

Written By
Christina Creado

DEDICATION

"Love is the emblem of eternity; it confounds all notion of time; effaces all memory of a beginning, all fear of an end."

- Madame de Stael

ACKNOWLEDGMENTS

To my husband and children, thank you for supporting me in my quest to check off a major item on my bucket list. You are my everything. I am blessed to have you in my life.

To my family and friends, to know that many of you are cheering me on has been priceless.

To my Literary Managers, Hazel Summer and Robert Riddle, thank you for patiently guiding me through this process. You both have been so wonderful to work with, and I hope to work with you again one day.

To my editor, Richard Court, thank you for editing Haven House and tolerating my many questions. You were kind in your words, patient, and professional.

And to my mother, my biggest support in life and the reason I actually put myself out there and published one of my many stories... thank you. Your constant support is immeasurable. I am so grateful for you.

PROLOGUE

"So, who shall I leave it all to?" Sir Oliver asked the person standing before him.

Sir Oliver

"You are asking me?"

"Yes, I would like your feedback."

"Wouldn't it naturally go to the family back home? To a relative in England?"

"There is only my cousin Frederick, who is older than I am, and his useless son, Cecil, who drinks, gambles, and has too many ladies to mention. He even sold his father's precious family heirlooms to pay off debts to continue his lifestyle. Irreplaceable items. I only found two out of the twelve that I know about. The will explicitly states what to leave any relatives that outlive me, and I had the best American and English attorneys assure me it is legally binding in both countries."

"Oh."

"How about you?" Sir Oliver asked.

With a shake of the head, "You always said Haven House needs a family. This house is too big and too much to maintain. Please think of someone else."

"Then I will build you one to your liking." Sir Oliver put up his hand to stop any arguments, "No one has been more loyal to me. Think of it as a thank you."

"I really couldn't..."

"Already decided. And I needed a new project. You know my mind doesn't realize how old my body is." He laughed, though he started coughing.

"Please rest, Sir Oliver. Please."

"I can't until it is all settled." He fretted.

"Let's think about it."

BIRDIE BLUE
AGE 10

"This is the most beautiful house I have ever seen!" Birdie exclaimed. Her father took her to the famous Haven House in South Carolina, built by the Astor Family in 1901. Unlike the many plantations around Haven House, this massive house did not use the land for growing; instead, it was just a single-family summer house once owned by an English Lord.

Birdie looked at the mammoth house before her. It was a tiered four-story house with multiple balconies on every floor. The second, third, and fourth floors each had giant front-facing windows, some with stained-glass roses and occasional blue birds detailing the intricate design. The colors of greens, reds, and blues sparkled in the sunlight even from afar. It was stunning, Birdie thought.

The bottom floor had large solariums on all four corners of the house connected by an opening on the porch. The arch of each solarium window had the same rose and bluebird stained glass design and was topped by a large balcony. The house was split into several sections: a four-story center, two three-story turrets with ornate finials on either side and one tall obelisk with a cupola on top for added architectural drama. The house's slate-tiled roof and black trim offset the beauty of this white house. And if that wasn't marvelous enough, the fragrant pink Old English Roses ascended lattices on each side of the house, adding a delicate touch. Birdie tried to capture every detail so she could paint it one day.

"Look at the birdhouse in that tree! It looks exactly like the real house." Birdie exclaimed in awe. Her father took the time to explain the architectural details when an older gentleman came over.

"Dalton Blythe?" he inquired. The man must have been in his late sixties or early seventies. He wore a tweed coat, had bushy white eyebrows, and was balding. He was very tall; Birdie had to look up at him.

"Yes, Sir Oliver Astor, I assume?" Her father shook his hand firmly.

"Come, come in. I find this time of year chilly in the mornings." Sir Oliver said. He led the way to the front door and opened it, gesturing them in. Birdie's gasp caught in her throat.

"Wow..." she breathed so softly that Sir Oliver's chuckle surprised her. He might have been old, but his hearing worked just fine.

"Like it, do you?"

"So much..." she said, taking in all the sites but mainly the enormous staircase that curved away from the door in opposite directions. To the left was a large formal living room, and to the right, a study or office, she could not tell. The ceilings were high, almost double what she was used to, with ornate architectural wood trim. But the show stopper was the beautiful curved staircase with its split end curving to either side of the hall. Sailor could not help but take in every detail.

"Which stairs do you use to go up?" she asked, forgetting her earlier talk with her father in the car. She was to be polite and quiet and to talk only when spoken to. Again, a chuckle from Sir Oliver.

"Why, it depends on my fancy." he laughed, "You are quite clever. Are you an artist like your father, little lady?"

Birdie quickly looked at her father before he nodded for Birdie to answer, "Yes, but I like to do murals."

"Birdie means she likes to paint all over my walls." her father laughed.

They all smiled, and for some reason, the twinkle in Sir Oliver's eye made Birdie happy. She could tell he did not see her actions as naughty as her father probably had; he just saw her love of art.

"I just happen to need a mural, but first, maybe a painting for my library... well, along with what your father plans to paint. Come look at this dull library and ballroom." Sir Oliver said, leading the way.

Birdie knew her father was there to paint a massive ballroom wall. The two men discussed the theme; her father showed renderings already in his portfolio. Sir Oliver and her father agreed that the work would start soon. Then he looked at Birdie. "And I need a painting from you, on canvas, of course, to hang in my library. Deal?" he asked with a kind smile.

"Deal!" she giggled, shaking his hand excitedly.

SAILOR WREN

"Mommy!" she called out. Her mom was painting, and her earbuds were in her ears; she was concentrating on the image in front of her. Sailor went before her to be seen, knowing she should never touch her mother as she painted; that would mean she would startle her and mess up her work. Her mother removed her earbuds, smiling, "Need me, Sailor?"

"You are on TV again; want to see?" she asked happily.

"Probably a repeat of the Guggenheim exhibit I did last month."

"It is, but you are talking in this one," Sailor said excitedly.

"Oh boy. No thanks." Her mom grumbled.

Sailor remembered being told by her mom that she had gotten cornered into an interview that night. Her mom usually avoids them like her grandfather did. She always said she preferred her work to speak for itself and stay anonymous. But Sailor thought it was awesome that her mom was on TV.

Before she could say anything else, she realized her mom's earbuds were back in, and her mom had her back to her again. She was back at work. The conversation was over. Sailor sighed and went back to their living room. She was proud her mom was famous. And proud to have an even more renowned grandfather in the art world. One day, she too would be an artist, she vowed. She wanted to be famous as well.

Lupe came into the living room, "Mamita, bathtime."

"Lupe, it's only..." She looked at the old grandfather clock, "It's not even nine yet-"

"Bath, bed. We leave early tomorrow." Sailor sighed and shut off the TV. Sailor knew the tone. Lupe may be her nanny, but she raised Sailor; not only that, but Lupe raised her mom, too. Lupe was strict about sleep, and Sailor knew not to argue.

They were flying to South Carolina tomorrow for another job with her mom. She has been talking to Sailor about it for weeks now. Her mother remembered going to some place when she was young and was anxious to return. She was so excited that she hadn't left the studio for a week. The thought of the place had inspired her to do oils again, her mom said.

"Hurry up. I need to get your schoolwork sorted. We will be there for a bit."

'A bit' was a vague term that has never actually had a definitive time. Sailor was used to being uprooted from one location to the other for her mother's jobs and had them traveling often. Sailor once heard her mother's manager, Frank, say she 'had a three-year waiting list and was in much demand.' Her mom did it herself, too. She never relied on her dad's last name. Most people only knew her in the art world as 'Birdie Blue' for most of her career, not by her full name 'Birdie Blue Blythe.' It only got out two years ago who her father was. Sailor's mom had not been happy because that made her even more sought after now. These days, the paparazzi are constantly trying to take pictures of her as they leave their house.

It was good to be so successful, Sailor thought, but it also meant her continually moving. Months here, months there, never seeing the same people. Last year, she spent six months in Dubai, another month in England, and two months in Las Vegas, where her mom painted an entire wall of a new casino. Luckily, Sailor attended a virtual school since they traveled so much, but it also meant that she had no friends as she never stayed anywhere long enough to keep any. She also hadn't expected to make any this time too. It was a lonely life at times. Oh, she had Lupe. She saw her mom between work, but she often felt alone. She wanted friends.

Sailor got up off the couch, showered, and said goodnight. She then prayed in front of Lupe as she lay in bed. Unfortunately, Sailor was wide awake. It felt like she was awake for hours; she yawned to the sounds of the cicadas outside and finally fell asleep.

BIRDIE BLUE

Birdie Blue

Birdie's cell phone rang as they drove; it was Frank.

"Hi, did the supplies arrive?"

"Yes."

"Did we double-check that everything is there? You know Haven House is in the boonies, and a decent art store is almost forty minutes away."

"Jason came last week and double-checked everything; it is all there."

"And did you find out who owns the house now? I searched online, but no luck. Did he have children that I did not know about? I never heard of any."

"There are still no leads on whether he had kids after his wife passed; he did not have children with Eloise Astor. I even reached out to the people who commissioned you. They have strict orders to hire you, show you the rooms they want you to paint, and give you Sir Oliver's wishes for each room; they did not tell me anything else," Frank said.

"So weird."

"What's weird, Mommy?" Sailor asked. Birdie silenced her with a quick finger to her lips, "One second, Sailor. I am so curious; maybe hire a detective?" she asked Frank, talking to him again.

Eloise Astor

"Birdie, Sir Oliver never remarried after Eloise Astor's death. No one knows of other children from other relationships, so maybe he bequeathed his estate to a firm. Maybe they will turn the mansion into a museum, which is why they are keeping with his wishes. Who knows? Want to know what I do know? They are paying you triple, and you bring in good money. TRIPLE. So smile, paint, and you can spend the rest of the year in Fiji." Frank laughed, "I can, too."

"You are the worst, Frank. Absolutely the worst. We all know you will have another ten jobs waiting when I finish at Haven House." Birdie laughed.

"Why Mommy?"

Lupe tapped her arm, making Sailor quiet.

"Let me go, we are near the airport."

Birdie looked at Sailor and squeezed her hand, "Excited Sailor? Remember I told you about this mansion I visited as a child? We will be living in it for a couple of months. A real live mansion." Sailor smiled at her before Birdie looked at her cell again, back to reading emails.

SAILOR WREN

Sailor smiled, more so because her mom was including her, and sure, staying in a mansion sounded fun. This would be different, Sailor supposed. Usually she stayed with Lupe in a hotel near the job. She would actually be staying in the very place where her mother worked. Maybe she would get more time with her mother instead of when she came home each day. Sailor missed her mother at times. Sailor knew she saw her daily, but she wanted more quality time with her. Maybe this would be the job where that could happen. It would be amazing to see her mother's steps as she painted in real-time.

"Frank just texted me that the caretaker and his family live in the Carriage House on the property. So maybe you can make some friends while I work just like I had when I was a kid. Sounds like fun, huh?" her mother asked her.

Sailor dutifully smiled. If only to assure her. But she knew the deal; she would likely leave before establishing real friendships.

They got out of the limo. They had six large suitcases, two art cases, and three leather portfolios. Oh, and Lupe had Sailor's roll-on school bag with her computer, books, and anything else needed for these next few months. The driver put them onto the tarmac in front of the private jet the customer had set up for them, and they were in the air before Sailor knew it.

QUINN RYAN

Quinn could not believe she was coming. Birdie Blue Blythe. Would she remember him? He had been checking off every item on his long list of things he wanted to complete before someone lived upstairs again. He was eighty percent done but needed to keep at it to finish on time. His other job, being an architect, would need to wait as he rushed around Haven House, finishing his to-do list.

Quinn

"Quinn. Eat. You haven't stopped in two days."

"Cora, I can't. They come tomorrow. I still need to oil the hinges and check all the drains."

"Eat now, I insist. Ten minutes won't harm anything." Cora Casey, Haven House's housekeeper and practically other mom to him said.

With a nod, Quinn washed his hands and sat. He grew up on the grounds of Haven House. His father was the original caretaker for over forty years before there were landscaping crews, electricians, plumbers, and so on to do much of the work his father did by hand back in the day. Even with help, his father handled everything he could until he died almost three years ago.

Cora Casey

Quinn had gone there to gather his father's things when Cora begged him to fill in as temporary caretaker until they found someone or he decided to do it permanently. He grew up helping his father with most of this, so he was the perfect person to do so. What he thought was a short-term job of maintaining Haven House, between his full-time job designing houses and altering people's floor plans, became his sanctuary. And his kids were thriving away from Miami. The iron gates surrounding the property protected them from their mother's fans.

Also, Miami has been priced out lately by all these rich people moving in, with increasing over-priced buildings going up. Though it was great for his business, the kids only sometimes had the latest gadget, toy, gaming system, designer clothes, etc. It was a place of constant competition and luxury. He had money, as business was excellent in Miami, but what were the kids learning to value? Things meant nothing at the end of the day, but happiness did. And after the messy divorce from his ex, he decided it was time for a slower life for him and the kids.

"Thank you for the sandwich, Cora," he said, smiling, taking a bite.

"Good boy, Quinn. Nancy made you all a lasagna, so don't forget to bring it home. Alright?" Cora smiled at him adoringly.

"Cora, please ask Nancy to stop. Just teaching me how to make some dinners was a huge help already." After a while, his kids were tired of pasta, eggs, and steaks. So, he attended cooking lessons from Nancy twice weekly for a few months until he felt more comfortable doing it independently.

In Miami, they had a cook from Monday to Thursday, many restaurants at his fingertips, and Uber Eats on speed dial, not to mention the cleaning staff for afterward. It had been a big adjustment coming here. Being a single parent was very different here on the estate without help.

"Hush." she waved him off, "We live to spoil you. And now the kids, too."

Quinn smiled; both sisters thought he was still a child. Especially Cora, as she lost her own son and husband in a car accident long ago. Being in Florida for the last eight-plus years before returning made them miss him terribly. Also, his father and Cora dated for the last ten years of his father's life. So she felt that he and his sister were her kids now, even if they did not ever marry.

"Has Sofía asked to see the kids?" Cora asked him.

"Sort of." he shrugged.

"What in heavens does that mean?" Cora scolded. Quinn knew Cora liked answers.

"She wants me to put them on a plane alone and send them to her in Spain for six days before her next movie starts."

"And you said?" Cora asked, annoyed.

"Send a five and a seven-year-old on a plane alone? No."

"Oh, thank goodness."

"I told her to come pick them up, and she had to care for them each day. She said it wouldn't be worth the short visit with jet lag and travel back and forth. Quote unquote. So I told her we are here, come whenever she wants; at least she calls them every week."

"Every week?" Cora asked in a huff.

"Most weeks, depending on her shooting schedule. Oh, and she asked about the Miami house again."

"You got custody and the Miami house; she got the three vacation homes in Spain, Colombia, and Italy; why does she want that home, too? Your business is there with Kiera. You both have homes over it. It's not like they make many Spanish-speaking movies here anyway! Doesn't she realize her kids need to live somewhere?" Cora huffed.

"She's Sofía." Quinn shrugged, "Thank you for the sandwich. I need to get back to it," he said, handing her the dish with a kiss on her cheek and taking off.

"Quinn?" Cora called out. He sighed; he was not in the mood for another Sofía bashing session.

"Yes?" He stopped.

"Did you or the kids happen to see the gold letter opener set Sir Oliver had on his desk? I don't mind anyone using them, of course, but I like to keep his desk intact."

Quinn came back with an odd look on his face. "Another thing suddenly missing?"

Cora sighed, "Or misplaced. Please ask the children."

"They are not allowed in his office alone. I made that very clear, but I will ask. Cora, this is the third item. All expensive items."

Cora's face could not hide the worry.

"Please think of cameras and security, maybe a dog to roam the grounds. I mentioned it last time."

She nodded, "But we found one item on the floor by the stairs, remember? So..."

"Cora."

She nodded, "Let me talk to the attorneys. Security is a big undertaking."

Quinn left, and he went straight to the kids. He asked them if they saw it. They hadn't. Both looked confused. He could tell if they were lying; they were telling the truth. They had not touched it. Could one of the groundsmen have taken it? Who else entered the grounds often?

BIRDIE BLUE
AGE 10

Birdie was jumping up and down excitedly. Today, she would accompany her father to Haven House to show Sir Oliver her painting. She had chosen the most giant canvas she could in her father's studio. He has been working long hours at Haven House, and when he saw the final piece for the first time, he seemed worried. "I don't think he meant for you to paint such a large painting. It may be too big, Darling."

"He has a giant house; he can find a spot, Daddy. It's bigger than the White House!"

"Not exactly." he laughed, "Just don't be disappointed if he asks for a smaller one. Us artists get paid for work; we must do it per the customer's specifications," he explained. "I have often had to redo work for a client."

"Oh," Birdie said, now worried too.

But when they pulled up, a happy Sir Oliver was waiting in a rocking chair on the porch out of the hot sun. "Hello, Birdie! Dalton. Have my painting?"

Suddenly, Birdie was nervous. She could feel her hands sweating—her first-ever requested painting.

"We do have it, Sir Oliver, but if sizing is an issue—say it's too big—she can redo it," her father said.

"Well, I was hoping for a big painting. I do hope it is somewhat big..." Sir Oliver said as if thinking out loud. Her father smiled and pulled the painting out of the car as Birdie beamed.

The back of the painting was to Sir Oliver, "Well, come show your work, Darling." her father said. She took the painting and was suddenly too nervous to move. What if he didn't like the painting of fairies reading books in his library? She had paid special care to take in as many details as possible during her first visit to the library, where he said he needed art. She made sure to incorporate the room's details into her painting. The three fairies with their delicate wings were lazily sitting around on chairs that looked like his library chairs, one having her feet up on a replica of the library desk.

Sir Oliver gasped. He seemed shocked.

"Did she create this? Herself? You did not help at all?"

"She did it alone, and you know I have all but been living here these last three weeks." Her father said, laughing.

"On your honor, you did not draw it first or ...?"

"I did it, Sir Oliver! My father did not help! He doesn't like fairies!" She was all but insulted.

"Birdie Blue Blythe." her father reprimanded.

"No, don't scold the child, please, Dalton. I am just so amazed. It is truly remarkable. But the painting is missing one thing." Sir Oliver added thoughtfully.

"What?" she asked worriedly.

"Your signature. All artists need to sign their work. I must have a signature on it. For you, my dear, have your father's talent. I shall see your name in lights one day."

She laughed. "I can add it. Daddy, can I borrow one of your brushes and paint?"

"I must insist on one more detail: use blue paint. I want you to sign it in blue. OK? Birdie Blue, only signs in blue from here on out. You are going to be as famous as your father."

With a shy smile, she nodded; he did like her work.

They signed it and hung it on the library wall beside the desk. Birdie made one hundred dollars, which was an unfathomable amount of money to her. Her father argued, but it went on deaf ears, and then Sir Oliver commissioned her to do another painting for his office. He wanted a proper mural done on the wall. This time, he had to see with his own two eyes if she had this talent at such a young age.

"Alright, I like painting on walls better anyway!" she giggled.

SAILOR WREN

Sailor looked at her reflection in the limo's window. Her blue eyes and sprinkling of freckles on her nose and rosy cheeks stood out, but the wavy, dirty blonde hair needed help. She tried to smooth the long hair down, but it popped back up. She knew her hair would calm down one day, as her mother's had over time. After all, how often was she told she was the spitting image of her mother? And that was a good thing, too, because she had no idea who her father was. It would have been weird looking like no one in the family.

"Mamita, come let me fix your hair," Lupe said, never missing a beat. She watched everything Sailor and her mother did. No one was more protective, attentive, and loving. "Mi hija, you too," she added. Her mom pulled out her brush and cosmetics case, also touching herself up.

"I don't think the paparazzi will be at the airport, do you? Did my coming get leaked?" Her mother asked worriedly.

Sailor knew her mother did not like the attention of many photographers and people screaming questions as she tried to politely get to where she needed to go.

As Lupe was brushing Sailor's hair and checking that she had no more smudged chocolate on her lips, she answered, "No. Frank stressed how private this was to the person commissioning this job. Hadn't they?"

"I guess..." she put away her mirror and brush.

Lupe, too, checked her hair. At fifty-nine, she still looked young for her age and had always joked it was because she 'took baths in Oil of Olay,' whatever that was. Sailor could see how much her face changed this year. Lupe used to be a touch overweight, or maybe thick is a better word, but had recently lost weight.

Sailor heard how Lupe had come from Mexico to live with her grandparents after her divorce when Sailor's mom was just three years old. Her grandmother was sick with breast cancer, she recalled. Lupe came to be a full-time nanny for her mother straight from Mexico. Lupe's husband left her because she was unable to have children. She 'showed him'; she would laugh, 'I had two beautiful girls after all' because she raised them as her own. Sailor's grandmother died when her mom was four. Her grandfather traveled everywhere and was always working. Just like her mom, come to think of it. She wondered if her mom was as lonely as a child, too. And if so, did she forget how it felt?

"Sailor, when we get there, we do not touch anything. Ok? It is an old home with fragile, expensive, non-replaceable things. Please, promise me. No touching unless you ask first."

"I promise," Sailor said, eyes wide.

"You know what I say about promises?" her mother reiterated.

Sailor nodded. She holds all promises sacred and expects everyone around her to do the same.

They pulled up to this massive wrought iron gate. It went on around the whole property. They drove up a winding path with beautiful Magnolia trees on either side. Suddenly, Haven House appeared right in front of them, massive in size. It was even more grander than it was in her mind. Her mom had shown her the house on the computer one time. It looked the same as the picture with the many windows and balconies. What had her mother called those round towers? Sunariums? The thought of reading in one of them got her excited. Maybe she can do her schoolwork there, too. The grounds were so pretty, she couldn't wait to explore around the house. All she saw were so many images she wanted to replicate with her pastels in her sketchbook. She needed to remember to tell Lupe she wanted to do that one day.

As the driver brought in bags, a middle-aged woman showed up with a big smile. Her black suit and severe updo hairstyle looked all business.

The woman went straight to her mom.

"Ms. Blythe, I am Martha Davis, one of Sir Oliver's attorneys managing his Will. Please come in. I can have you read the contract and sign off, and then you may get settled. I asked Mrs. Finnley to get us tea and coffee on the fire. Maybe a glass of milk with some cookies or brownies for your daughter?"

Sailor smiled, nodding happily, as Lupe held her hand to keep her from rushing in.

BIRDIE BLUE

Birdie followed Mrs. Davis to a Parlor, and Lupe and Sailor went to the kitchen. The Parlor was one room Birdie had never seen before. The rich mauve velvet and satin wallpaper looked delicate and rich in its brocade. The floor-to-ceiling silk curtains showing off the room's height were exquisite. The ceiling inlay and its architectural detail were stunning. The dusty rose velvet settee with Chippendale tables and chairs looked out of an old-fashioned movie. Birdie was in awe. And then she saw it. She was shocked. One of the first pieces she ever sold in the thousands of dollars was there. She had called it 'The Circus'. When starting her career, she had done paintings on wooden screens, some on canvas, and many murals on walls of businesses before her work got noticed.

"The screen..." Birdie said, stunned.

"Yes, he had some time finding the original purchaser. You will see many Blythe works around the house—yours and your father's. Does your daughter dabble in the arts, too?" Mrs. Davis asked, sitting down across from her. Birdie's mind was racing. Sir Oliver searched out her art. He tracked down the screen's owner to buy it. She sat there numb for a second before shaking the thoughts away.

"Sorry? Oh, uh, yes, she uses mixed media, not just paint as my father and I mainly use, but she does art too. She's only eight, so time will tell."

"You, my dear, were not much older when he fell in love with your work." Mrs. Davis smiled.

"But... he only bought a canvas and a mural-"

"Oh, much more than that. Sir Oliver has four other pieces. He would have bought more, but the murals could not be removed from where you painted them without damaging them." Mrs. Davis laughed.

Birdie just nodded, surprised.

"He was a writer of sorts; his will comes with some twenty-plus pages of handwritten details as to why he wanted what he wanted completed. So, I feel as if I knew him. He was quite candid. So, as an executor, I must read out every word to you. There are several areas we need you to sign. I am afraid this will take a bit. He had very distinct wishes. Mr. Altman already reviewed this, as I am sure he told you." Yes, Birdie thought. Frank saw it before she did.

After what felt like a lifetime, Mrs. Davis asked Birdie to touch up any Blythe painting or mural as needed. That was easy. She had done that for her father many times and obviously for her own work. She was also to paint an entire children's room and a Nursery. Again, it was easy and her favorite type of work. She was to paint the floor of all four of the Solariums. That was new, but she could not see a problem if she put many layers of clear sealer over it. She was to paint an ethereal theme on the ballroom ceiling. That one worried her. She never painted a ceiling.

"So this one will require my team to rent platforms when you are ready. You can just give me details, and we will get it. Though Sir Oliver wanted this badly, this one is not a deal breaker. He agreed that we could paint it sky blue by a painting company if you fear heights. Only sign if you can commit to it." Birdie signed. She thought that sky blue next to her father's original work would be boring.

"Final point of business. We have many valuables here; everything is itemized and insured with pictures taken. We had to do this for Sir Oliver's will and to make it a historical home. I understand you brought your nanny, but there are some rooms in the house I request your daughter stay out of unless you or the nanny supervise her. These rooms are Sir Oliver's office, the art wing for obvious reasons as he was a great collector of priceless works, and the basement as no one goes down there except the caretaker. Speaking of the caretaker, Mr. Callahan has full access to the main house and checks it daily. If there are any issues in the house, contact him first. We also have other staff here. Mrs. Casey is the housekeeper, and once a week, a full cleaning crew comes in to refresh, dust, and that sort of thing. This day is Saturday. We ask that you allow them access to any room, including yours. Mrs. Casey will show you the room's safe to lock up anything of value."

"Can they stay out of any room I am painting?" Birdie worried about wet paint drying untouched.

"Of course, no issues. I will let Mrs. Casey know. Also, Mrs. Casey's sister, Mrs. Finnley, has been hired to cook during your stay. She will need a full listing of allergies, likes, dislikes, and so on from you."

"Oh… Thank you. Lupe will appreciate that. We have no allergies. We eat almost anything."

"All part of the contract. And let's also agree that everyone stays out of staff rooms as well, please."

"Of course."

"Any questions?" Mrs. Davis asked.

"Many." Birdie laughed. "May I ask who is financing this?" Birdie asked.

"Sir Oliver… well, his estate is." she laughed.

"Did he have children, family? Are they running the estate?"

"My firm is handling legal issues, and Mrs. Casey is running his estate since his wife and sister died before him; he did not have children. We will both manage this list of to-do items until it is complete. Sir Oliver's wishes per his will are that we bequeath the estate to predetermined heirs, but that matter is private at this point. Mr. Altman told you this could be many months, right?"

"Yes. This list is a lot of work and will require time. These rooms are huge."

"Good. Make yourself at home. We have wifi, satellite cable, central air per room so everyone can be comfortable, and a full kitchen of food, snacks, and drinks. Help yourself any time.

My phone number is here on this paper. You can contact Mrs. Casey, Mr. Callaghan, and Mrs. Finnley via intercom or cell. I also listed their numbers." She handed Birdie a paper.

"Thank you."

"Shall I tell you the history of the house? Maybe it will play into your work?"

"Sure."

"Lord Charles Astor and Lady Elizabeth Astor, Sir Oliver's uncle and aunt, built this house as a summer house to visit when in the States. It also has a four-car garage hidden at the very back of the property. At the time, the house did not have the solariums and wrap-around porches; Sir Oliver added those, changed windows, and made some interior modifications." Mrs. Davis pulled out some notes, found the paper she wanted, and began to read. "Lord Astor was very fond of Sir Oliver and had him and his sister visit many times over the years. Sir Oliver then inherited it when his aunt and uncle's son died prematurely at the age of twelve from an asthma-related illness. Lord Astor also had a brother, Charles, referred to as the black sheep of the family, who was not happy that he did not naturally inherit this property and money. He was shocked when all assets were bequeathed to Sir Oliver, minus the title and the English Manor. As you can imagine, Old Manors cost money to maintain. Though his brother, Charles Astor, did get the title, he himself died in a horse riding accident shortly afterward and the title went to Sir Oliver's cousin, Frederick. In 1982, Frederick died of ALS, and the title and Manor went to his son, Cecil Astor. Cecil is a bachelor, so who the title goes to next remains a mystery as the family has all but died out. We did some research, and we cannot find any other family with the Astor name."

"Wow. And the rest of the buildings, did Sir Oliver have that built too?"

"Yes, he built them afterward to match Haven House. The two buildings are a Carriage House and a shed. Though shed may not be the proper term, as it is massive." she laughed.

"Speaking of the Carriage House, Mr. Callahan and his family live there, so please respect his private home. Mrs. Casey lives here now, and so does her sister some nights for as long as we need her. They have rooms off the kitchen; again, those rooms are private. Otherwise, look around, see the art, enjoy the views, smell the flowers. There is no time limit, though this should not take as long as a year, right?"

A year? Birdie thought it would be two to three months. But before expressing her concern about her waiting list, Mrs. Davis started talking again.

"Sir Oliver added the gardens in the back for his wife Eloise, added magnolia trees lining the driveway, and finally, a fountain out front for the birds to play in. He did that in honor of his little sister, Sarah, who died of Polio when she was seven. You will see birds throughout the house's design, especially blue ones, everywhere, like little easter eggs for you to find. It's in the carvings, paintings, stained-glass decorations. Birds were her favorite. The will has an allowance for bird food until it is endowed, so real birds are always around, too. You may not appreciate it at dawn, but the sound is lovely during the day as you stroll through the gardens." Mrs. Davis laughed.

Sarah Astor

Birdie smiled.

"Do you have any other questions? I'm sorry. I have a three-o'clock appointment back at my office, but I want to make sure I answer everything."

"What am I to paint? My father did one accent wall of the ballroom, so I will stick with his theme yet add an ethereal ceiling as requested, but for the other rooms, was there a theme I needed to adhere to?"

"His wishes were to let you have free rein. Though I do hope you keep in mind the historical nature of the house and keep it cohesive."

"Wait, he wanted ME to have free rein?!"

"Yes, you. You reminded Sir Oliver of his sister. Her favorite birds were," she rustled through her notes again, "Indigo Buntings and Eastern Bluebirds. So when you came to see him all those years ago at a similar age as his sister, then he heard your unique name -"

"You mean an odd name." Birdie laughed. "It's my real given name, though. My father used to say I came out of the womb blue and looked like a baby bird." Birdie hadn't liked that analogy long ago, but she always smiled at the thought of her somewhat stuffy father's attempt at a joke.

"Well, 'Birdie Blue' and Sarah's love of bluebirds, he felt it was a sign from her that she was alright. He thought he was being nice by asking you to paint something, but he was stunned by your work. He thought your father did it, so he asked you to do the mural in his office. He couldn't believe you were so talented at such a young age. He wrote all about you when writing his wishes." Mrs. Davis smiled.

Birdie sat there surprised, but she guessed it made sense. And weirdly, Birdie had felt a connection to him. Like they thought alike and knew what the other was thinking, he had come twice daily to peer in on her progress as she worked. He did not disturb her if the paintbrush was in her hand. He respected her need for concentration. When she did get to speak to him, she could see his constant awe and approval. At the end of each day, they would sit at the kitchen table with Lupe and dunk cookies in milk, discussing the next scene she planned to paint. He had been so easy to talk to. Lupe had thought it was because he was alone now and missed companionship. But Lupe liked him too. She had always said she had a sixth sense about people and their intentions and that 'he was a good soul'; Lupe was usually right about things like that.

QUINN RYAN

She's here, Quinn thought. Right now, Birdie is back at Haven House, and he is too. What were the odds? He had a crush on her when she was here last. It was not as if she knew or he would ever date again, so why was Quinn thinking about that? Sofía had been enough female drama for a lifetime. But Birdie had been so exuberant and fun. Happy. Something Sofía only truly was when a camera was on her. Birdie was an unbelievable painter, too. He would sneak in one of the hidden 'servant' passages and stare at her work as he cracked a panel open just a bit to see her paint. His younger sister, Kiera, was great friends with Birdie, too, and when she was not painting, the three of them roamed the grounds, laughing and playing together. He knew the attorney would be with her all day and didn't want to interrupt, so he used this time to catch up on his other work. Or try to.

SAILOR WREN

Sailor had her very own room. It was big and beautiful. Everything was a pale buttery yellow. The room was warm and inviting. The massive king-size canopy bed beckoned her to lay on it as the quilt was so thick and cozy looking to Sailor. She especially loved the embroidered bees, bluebell flowers, and little blue birds all over the canopy, pillow shams, quilt, and bed skirt. She could only imagine how fun it would be to jump on that bed when no one was looking.

She had a large window that overlooked a giant fountain. Next to it was an ornate wrought iron pole holding a large plate-looking bird feeder that hung in the air so only birds could get to the food. She could see birds playing in the fountain and sitting at the feeder. Their chirping could be heard from inside, making her smile. She decided to draw the beautiful scene before her first. For once, she looked forward to staying somewhere that wasn't her home.

Lupe's room was attached to hers. "Mamita, let's unpack your clothes."

Every room had an adjoining bathroom, which was nice. Even if the bathtub did look old, it had silly gold-clawed feet on the bottom, which Sailor thought looked weird. They had spent an hour setting up the desk for her schoolwork in front of the window, unpacking toiletries and clothes before finding her mom. Lupe helped her mom next as her mother sat in an overstuffed chair, sketching ideas in a sketchbook.

"The ceiling of the ballroom is easy. I already know what I am doing for it." She showed her sketchbook, which was in colored pencil so that Sailor could see her mom's vision. How her mother so effortlessly drew such a complete vision so fast awed Sailor. She often borrowed her mother's sketchbook and tried to copy the work on her own. She could not wait to try to copy this one, too. Lupe always told Sailor, 'Practice makes perfect,' so she was encouraged to practice art whenever possible. Her mother told her she, too, had the artist's gift, that it ran in their genes. Sailor hoped so. She really loved doing it as much as her mother did.

"You need to add a bluebird." Sailor said, giggling, "I see them in every room."

Her mom laughed, "Apparently, Sir Oliver has them put on everything: flowers for his wife Eloise and birds for his little sister. You are very right, Sailor!" She got up and kissed Sailor's head. Sailor smiled. She knew her mom loved her, always kissing and hugging her when she was not working. But her mom worked a lot. Sailor knew it was to give her everything she needed or wanted, but Sailor always tried to capture moments like this when she could. They were precious to her, just a simple moment between them. Once her mom started painting, she knew she would be unavailable for the most part. Sailor was pleased when she saw her mother reach for the blue-colored pencil and start drawing. Her mother valued her idea, and it made her feel proud.

They toured the gorgeous house, and Lupe never let go of her hand. Sailor's favorite room was the long 'Art Hallway'. There must have been some two-hundred-plus framed art pieces behind a protective glass. Some were of horses on a prairie, dogs in a hunting scene, a ton of bird pictures, landscapes, and many whimsical pictures, too. In the center of the hallway were vases, sculptures, and fascinating folk art in sturdy glass cases.

"No wonder they were okay with Sailor coming in here. I recognize the label on the glass," her mom said to Lupe, pointing to a label in the bottom corner. It said 'Firebox RE11 by Fredricson.'

"Fredricson makes fireproof glass, and it is also impenetrable. Most definitely alarmed, too. This system is super expensive."

"Look, Mi hija. Your bench." Lupe pointed to a roped-off section at the end of the corridor. Sailor looked at the colorful bench with a beach theme.

"He got that too?!" her mom laughed. "I never liked it. I hated the crabs they wanted all over it. A major retailer with crab houses nationwide asked me to do it, so I did. But I was crabby about it." she told Sailor, wiggling her eyebrows. Sailor giggled at her mom's silly pun. Her mom could be super silly sometimes, and it always tickled her.

Her mom put her arm around Sailor's shoulders and led her out, "Let's go find Mrs. Finnley."

BIRDIE BLUE
AGE 12

"Darling, you have another letter."

Birdie ran over excitedly. She had a school project last year where they had to ask someone to be a pen pal and write them once a month for that entire school year.

Of course, the teacher hoped that the children in her 'class' would write to a classmate as they all lived far from each other and were sent work every month by the teacher. But Birdie had chosen Sir Oliver. And though her father said he would probably be too busy to write back, he always had.

She ripped it open and read it.

Dearest Birdie,

Thank you so much for the drawing you sent me. It looks exactly like my sister's favorite bird. I framed it and put it on my desk.

I have news to share. Kitty had kittens: two calicoes, one white with a bit of black speckle on its nose, and a tabby. Kitty did not listen when I said I would make an exception for her, as she did not try to kill the birds. Now we have five cats! Most likely, six, as there is a daddy cat somewhere. I will just need to teach these little ones the rules fast - to always be kind to the birds. So I need names for the two calicos and tabby. I named the white one "Speckle'. She is just too cute. I may be a cat person, after all.

Kiera and Quinn asked about you again. I told them that if your father ever has a chance, you both may come again.

So, if you are ever in South Carolina, we expect a visit. Tell your father.

I hope you are still painting, for a talent like yours is a God-given gift and should never be wasted. Oh! I thought of what you asked. A circus theme. How interesting would that be?

Sincerely,

Sir Oliver Astor

Birdie beamed. That is what she would do. She will paint her screen with a circus theme.

"And?" her father asked, "What is new with Sir Oliver?"

She handed him the letter, "He has four kittens!" she laughed.

"Oh boy, kittens and birds do not go together." Her father laughed.

"He's going to teach them to be kind to birds."

He read the letter with a chuckle and handed it back to Birdie.

"I better keep these with the others. When can we go back to Haven House?"

"Darling, one day. We are traveling to Washington, D.C. first. I am to paint a room in the White House and then go to a diplomat's home to paint while there. We shall see."

Birdie sighed, 'We shall see' was never good.

SAILOR WREN

It was nine-fifteen at night. The room was dark now, a bit scary, if truth be told. She has spent nights in many places, some spooky even, but the quietness and the complete blackness of the room was a little daunting. So very different from the mornings. Sailor knew she just needed to get used to it. Especially since Lupe usually had a queen-sized bed next to Sailor's in a hotel room. She just had to get used to it, Sailor thought. She was big now, eight years old and Lupe's room was right there through an opened doorway, she reminded herself.

When the clock chimed, she jumped out of bed, startled. She peeked in Lupe's room. It was dark and empty. Where was she, Sailor wondered. She was afraid and needed to know someone was around her, to know that she was not alone. Sailor quietly opened her bedroom door and looked across the hall, where her mom was staying. The door was ajar a bit; the lights were on. She heard voices murmuring, Lupe's and her mother's. She felt relieved she was not alone. Curiously, she snuck to her mother's doorway.

Her mom was crying! Why was she crying, Sailor wondered.

She peeked; her mother was lying on the bed next to Lupe, her head on Lupe's lap, as Lupe soothed her hair over and over reassuringly.

Lupe

"...I'll never trust men again. Ever."

"Mi hija, one boy cannot ruin the rest of your life. I won't always be around. Sailor needs a mom AND a dad."

"But... Steve, he just left me there. Five months pregnant. Do you know how hard it was to return to you and Father?" she sniffed, "I was so scared. Ashamed."

Sailor knew this story. Her mother had been honest with her. She did something too young and got pregnant. That was why Sailor did not know who her father was. He was too young, too, and went back to his parent's house. Her mother told her that she had loved Sailor so much, she did not want to share her with anyone anyway. Sailor always smiled when her mother said that. The only thing she knew about him was that he was an artist, too. Charcoal was his favorite medium. Other than that, he was never spoken about. Ever. Lupe would get very mad if she heard talk of it. So she just let it go. Not like he tried to see her anyway, Sailor thought. Lupe was probably right.

"I know. You were too young to understand what you had gotten yourself into, what you faced. But not all men are like him."

"Look what Rafe did to you. Men are bad!" Birdie sniffed angrily.

"Now, now. In my day, back home, my job was to give him kids, not like now. I failed him as a wife. His new wife gave him seven children to help run the farm. My cousin told me they all still live in his parent's two-bedroom house, working on the farm. His kids will probably do the same. Look at this amazing life I have because of that." Lupe smiled. "I live in luxury, and I get to see the world; I get to mother you-"

"And Sailor." Birdie smiled.

"YOU need to be a mother to Sailor. It is important. Your father did not know how to raise a young girl, but you know what a girl needs. You must. We have been having this conversation too often lately. She needs you."

Her mother sat up fast. Lupe was scolding her. Sailor was shocked. Lupe was right; she had needed her mom more lately.

"I love Sailor! I didn't put her in the boarding school Father suggested years ago to keep her close. I made changes to bring her to every job, unlike when I either stayed home with you waiting on Father to finish a job locally or at hotels for weeks at a time if far from New York. I give her the best of everything, Lupe!" Her mother said fast, wiping her eyes angrily.

"She doesn't need things. She needs her mother every day, not just between paintings. You know this. She desperately misses you."

How had Lupe known this? It was exactly how Sailor felt. She never told Lupe this.

"It is why I selected this job before the others, Lupe; we will be together here where I paint."

"Being in the same building and being together are two different things. You will miss out on her childhood and regret it forever. I need to push you. I will go away every Saturday, maybe another day too -"

Her mother looked panicked, standing up quickly, "Where will you go?!"

"I have no idea. But you will be forced to care for, feed, and put Sailor to bed those days." Lupe said firmly.

"But this commission, I have others waiting..."

"Your daughter is more important than a job, more than money, which you have enough of. She is more important than anything. You miss this stage, and you never get it back. You will regret it. She longs for you, Mi hija; she just wants to be with you." Lupe all but begged. It sounded as if Lupe's voice broke when she said it. As if she cried when she said it, Sailor thought.

Then she heard her mother crying again, "I want to be with her, too. I will make a concentrated effort to fix this, but I cannot paint with anyone there. I need to concentrate. I can't have questions and interruptions, as any child would do. I am here to paint. I signed a contract. Lupe, you do know that I love Sailor, right? She is the best thing that has ever happened to me, and I love her with all my heart. You know this. She knows this."

"Lately, I think she is questioning it," Lupe said flatly.

Her mother looked shocked. Sailor felt her own eyes welling. How had Lupe known?

"Don't you remember missing your father? You asked when he would be home over and over. You only had one parent, too," she said softly.

"But I had you. Sailor has you."

"I am older now. I should be acting like a grandmother. YOU are her mother." Lupe said firmly. "You don't paint Saturdays and maybe Wednesdays half a day. Stop working at one o'clock. You need to spend that time with Sailor. You also stop working at dinner and spend each night with her. You tell her to take a bath. You tell her to go to bed. It will be up to you. After she is in bed, you can go back to painting. And I mean it." Lupe said firmly, standing up. Sailor took off, heart beating fast. She slipped under the covers before Lupe stuck her head in to see her asleep, then left.

Sailor was afraid to open her eyes but waited until she heard Lupe in her room. Once the sound of the shower turned on, she opened her eyes. Sailor had so many thoughts going through her mind. For one, she was shocked that Lupe had told off her mom on her behalf. She had never heard that before. Lupe babied her mom. Sometimes, she was jealous of how close the two were. And Lupe gave it to her. But what she was mainly feeling was giddy. Her mom usually listened to Lupe. Would she get time together every Saturday and a half day on Wednesdays? She was afraid to hope. But she did fall asleep with a big smile on her face.

BIRDIE BLUE

Birdie felt terrible. She knew Lupe was right. It was as if Sailor were her little sister and not her daughter. She needed to fix that. She allowed Lupe to decide schedules, correct bad behavior, and supervise essential motherly duties. Lupe was correct to point it out. It had been hard to hear, but she needed to fix it.

She almost laughed at how innocently the conversation started about her giving dating a chance again. Theo called for the third time while Lupe was in her room unpacking with her. He wanted to come down to see her, but she made a flimsy excuse, citing that no visitors were allowed. She had no desire to date. She needed to tell Theo her decision. He wasn't suitable for her. Lupe asked her to give someone a chance again before the conversation segwayed into Sailor, where she needed a dad one day. Then, she commented on how she needed to step up more as a mother to Sailor.

Her beautiful, intelligent, funny, sensitive Sailor felt it. She did remember how it felt. Why hadn't she thought of it herself? Lupe was always the one who opened her eyes to things. Even if her father had been home more, he couldn't have given her what Lupe had. The maternal hugs, reassurances, and attention to detail regarding what she liked and disliked, nor could he give her a mother's love. Birdie felt her eyes well again. She had been a distant mom, even if she hadn't meant to be but no more. She vowed to find a way. Lupe gave her a good start, too. Lupe would step back. She insisted on scheduling times together, which was good for her and Sailor. After all, she had a year to complete this contract if needed. Longer if necessary. And this would be a perfect place to be together. She would fix this. She had to make another phone call, and she dreaded this one. She picked up her cell and dialed.

"Hello, Frank..."

SAILOR WREN

"Get up, sleepy head!" her mom laughed in bed with her. Her mother was in her bed?! When was the last time they had been in bed together? Sailor smiled broadly. She remembered the conversation she overheard from last night. Her mother had heard Lupe, after all.

"Come, let's wash up, have breakfast, and explore the grounds. I also need to run some ideas for the Solarium floors with you."

"Me?!"

"Yes, you silly! Only a true artist can help me come up with ideas. Face and teeth washed, chop chop." she laughed, leaving the bed and opening the curtains. "I'm so jealous! You have a better view than I do."

"Mommy, you have the view of the beautiful gardens."

"But you have the birds and the fountain. And you can see everyone drive up." Sailor's mom said happily.

"You can have my room, Mommy. I can switch with you." Sailor offered.

Her mother came and hugged her, "No way. I insist my little girl gets the best room in the house." She kissed Sailor's head and led her to the bathroom.

BIRDIE BLUE

Birdie had no idea how she was so awake. It was eight a.m., early for her as she was usually a night person. And she hadn't slept much last night, thinking of all she needed to fix with Sailor. She also rehashed Frank's arguments regarding the waiting list and her decision to be here for at least six months. But she needed to do it until she and Sailor fixed their relationship. And she was happy here. She felt Sir Oliver here.

What was the rush on her part anyway? Birdie understood that Frank only made money when she worked, but she had been working with him non-stop since she was nineteen. She was due a break. And let's face it, Lupe was right; her father left her plenty of money. PLENTY. She was a millionaire herself, not counting his funds.

Here was a once-in-a-lifetime opportunity to have her three constants in life meld perfectly: Art, Sailor, and Lupe. She would also be more open-minded to dating one day, as she had decided last night, just not with Theo. The way he pursued her was annoying and icky. Maybe he saw her as a way to be famous or rich, but one thing was for sure: it wasn't right. Regardless, she had to let him know.

Six months in a beautiful historical house, painting whatever theme she wanted, was beyond perfect. She may have gotten pregnant as an unmarried teen, not been the most attentive mother, and needed to learn about men, but for the first time in a long time, she felt like she was back on track and her world was re-aligning itself.

Happiness was exploding out of her, as it had been when she first came to this house as a child. Haven House was a magical place. She could feel Sir Oliver smiling down on her.

Birdie and Sailor

SAILOR WREN

Sailor was so happy to have spent the whole morning with her mom. They toured the outside first, smelling all the flowers in the gardens and adding bird food to the feeder from the lock box next to it. They checked out the birdhouse, too. The likeness to Haven House was even more prominent up close. They ran through the grounds holding hands and laughing, which Sailor was sure she would never forget—the morning had been magical to Sailor. She loved it here. Then, both went back to their favorite place, the art hall.

"Why is this one so messy?" Sailor asked her mom.

"That's a Jackson Pollock piece. It's supposed to look like that." Then, her mother pulled out her phone and showed Sailor many images of his work.

"Oh, it doesn't look very hard to do," Sailor said innocently, making her mom laugh so loud it echoed.

"I always thought the same thing." Her mother winked at her in a whisper.

"And this one is weird; who wants so many images of Campbell soup cans?"

Again, her mom laughed, "I must educate you on art history. This work was made by an artist named Andy Warhol." Her mom explained who he was, his work, and other things he did in 'the name of art.'

"Who is F Marc?" Sailor asked, moving to the next artwork.

Her mother came over and looked at the painting of blue horses. She pulled out her phone from her back pocket again.

"I have an app that allows you to scan the art or signature; then it tells you details about the artwork. Let's see."

They waited for it to process. "Franz Marc. This one is old; it's from 1911. I never heard of him. See? I have much to learn, too." Her mom smiled.

"Xavier Casalta! I have never seen one up close." her mom gasped.

"Why is a photograph framed with the rest of the art?" Sailor asked, peering at the six-by-six frame next to the others.

"It's not a photograph. That's stippling. Using only dots to make a picture." Sailor's mother scanned the image, bringing up a video of all his works.

Sailor was stunned. "Wow. It looks just like a photograph."

"One day, we should try it," her mom said. "But now, I am afraid I need to work, okay? So come along. I need to know if my ideas will work."

"Me? Come too?" Sailor asked, shocked. She thought her mom was going to drop her off with Lupe like usual.

"Yep, until we finalize what I need to paint. I must be alone when I paint, but now we are planning. Still work, but you can help." Sailor beamed up at her mother.

QUINN RYAN

Quinn watched her run through the gardens, holding her daughter's hand while laughing from his bedroom window. Fame and money hadn't seemed to have changed her at all. She looked as young and carefree as ever. He couldn't stop watching if he tried. Seeing her daughter at first had made him do a double take. It was as if he were looking at Birdie at the same age years ago. She was a carbon copy of her mother—same wild, dirty blonde hair, same rosy cheeks, blue eyes, and just as petite. Even the laughter was the same.

Quinn wondered if it was too soon to say 'hi.' She was famous now, sought out by many. Would she even remember him?

Quinn had no real reason to go there today since he did everything at Haven House these last few days and needed to catch up on his architectural work. But he wanted to say 'hi' badly. Quinn didn't, of course. He wanted to let them have their first day here alone together.

With a sigh, Quinn returned to the plans before him. He knew it would soon be time to pick up the kids from the YMCA swimming class.

BIRDIE BLUE

Birdie felt like she was a kid again, like Robin Williams' character in Hook, remembering that he was once a lost boy. It was freeing, running through the gardens as she once had with Kiera and Quinn. They had played non-stop between painting and occasional schoolwork. Even if Quinn was older, age twelve, and Kiera the youngest, age eight, though age hadn't mattered then. They just simply got along effortlessly. Had they known they were her first-ever real friends, Birdie wondered. She wondered whatever became of them. Quinn used to say that he would be an architect and design famous houses for rich people. Kiera said she would do interior design for him or be a teacher; she had been conflicted. But they all agreed that Birdie would do murals on every wall.

She saw Lupe smile at her as she sat on Lupe's bed after Sailor was asleep, "Finally, you heard me. Good job today, Mi hija."

"Lupe..." Birdie all but pouted, "I heard you before."

"Her smile said everything. She enjoyed her time with you. You couldn't wipe the smile off her face if you tried. That is how you know you are doing it correctly; this better not be a one-day thing."

"I know."

"You had fun, too. Your smile was just as wide." Lupe laughed.

"Saturdays and Wednesdays. But tomorrow is Sunday. I need to sort out the stuff I need in the shed where it was all delivered. Mrs. Casey said Mr. Callahan would bring whatever I needed so she could come again for an hour or two, but I was clear when I start painting again, I will need concentration."

"I also explained that. And Sailor will have to do work too. We will find a way." Lupe agreed.

"Yes." Birdie smiled, yawning. "I think I tuckered myself out." Birdie laughed, hugging Lupe 'goodnight' and going to her room; as she lay in bed, Birdie thought of the fantastic day. So similar to the ones she had at ten years old with Quinn and Kiera. She hoped Mr. Callahan had kids that would want to play with Sailor, too, as Mr. John had.

QUINN RYAN

Quinn answered his cell; it was from Haven House. "Hello," he said, thinking it was Cora or Nancy.

"Oh, hi. Is this Mr. Callahan? I'm Birdie Blythe, the artist." "Yes," Quinn said. Quinn took in a breath; he was talking to Birdie again. Did she recognize his voice, Quinn wondered. Then he thought his voice must have changed somewhat, getting deeper like his dad's. Probably not.

"Could you please meet me at the shed to help me bring over paint cans?"

"Sure, now work?" he asked. Quinn wondered why he was so nervous talking to her.

"Perfect! Thanks." She hung up.

Quinn ran to the bathroom, washed up, brushed his teeth again, and sprayed a bit more deodorant; should he shave, he wondered before stopping. What was he doing?! After Sofía, he wanted nothing to do with females. No, Quinn thought, I just miss my friend. Quinn was nervous because he would see a friend he missed, assuring himself, looking in the mirror one last time to ensure he looked alright.

"Kids, come take a walk to the shed. I need extra muscles." Quinn said, shutting off the television.

"I'm strong, Daddy. I will help you." Quinn heard his son, Tommy, say.

"Yes, you are. It's a good thing I have you," Quinn winked, looking at his mini-me.

"Hey! I'm strong, too. Right, Daddy?" Lucy asked madly.

"Yes, my girl, of course you are. Come on now, Ms. Blythe is waiting on us and our muscles." he teased, making them smile.

The shed was behind his house, so they waited when Birdie and her daughter walked up smiling.

"See? Kids! I told you there would be kids," Birdie happily told Sailor. Then she looked up at Quinn.

Quinn was unsure how to address her but decided he had to be professional. "Good morning, Ms. Blythe."

Quinn noticed Birdie pause as if remembering him somehow but couldn't quite tell from where. Did he look so different, Quinn wondered? He thought he still had the same unruly brown hair, hazel eyes, and smile. Maybe working outside made his skin darker? He hadn't shaved that morning; could the stubble on his face have thrown her off? He was more muscular now from doing all this manual labor in the gardens; that had to be very different from the gangly tall boy she remembered, he thought.

Remember me, Quinn silently begged. Quinn noticed he was holding his breath. Remember me, Birdie, he thought, because Quinn never forgot her.

"Have we met before- Quinn?!" Birdie said, eyes widened in shock.

Quinn smiled broadly; she had remembered him, after all.

She was still gorgeous. Her blonde hair was straight now, her blue eyes even bluer somehow, and the same sprinkling of freckles over her nose. And she was still petite. Quinn almost laughed out loud; she hadn't grown as much as she had always hoped. He felt as if he had towered over her now.

"Wasn't sure if you would remember me, as it was ages ago. Hello again, Birdie, uh, Ms. Blythe," he stumbled awkwardly.

Birdie laughed, "Birdie. I thought your last name was 'John' all these years! It's Callahan??" Birdie laughed and hugged him before he realized what had happened.

Quinn was surprised by the hug; he almost stopped breathing, shocked. He could smell her perfume, and he gulped quickly, gathering himself.

"My... dad was John Callahan. You called him 'Mr. John' as in his first name," Quinn mumbled nervously.

"Was?" Birdie's face clouded over.

"He died almost three years ago. I sort of temporarily took over." Quinn finished again super awkwardly.

Birdie said, "I am so sorry, Quinn. I loved your dad. He was always nice to me." Another hug. This time, he knew the hug was coming. He took the opportunity to breathe her in and hug her back. Possibly too long, then realizing what he was doing, letting go. He felt his face get heated.

"Thank you... These are my kids Tomás and Lucía, but we call them 'Tommy' and 'Lucy' around here." Quinn said, looking at his kids. Quinn tried to see them as she would. Tommy was tall and slim as he had been at that age—same brown wavy hair, same hazel eyes, but with Sofía's nose and olive skin coloring. On the other hand, Lucy was a spitting image of her mother; she was brunette, had large brown almond-shaped eyes, the same nose, olive skin, and was petite.

Tommy   Lucy

"It's lovely to meet you. Meet my daughter, Sailor. Please call me Birdie," she told the kids, smiling.

Quinn was looking at a younger version of Birdie, but she seemed more reserved and shyer.

"Ms. Birdie." Quinn corrected.

"Nope, can't do the whole formal thing. My name is unique enough. Then I did the same thing to her." Birdie laughed, nodding toward Sailor.

Then Birdie bent down to his kid's level. "Her name was going to be 'Scarlett,' but at the last minute, I decided it was too common for a Blythe," she teased his kids. "She is surprisingly named after artwork I saw on the maternity suite wall. It was of a person sailing on the ocean, and bam! Sailor." Birdie laughed.

Quinn was enraptured all over again. His kids were, too, as they hung onto her every word. Their faces beaming up at her mesmerized. On the other hand, Sailor had a death grip on Birdie's hand and barely looked up at him, though Quinn noticed she shyly peered at his kids. There was a story there, Quinn thought. Sailor did not look comfortable around men. He knew to be gentle around her and give her plenty of space until she realized he was safe.

Quinn scooped up Lucy, smiling, "Let's lead the way, my girl. Then maybe we can all have ice cream together at the main house. Nancy always has extra, and we can all become friends."

As they sorted through a massive pile of paints, they spoke casually.

"I cannot believe you stayed here all this time. Raising a family here must have been magical." Birdie had said, stopping to look up at him.

"No, actually, I went to school at FSU in Tallahassee, Florida. Then, I got a job down in Miami. I made my life there. I only did this job once Dad died. And it was supposed to be for a few months around my other job."

"Which is?" Birdie asked Quinn, intrigued.

"Architect..." and somehow Birdie finished the word with him, saying it simultaneously.

"You remembered," Quinn said softly. He was happy she had remembered all these years later, and her remembering somehow made him less nervous.

"You were going to design houses, and I was-" Birdie started to say.

"Going to do all the murals in them." he finished laughing.

As Quinn pulled a trolley full of paint cans, a familiar lady stepped out of the front door. "Mi hija, I need you," she said in Spanish, hoping for privacy. Quinn thought the lady looked guarded. He wondered why. Wait. Could the lady be Lupe? She looked so different. She had lost a lot of weight since he last saw her.

"You speak Spanish, too?" Tommy asked in Spanish excitedly.

Lupe looked taken back.

"Their mother is Italian and Spanish but was raised in Colombia since childhood." Quinn said awkwardly, "Both are fluent in both languages."

Lupe looked as if she had relaxed a bit. "How wonderful. I can take Sailor if you want now, Birdie, so that you can work."

"Oh! Where are my manners? Lupe, you remember Quinn, right? One of the two kids I played with here as a child all those years ago?" Birdie asked excitedly.

"Quinn?! Kiera here too?" Lupe asked happily, actually surprising Quinn by hugging him, too. Her face was now warm and inviting.

"No, she is working at our place in Miami. We went into business together. She is an architect, too. Kiera tends to love designing the spaces afterward just as much. She is married now with a daughter. Amanda is two and super cute." he said. Quinn wanted to smack himself; why was he talking so much?

Amanda

"Kids go to school around here?" Lupe asked Quinn.

"Yes. Tommy and Lucy start on August 12th. The bus picks them up and drops them off at the main gate." Quinn inwardly groaned; why was he volunteering so much information? Why was he getting so nervous again?

"Sailor would love friends, so if your wife wants to set up a playdate, please have her speak to me." Lupe smiled.

"No wife, uh, she lives abroad. We're uh-"

Quinn wanted the floor to open up. Great! The first five minutes of seeing them again and his failed marriage is topic number one.

"Did I tell you their names, Lupe? Tomás and Lucía, but everyone here calls them 'Tommy' and 'Lucy.'" Birdie said fast. Quinn looked relieved.

"Then who watches them when not in school?" Lupe asked.

Quinn shrugged, "Me."

"They are welcome with us any time. I would love to have Spanish-speaking friends nearby. Any time you need a break, my Sailor would love the company. Right, Mamita?" Lupe said, kissing the top of Sailor's head adoringly.

Sailor smiled shyly, leaning her body into Lupe's legs. Quinn caught the hopeful smile on her face.

"Thank you," Quinn said to Lupe.

"No, thank you. Sailor needs friends just as Birdie had. You and your sister were wonderful friends to Birdie. Sailor can benefit from the same. I mean it when I say any time. We will do her work around playdates. And I get to speak more Spanish. Win-win!" Lupe laughed.

Birdie laughed, "She only gets to use it when I am in trouble now."

Lupe laughed, "If you do not get to work, you will hear it shortly."

All laughed again as Lupe winked at his kids so they knew she was joking.

"Let me just bring this up for you. What room are you doing first?" Quinn asked Birdie.

"But Daddy, you said ice cream," Lucy said sadly.

Lupe interjected quickly, "Of course, there will be ice cream. While the grown-ups work, let's see if Mrs. Finnley has some. Will they come with Sailor and I to the kitchen?" Lupe asked Quinn.

"Yes." Then he added, "Manners," whispering to his kids and looking at them knowingly.

"Thank you!" Lucy exclaimed. "Auntie Nancy got me the chocolate chip flavor I liked last time. Do you like chocolate chip ice cream?" She asked Sailor.

Sailor nodded shyly.

"Come kids, let's go together. They won't be out of my sight, I promise." Lupe assured Quinn.

"Actually, Cora... um, Mrs. Casey, the housekeeper, is their 'grandmother' of sorts... Nancy, um, Mrs. Finnley, the cook, is like a great aunt. So they are always in the kitchen being spoiled rotten by both." Quinn explained.

"Grandmother?" Birdie had asked him, intrigued.

"Dad and Cora were a couple for ten years before he died."

"Mr. John and Mrs. Casey. Lovely." Lupe smiled.

"Both were widowed; she helped raise my sister and me. I guess feelings grew. We are both super close to her." Quinn shrugged, "Shall we bring all this up?"

BIRDIE BLUE

No wonder she never found him on social media, Birdie thought. And she had searched—many times over the years. She searched for 'Quinn John Architect,' as she had thought his name was, or 'Kiera John Interior Designer or Teacher' in South Carolina. Birdie wondered how they ended up in Miami, of all places. He couldn't find an architectural job here in South Carolina?

"So you only need the five colors?" Quinn asked, looking at the giant white, black, yellow, red, and blue paint tubs he put down on the Nursery floor.

"Yep."

"What if you need green or orange or.."

She smiled, "I mix the color I want. Surely, as an architect, you took some art classes? Most colors come from red, blue, and yellow." She teased.

"Primary colors, yes, I recall." He laughed. She liked his laugh, Birdie realized.

"And the secondary colors are?" Birdie jokingly tested him.

"Green, purple... orange. Right? You mix the two primary colors to get a secondary color. Flashback to Ms. Higgins' Studio Art 101 Class." Quinn laughed.

"Very good. I must let Ms. Higgins know that you paid attention in class." Birdie teased him. It felt good to laugh with him again. It had always been so easy with him, and it still was.

"So, if you need anything, just call my cell. You have my number, right?"

Birdie wanted to laugh at his nervousness. Of course, she had his cell. She had called him earlier.

"Yep, but in my room. I called from the house phone earlier. Shall I put you in my cell? Then I will text you my number?" Birdie asked. Birdie felt so odd asking for his number. Quinn nodded as they exchanged numbers.

"Great. Thanks Quinn. And I hope the kids become fast friends. Sailor is shyer than I was."

"Anyone was more shy than you were," he teased. He looked shocked that he had said it out loud, and Birdie lost it. She had a full-on belly laugh, bent over with tears.

"I've been wondering when my Quinn would be back. This formal stuffy man-version is boring." She teased back. Did she just say 'my Quinn'?! She panicked.

She could see his face blush, but she kept talking, so hers didn't match his.

"We always roasted each other and laughed. And we were always blunt with each other. Why haven't you asked me any questions? Some are painfully obvious." Birdie said, sobering a bit but forcing a smile.

"OK, are you married?" Quinn asked.

"You were always a terrible liar, Quinn. Everything about me is public knowledge, but one thing: Sailor's dad. Steve. His name was Steve. I had her at seventeen after running away with him. He left me miles away pregnant, without money to pay for food or a place to stay once his family knew we were in their summer house. Came home with my tail between my legs." Birdie said matter-of-factly. Then she pointed at his chest firmly, "Steve's name gets out. I will hunt you down. Only Lupe knows. Well, and Steve." she grumbled.

Birdie was surprised that she trusted him with this information. After her father and Sir Oliver died, she trusted no one except Lupe. Even Frank did not know, and he had asked many times. "You and Kiera were my only friends growing up, Quinn. ONLY. Friends tell each other stuff. I miss having friends."

Did he miss her? Does Kiera miss her too?

"Your turn."

"I told you all before; I just spewed it out like a moron," Quinn grumbled, and again Birdie roared. "You always did that when you got nervous, Quinn. You always squealed like a pig. Note to self: do not go on a crime spree with Quinn." she teased him.

Quinn laughed. She could see that he knew what she was referring to. They had once snuck off the grounds to see if they could. It was a big no-no for all three of them. Of course, it had been her idea. She knew they would have followed her anywhere back then when she suggested the quest to see if they could make it to town. They had. The only problem was as they were about to go back, they ran into Mr. John. Of all the times for him to be in town to get supplies. Still, to this day, she did not know who was more shocked, Quinn or Mr. John. Quinn had guiltily confessed all except it being Birdie's idea. As the oldest, he bore the blame anyway. Birdie insisted it had been her idea and forced them. Anything to get Mr. John to stop being so angry with his kids, but Quinn still got in the most trouble. He had to help around the grounds for three days instead of playing.

"Are you still married? Separated? Divorced? Dating now? Details, Quinn Joh- sorry, Callahan. I will never get used to that being your last name."

"Quinn Ryan Callahan. Hope adding a middle name screws with your head a bit more." Quinn had teased her back, laughing. He was finally relaxing around her, she thought. She missed their banter.

"DETAILS!" Birdie huffed, intrigued.

"Divorced. You?" Quinn asked back.

"Asexual." she laughed jokingly. "Seriously, no one worth mentioning. Dating?"

"No one worth mentioning." He gave back.

"Touché," she smiled. "Let me get to work before Lupe comes. Thank you, Quinn, for helping me bring all this up those long stairs and for opening up," she said, smiling softly.

SAILOR WREN

Lucy was very talkative and bossy at times but fun, too. Tommy was calm and super kind. She liked them both, but Tommy was more her speed.

"Did you see the children's room upstairs? We can play there. Sir Oliver made it for all children." Tommy said, excited to show her. Sailor looked up at Tommy, who was about five inches taller than her, nodding but then turned to look at Lupe first.

"Can I, Lupe?" Sailor asked her. Lupe looked at Cora.

"Sir Oliver wanted this house to be a home. He allowed the kids almost everywhere, even the art hall, as it is all protected." Cora said, waving them on.

"Mrs. Davis said no going-" Lupe started to say.

"I run this house and have for thirty-two years. I was only gone two months to care for my mother when you came all those years ago. The attorneys are just being over-protective.

Sir Oliver very clearly told me his wishes. He even made some rooms for children, such as the playroom, the library, which has an entire wall of children's books, a nursery, and even the solariums off the decks to play. Short of whichever room is being painted, the rest of the rooms are to be lived in and used, per Sir Oliver. He was quite clear on that. I even have it in writing."

"Oh." Lupe said, "Mrs. Davis said it's a historical home now..."

"Mrs. Davis is an attorney who never met Sir Oliver. He would hate this house being a shrine and not a home. I am in charge of Haven House and grounds until the new owner is revealed, which is in writing, too. He tried to leave the entire thing to me and Nancy. We said no. This beautiful home needs a family living in it. I shall keep my room here as long as I run this house, but he built me a house in Bal Harbour, Florida, years ago. Just close enough to Kiera and Quinn, if he goes back, but still let them live their own lives."

Sailor needed help understanding everything the adults said, but the tone was unmistakable. Cora was in charge; this house was child-friendly.

"Nana, can we go up to the children's room now?" Tommy asked.

"Go on, love."

Sailor looked at Lucy, who pulled at her hand. "Come on, I want to show you the rocking horse."

Sailor panicked and looked at Lupe for permission. Lupe nodded with a smile. "I would like to see it, too. May I join you all?"

Sailor felt relief at Lupe's words. She needed more time to get comfortable with the kids alone yet; but for once, she wanted these children to be her friends.

Lucy nodded and then pulled Sailor up out of her seat.

"Lucy Callahan, manners. No pulling." Cora said firmly.

"Sorry, Nana." Lucy pouted, letting go.

"Good girl. Let her get used to you both. I know you miss having a female friend nearby." Cora said softer. Sailor looked up, shocked. Lucy wanted her as her friend as much as she wanted them to.

The playroom had different things in each corner and two alcoves. One corner table had blocks and legos on a table, and another had the rocking horse that was Lucy's favorite, which she ran to and jumped on. One alcove had a large window and two long seat cushions facing each other with cozy pillows. It was a reading nook, she realized.

The thought of cozily sketching there appealed to her until she saw an art easel with every art supply possible. Paint, pastels, watercolors, colored pencils, crayons, paper, and paint brushes than Sailor had ever seen in one room. Which said a lot, as her mom and Grandfather were real artists! She already knew her favorite spot, the art corner. The final corner had toy cars, trucks, and ramps to play with. The second alcove showcased an enormous dollhouse with one side open. It looked just like Haven House from the outside, Sailor realized. The inside had some similar wallpapers, rugs, and sofas; it was gorgeous. This doll house looked old, but with all the dolls thrown about, she could tell children had played with it recently.

She looked at Lupe for permission before touching anything. "Mrs. Casey says it is alright. Go on," she said.

Sailor took off to the art table before she heard, "Come try this first, Sailor. It's fun," Lucy said from the rocking horse. Sailor smiled and went to her new friend. She tried it, and it was fun. She was going to like it here.

Over the next few hours, Sailor got more and more comfortable with Tommy and Lucy. Both looked as happy to have a new playmate as she did. Tommy showed her everything with such excitement. He really knew Haven House well, Sailor thought as he took her, with Lupe following quietly all over the house and grounds.

"We live there. Want to see it, too?" Lucy asked, pointing to the Carriage House.

"No need, dear, that is private." Lupe finally said, "I think it is time for lunch anyway. Thank you both so much for the terrific tour."

Lucy and Tommy beamed at the compliment.

Sailor was sad to leave the kids, "Can we meet again later?" she asked.

Tommy nodded, "OK. Let's eat fast, Lucy. "He grabbed her hand, and they took off, making Sailor smile.

QUINN RYAN

Quinn returned to the shed to bring in the next pile of cans. So many random thoughts bounced around his head as he loaded the cart. Birdie trusted him with sensitive information, such as the name of Sailor's dad. That had touched him. Probably because he and Kiera were her only childhood friends. How could that be? She was so friendly and bubbly. She had been so easy to befriend. She hadn't made other friends as a child in all those years? That just did not make sense.

Then he groaned at being caught lying. Birdie called him on it, too. She guessed he probably knew everything about her since she was so public. And if truth be told, he had googled her many times. He saw pictures of her in galleries, read write-ups about her, and watched an unauthorized biography of her and her father.

He knew she had a child early, which shocked him when he first heard about it. He always thought he had been young, but Birdie had been inappropriately young—way too soon to be a parent; she was still a kid herself then. He always wanted to know the details, especially since he knew how protective Lupe was back then and how much she adored her father and Lupe when he had seen them together.

He had many other questions, like what made her run away in the first place? It seemed as if she had an idyllic life as far as he was concerned. She was famous, rich, talented, and beautiful. Why run away? So it couldn't have been as great as he imagined; she had run away from something. Or to something.

He also knew she was still unmarried but could not understand why. He had not seen any comments in the media about relationships lately, either.

Yes, he knew much about her. She was correct; Quinn thought he was a terrible liar, flushing.

Quinn managed to get it all on the cart but then took half off as he wanted a reason to keep returning to see her. Hopefully, talk to her again.

As Quinn brought up the second batch, he stopped in the hallway. He could hear her having a conversation. These rooms were empty of people and everyday noises. He wasn't even near the Nursery door yet, but her voice rang out in a hollow echo down the hall. He should make himself known, Quinn thought. He shouldn't listen but couldn't stop himself.

A loud peal of laughter rang so freely, and it almost startled him. "Come on! Please, Frank…. I need it." He heard her plead. Quinn felt himself get sick. Who was Frank, and why was she begging him?!

"I love you…" she sang out to him hopefully in a flirty sing-song voice.

"Just for the day, please? Even a couple of hours. Yes! Thank you, Frank. I am so excited to see you. Yes. Yes. It's in my bedroom drawer. Go look now." He heard the one-sided conversation.

WHO WAS FRANK? Quinn seethed. WHY DID HE HAVE ACCESS TO HER BEDROOM? Quinn felt sick. Had she lied to him? Was she in a relationship? And then it dawned on him that his 'crush' was never a crush. He always loved her, even at the young age of twelve. Even after marriage to Sofía, he could feel he was headed for heartbreak again.

Quinn resolved to taper any feelings. His life was full enough with kids, two jobs, and Sofía drama. No, he had to be smart. He was older, and he knew the deal. There was a 'Frank,' also known as 'no one worth mentioning.' He stomped purposefully in the hallway, so she turned around and smiled at him.

"Let me go." She hung up and smiled at him. He saw her usual happy-to-see-him smile. Maybe she did that to everyone?

"Thanks, I have enough to get started. If you want to leave that in the hallway, please." Birdie smiled at him.

"Sure," Quinn said quietly, "I need to do the gardens anyway." Without another word, he took off before his resolve melted.

SAILOR WREN

Sailor, Lucy, and Tommy all sat at the table drawing. They used crayons, and she used pastels. Sailor was drawing a picture of the rocking horse.

"How do you draw so well?" Tommy asked, awed.

"My grandfather and mother are artists. I guess I learned from them. I can teach you... if you want?" she asked shyly.

She looked over at Lupe, sitting in the reading nook, glancing at her phone. Most likely, it was purposefully encouraging Sailor to make friends without her help but still within earshot if needed. Lupe hadn't seen her worried face; Sailor did not know if offering to teach them how to draw was pushy. Sailor tended to look up at Lupe for encouragement when overly concerned. She realized she would need to figure this out on her own. Lupe was busily looking at something. She had her 'concentration face' on when reading something important.

"Yes! I want to draw just like you!" Lucy said passionately, "Jazmín can draw well, too, but she likes to draw clothes. She wants to be a fashion designer."

"Who's Jazmín?" Sailor asked.

"My sister! She's big. She's thirteen." Lucy said.

"She's not that big, Lucy. She just thinks she is." Tommy rolled his eyes, "She thinks she is such a big deal artist, but just your quick drawing of the rocking horse is ten times better than anything she ever drew."

"Because she draws clothes!" Lucy defended, face in a mad pout.

Sailor looked at Lupe coming over. "Everything alright?" she asked gently. She saw Lupe hadn't paid attention to the conversation, but she heard the bickering tone and rushed over, probably thinking they were fighting with Sailor, not with each other.

Jazmín Colon

"Look! Sailor draws like a real artist!" Lucy exclaimed, quite pleased.

"Well, some things are talents you were born with. Sailor comes from a long line of artists." Lupe explained, smiling.

"Yep, and Sailor said she would teach us!" Lucy squealed, echoing around the large room.

Sailor smiled broadly, then looked up at Lupe happily.

"That was nice, Sailor. Only if they want to learn."

"We do, Ms. Lupe. Lucy always wanted to draw better, and now, seeing Sailor's horse picture, I do too." Tommy said politely.

"You may call me Lupe. My Sailor is a very patient teacher. Although she may seem shy at first, she will be good at explaining how she starts her drawings." Lupe smiled, seeing the three kids smile too.

"Dad used to say I was shy. After I turned six, Dad said I changed and got bolder. So maybe you need to be six first." Tommy told Sailor seriously.

Lupe laughed, "You are the sweetest, Tomás. Maybe six is the magic number for boys, but Sailor is eight now and still shy. Maybe her number is nine?" She winked at Sailor, who giggled.

"You are eight?!" Tommy asked, shocked.

"But you are smaller than Tommy..." Lucy said, confused.

"She's petite like her mother, and Tommy is big like your father," Lupe smiled.

"I've always been tiny..." Sailor said, laughing, feeling more relaxed and speaking for herself, "Mommy calls me Tinkerbell."

Sailor spent an hour explaining how she observes the item she is about to draw, notices the outline, takes one section at a time, and tries her best to copy it. Both Tommy and Lucy tried. It came out a bit wonky, but the shape was a horse in both pictures. Both were super pleased with themselves.

"You just need to keep practicing until you get better at it." Sailor said, "I practiced a lot." And she had. What else did she have to do when in strange places?

"Like you do with soccer, Tommy." Lucy said to him, agreeing with a giggle, "I need a lot of practice."

"We both do." Tommy laughed.

BIRDIE BLUE
AGE 13

Another letter came, and Birdie squealed. Lupe handed it to her. She could see the envelope was already read, as Lupe did not allow communications with adults without previewing them first. Unlike her father, even if Lupe thought Sir Oliver was 'a good soul'.

Dearest Birdie,

How was California? I read about your father's installation in the paper. What work! The talent in your family is astounding. Kiera wanted to thank you for the bracelet you made for her. I had never heard of clay beads before; that you mixed the clay yourself and created such delicate flowers in the round beads was outstanding. Kiera wears it every day. Quinn, like myself, loved the belts you made us. The intricate stamping you put into the leather must have taken a long time. You learned exciting new things at this summer art camp. Do you see yourself doing more of this? You didn't sound like you loved it as much as being home with Lupe, but sometimes we learn new things from different people, so maybe give new experiences a chance.

I do hope you are still painting your murals. I was thinking of creating a children's room on the third floor. Maybe one day you can fill its walls with your beautiful artwork.

Anyway, sweet child, my health has not been good this month, so I apologize for the delay in getting this letter out. This flu did not want to leave my body, and I was bed-bound for three weeks. Luckily, I feel better now and am anxiously awaiting your following letter.

I cannot wait to see your name in lights.

Birdie hugged the letter to her chest. She had hated the art camp her father insisted on. She felt out of place, and no one painted! How can they not paint at an art camp? They made beads, tie-dyed, macrame, stamping leather, and found stuff around the camp to create art. She had won first prize for the mosaic, as it was the only project that caught her interest. She found an old box of bottle caps and twelve large yellow, red, and green tiles. She broke the tiles into pieces and created a mosaic of the gardens of Haven House. It had been the only time she smiled the entire two weeks. She hadn't made any friends. Again. Not that she tried. Birdie knew it was only for two weeks, so why bother?

She begged Lupe never to send her away again, but Lupe explained that it was her father's choice. Lupe had used that time to return to Mexico to see family she hadn't seen in years. But if truth be told, Birdie thought Lupe looked like she missed her more than she had Lupe.

QUINN RYAN

Quinn's phone rang. He looked at it and groaned. Sofía. What now, he thought. He put down the shovel he was using to replant a lavender bush so he could give it more room to grow.

"Hello," Quinn said.

"Is she there?" Sofía asked furiously, then a barrage of Spanish so fast he hadn't gotten every word. He was almost fluent in understanding Spanish now but stumbled sometimes when speaking it back to fast talkers like Sofía.

"Who? Kiera?" Quinn was suddenly tired. "Kiera is not here, and NO, you may not have the Miami home. Stop asking. You know our business is on the main floor, with the second and third floors being our homes. Half of it is Kiera's," he said. The two did not always get along. Why would she want to know if Kiera was here, Quinn thought?

"I am moving to Star Island. Who cares about that place! My daughter, is she there?"

Star Island was a crazy expensive and exclusive place. He had done many jobs there.

"Of course, Lucy is here-" he said, annoyed before being cut off. "Not Lucía and we spoke about not calling her 'Lucy'!"

"Come raise her, then call her what you want. Oh, that's right, I have full custody. Her mother is too busy acting in telenovelas for Abuelitas."

"Pendejo!"

"I could legally change her name if I wanted to, as I am her full-time parent." He argued back. He knew he sounded immature but didn't care. Quinn was always so triggered by her. He was being petty and knew it. Sofía just made him furious.

"Put her on the phone. I know she is there." Sofía ignored him.

"Where else would she be? With her mother?" he asked acidly.

"Carajo, pay att-."

"Goodbye, Sofía." Quinn hung up.

His phone rang another three times, and he forwarded it directly to voicemail each time. Finally, he got a text.

'Jazmín is missing. She left her boarding school.'

Shit, Quinn thought. It was one thing to love aggravating Sofía back, but another thing to not know where Jazmín was. Not that she was his responsibility. She was Sofía's child with her first husband. Jazmín's absent father, Julio, has never met Jazmín or tried to contact her. He hasn't reached out to Sofía either, not even for money when she got famous.

No, Quinn was the closest thing to a father Jazmín ever had. Not that being her father for five and a half years meant anything to her. And she, sure as shit, did not listen to him at all, Quinn thought. She constantly argued with him and his 'barbaric rules.' Not that Quinn thought his rules were ridiculous. All he asked of her was no cursing, staying up to three a.m., or sleeping all day. He asked Jazmín to do schoolwork and help clean up after herself. These were barbaric rules, Quinn thought to himself, shaking his head. No way would Jazmín run to him. Though, she had before. Twice.

He tried her cell phone.

"Hello! I was just thinking of you." She laughed.

"Where are you?" Quinn demanded.

"That's how you say 'hello' back, not very nice, Daddy Dearest." She laughed naughtily.

"Don't 'Daddy Dearest' me; you only call me that when you want something. Where are you?" He asked firmly.

"Um…. excuse me, where are we?" Quinn heard Jazmín asking someone.

"Who the hell did you just ask that to?" Quinn seethed. That was it, daughter or no daughter; if he saw her again, she was getting the speech of her life.

"The limo driver, geesch Quinn. Be nice to me." Jazmín huffed.

"Where are you?" He demanded.

"Columbia."

"As in the country or South Carolina?" Though spelled differently, both sounded alike. Could she be visiting her mother's family in Colombia? Or was she in Columbia, South Carolina? If so, Quinn calculated she was forty-something miles away from Eastover.

"South Carolina. Surprise!" she laughed.

"You are on your way here?" Quinn sighed.

"Only if you aren't angry. I miss my siblings." Jazmín pouted, "But if you are angry, I will go somewhere else."

"You mean like school?"

"I sort of got sent home… I only went to Cabo for a few days; it's no big deal. They overreacted."

Quinn could feel his blood pressure rising. He hadn't been her stepfather in a while now, and he had to tell himself he legally had no rights over her. She was not his problem now; he kept telling himself repeatedly. It was not his problem… Now, to believe it, he thought. "Call your mother." He said between clenched teeth.

"No." Jazmín huffed.

"If I call too, then when you come, you are in for it, and I mean it. Call your mother."

"Getting cranky in your old age, Quinn." she teased. "Jazmín Sofía Colon, call now."

"Fine, but I am still coming. Tell the kids. See you soon."

Just what Quinn needed. And Birdie was here. She would need to concentrate. Maybe he should tell Jazmín not to come, he panicked. But then, who did she have? Sofía was just as absent with her as she was with his kids. His kids at least had him, Kiera, Jason, and Amanda, not to mention Cora and Nancy daily. Jazmín had no one but Sofía. Not that he hadn't tried to stay in touch, making sure the siblings had relationships. He and Jazmín had a relationship, too, though it was hit or miss with her. Sometimes Jazmín loved him, sometimes she hung up on him or did not return phone calls. He never knew what she wanted from him or how to give it to her. And he tried. For a short time, they were good. She seemed to trust him, then suddenly, 'he wasn't her father and didn't have to listen to him' and would want to do her own things and ignore him. He just never found the right balance. However, he couldn't turn her away. Besides, Jazmín and the kids adored each other for the most part, especially Lucy adoring her older sister. He had to try.

He called Sofía, "Did you hear from her?" Sofía demanded.

"She didn't call you? I just spoke to her. She is on her way here." Quinn sighed. He heard Sofía exhale deeply. Relieved. Then he could literally feel her getting mad. The long pause gave her away before the explosion.

"Punish her! The school just called; they are expelling Jazmín. Just like the last school. Expelled again, Ave Maria, this girl is putting me through this again!"

"AGAIN?! She was expelled before?" Quinn asked before he tried to calm himself. Why hadn't he heard about the first one?

"Yes, for the same reason; she just takes off when bored." "Will you listen to me now? No thirteen-year-old needs credit cards and unlimited freedom to do as she pleases. She needs structure and daily guidance from a parent, not a teacher. She needs to be told 'no.' Stop all the credit cards and enroll her at the local school here or she cannot stay. I won't even let her in the gates," he said. Sofía had no idea Quinn was bluffing. He could never turn Jazmín away; she had no one else in the country.

"Fine. Constance will stop the credit cards after she gets there."

"And start acting like her mother, not her friend."

"Don't you start-" another barrage of Spanish saying she was trying to do it all, that this was her last chance at her career in Spain before she attempted acting in America next, like

Penelope Cruz or Colombian-born Sofía Vergara. She added she feared they would be killing off her character soon in a sob. Quinn could not believe his ears. Her selfishness always caught him off guard.

Quinn thought back to when they were first married when her career was on an upward trajectory. It was a long-distance relationship at times, but it worked. The Spanish press adored her. They had followed her pregnancy like they couldn't get enough of her. She felt beautiful while pregnant. She was loving all the attention. When Tommy was born, she did a Spanish Vogue cover carrying Tommy as an infant, and it sold so well that suddenly all the papers wanted her on their cover. She had been so happy.

Sofía Colon

Then, she started making more appearances around the telenovela. She was coming home less and less. When she would go home, they could not keep their hands off of each other. Sex and desire had never been a problem for them. The chemistry was easy, but the relationship was complicated. Then, she was with child for a second time. Once again, pregnant Sofía was on every magazine cover. The paparazzi was even more insane than before, if possible. But she was happy, and when she was, she glowed and looked more beautiful; he just wanted to be with her, only seeing the good in her. And there had been good, too, Quinn thought, being fair. However, the little she gave them was not enough after a while. He needed help taking care of them. Didn't parents raise children together? Didn't mothers want to be with their babies? He grew resentful. Starting up a new company needed attention, too. He was already home with the kids working around naps and, thankfully, with the help of the baby nurse. Then, one day, the nurse said she needed to leave, and Quinn panicked. She did not want to chase after toddlers; the hours were too long. He called Sofía, begging her to come home more, not every day, but just an equal split between home and abroad.

She insisted the only solution was for them to go there as she had made more money. Quinn thought about it. He had. He knew Spanish now. Thanks to four years of Spanish in high school and being married to her, it was her native language, and they spoke it often. Of course, living in Miami, a.k.a. Little Havana, he was always immersed in Spanish, and surprisingly, it came easy to him. He thought he could move the business there since it was just starting, but he would miss his family. He would miss Kiera, specifically. He had been excited to start a family business with Kiera and get her on her feet. They had always been close. He knew she would not move, and his Dad was older. He could not leave him either.

Also, the two visits he made earlier in her career to Spain with a nanny and kids in tow were insane. He hadn't felt safe. They were swarmed by the press wherever they went. They swarmed their car once, which was super scary for the kids. Another time, a photographer grabbed Quinn's jacket sleeve of the arm holding Lucy. He tugged so hard to turn him around for a shot that Quinn almost dropped Lucy. Quinn hadn't expected it but managed to pull his arm away and grabbed her tight. He was livid. Luckily, the nanny had Tommy safely tucked in her arms, but she looked just as scared. Sofía was holding Jazmín's hand, talking to some of them by name, posing, not knowing what was happening behind her. Had he not been protecting his daughter and needing to get his family to safety, he would have been in jail that night. He knew that for a fact. Quinn did not lose it often, but mess with his family, specifically his kids, it was game over. He saw red.

He packed their stuff that night while a sobbing Sofía said she would do a press tour to tell them what happened and it was not acceptable in the future. They would listen to her, she said. She would create change in the laws. They all knew her, knew she allowed photos in the past. She tried to get him to see it was just one person making a mistake. Nothing worked on him.

Then she started to get angry at him for not listening to her. He kept packing. Instead, he asked her to leave with them. He insisted. But she was hosting a big award show in two days, which was why they had come in the first place. She felt obligated to stay, or she chose to stay. He wasn't sure which one was more true. He, the nanny, and the kids all left as she screamed at the top of her lungs to stop overreacting.

After three days, she must have cooled down. She called Quinn in a lovey-dovey voice, apologizing, and asked him to please come. She would have bodyguards and a super-protected villa for them. They could make it work. Though he calmed down, all he could think about was how the paparazzi had almost dropped Lucy and the crowd could have trampled her. He would never feel the kids would be safe there. He told her no.

Sofía was not one to hear the word 'no' gracefully. They ended up having another fight. He offered a compromise for her to work in the states with laws to protect them. He said he would do everything to get her working in America, trying to find a compromise. She pointed out the lack of Latina roles. They fought for weeks about this. Then she just refused to come home. He guessed it was due to her being adored there while being a no one in America. She would not come back, not now. But she had been willing to look for parts in America if he agreed to move to Los Angeles when the time came. Quinn knew she would not try. Not for him. Not even for the kids, but he agreed.

Jazmín felt the rejection the worst. She was old enough to understand. She only talked of her mother's selfishness. He made plenty of excuses for Sofía, but that made Jazmín angrier; angry at him, too. More defiant. Jazmín had reverted back to the angry, disobedient child he first met. The same behavior he had worked so hard to improve over those six months of her living with him and going to a regular school. He tried talking to Sofía about it. Instead of hearing that her actions were part of Jazmín's behavior issues, she heard what she wanted. Sofía insisted on another boarding school for Jazmín. This one in Spain.

He had no choice but to agree because Jazmín was her daughter. He hoped that being near each other would make mother and daughter closer. Hadn't every girl needed a mother at that age? He hoped Jazmín being in Spain would mean seeing each other often, but after many phone calls to Jazmín, Quinn heard that Sofía only went twice to see her in as many years. After that, he kept asking Sofía to allow Jazmín to return to live with them. She was alone, four hours away from her mother. Sofía insisted she was doing her best for HER child. She was Jazmín's parent, and he had no say. He should have fought harder. He regretted that.

The most significant change was in Sofía. It felt as if she were addicted to being famous, and the kids were used as bargaining chips or props in pictures to get love from her audience. Quinn then stopped allowing Tommy and Lucy's pictures to be in magazines. Again, another huge fight. These were not paparazzi, she argued; they were professional photographers. She needed pictures with them. They kept asking her for more. He said no. She conceded. She knew he would not budge and to give in to get him to forgive her. Butter him up. She would do something sweet for the kids, send gifts, chocolate-covered strawberries, and even a rare surprise visit, and it worked.

The following year, things started to go wrong for her. She was cut from a movie she had been super excited about. According to the rumor mill, she was too demanding, her way or no way. Then, another huge blow to her ego came. She started only being cast as a mother figure, which she hated. She felt she still looked young. After that, she no longer wanted the kids in the papers—to only be considered a mother.

She got plastic surgery to make her body and face seem younger. They were just not as into her as they were before the surgery. She also hadn't even told Quinn about the surgery. He wasn't there for it because she told him afterward. She hadn't asked him his opinion, as if he did not matter in any of it. It seemed sometimes she forgot she was married, a partner to someone. That is unless she needed something from him. Or that was how Quinn felt.

The constant ups and downs and fights were too much. He was relieved at times she was so far away. Busy, but less drama. There was so much tension. He could feel his normally easy-going personality changing. He did not like this angry side of himself when dealing with Sofía. He has been angry lately, especially when the kids asked for her. It felt like a disease consuming him.

The roles offered were fewer and fewer, so she was worse to deal with, too—until she got hired in 'Fuego,' Quinn thought. Her role was the head of the family, a no-nonsense matriarch who was older but a lead role.

Once again, stardom. Sofía had the hit show she wanted, but at a cost. They divorced when Quinn learned she signed a five-year contract without even talking to him about it. She had been doing it for four years now, leaving all three kids behind.

He was left long ago if he listened to the rumor mill about her and her bodyguard. That hurt him if Quinn had been honest. But it hurt his pride more than his heart. Quinn was super angry at first, but what got him was how she portrayed herself to the press when he heard her talk about the kids. She would say things like she 'often put aside her feelings to make her kids' needs a priority' as she told one article. Jazmín was finally 'getting an education she always longed for at a private boarding school,' and the other two kids 'were being raised by their adoring father away from prying eyes.' She also went on and on about their safety, 'the paparazzi was doing crazy things to take pictures of the kids." Luckily, the paparazzi that followed her were in Latin countries, not here. Thank God, Quinn thought.

She would really play it up, he shook his head. She 'had to put her family first, to keep them safe.' Now, 'they were no longer allowed to be photographed' as if it were her idea or maybe re-stating his rules; he wasn't sure. This lovingly concerned, protective parent didn't know anything about her kids.

Tommy hated chocolate, and she did not know that Lucy was allergic to strawberries and that Jazmín used to scratch Sofía's face out of every magazine and picture they owned until he scheduled weekly therapy for her before she was taken away from him and sent away to school.

No, she can act how she wants for her fans. Her roles are fake, but so is her life. Quinn no longer cared. Let her say what she wanted. He knew the truth; more importantly, the kids did, too. They could see who truly cared about them. He knew she loved them but would not raise them as an average parent would by being there daily.

He promised himself never to say a mean word about her to them, never to critique her mothering out loud where they could hear it. She chose her career and fame, and he chose them.

He had to call Cora. Oh boy, this was not going to be good.

BIRDIE BLUE

Birdie knew what she would do for this room. She sketched the four walls onto her sketchbook. It was the story of Peter Pan in four scenes. Something for a boy or a girl, as Wendy and Tinkerbell played a large part in the story. It was dainty, elegant, and whimsical in soft pastels. She was excited to start.

"Birdie, it is six twenty. We spoke about you being at dinner and supervising bathing and bedtime." Lupe said firmly. Birdie looked up; Lupe looked tired.

She rushed over, "Are you feeling alright?"

"Just a headache." Lupe dismissed.

"Let me take care of the brushes, and I will be down in five minutes."

With a nod, Lupe left.

Birdie quickly took care of her tools, closed paint cans, and washed them up. Lupe just did not seem right; she worried. Birdie thought she would insist she go to bed early.

QUINN RYAN
AGE 14

A belt? Birdie had made him a belt. The brown leather wasn't that nice looking, if he had been honest, but it was from her, so he treasured it and would wear it every day anyway.

He wondered if she would come back soon. He missed her laughter and their candid talks. Kiera missed her, too.

Just last week, Kiera had been crying in her bed out of nowhere for her. Or maybe it was because their mother had died six weeks prior, and she missed her, too, as he had. No mom, no Birdie; it was sometimes too much to bear. Both his mom and Birdie were suddenly gone without warning. Birdie would have made the sad time tolerable, Quinn thought. Luckily, Cora was there when he needed to talk.

SAILOR WREN

"Can't catch me."

Sailor called out to Tommy and Lucy as they ran around the shed towards the front of the Carriage House. Lucy was on her heels, running as fast as she could. But then Sailor stopped. There stood a beautiful teenage girl with long dark brown hair, dark brown eyes, a beauty mark on her cheek, and a face full of makeup. Sailor thought she looked like a model. She was that pretty, she thought.

Lucy all but crashed into her, and Tommy tagged Lucy before he noticed the teenager.

"Jazmín?!" Lucy squealed, throwing herself at her.

"Hey, squirt." Jazmín hugged Lucy, then Tommy.

"We didn't know you were coming," Tommy said, surprised.

"Who's the girl?" Jazmín asked in Spanish.

"Sailor, the artist's daughter." He answered back in Spanish. Did they not realize that she knew Spanish, too? Sailor wondered. Lupe raised both her and her mother to speak Spanish. Now that she had mastered Spanish, Sailor was also learning Italian during her summer months.

"Sailor, this is our sister Jazmín. Jazmín, this is Sailor Blythe. Her mom is a famous-." Tommy introduced them.

"As in Birdie Blue Blythe??? Is Birdie Blue here, too? I love her work!" Jazmín said, shocked, looking around.

Sailor smiled shyly. She was used to her mother's fans reacting like this.

"Yes. Birdie was Daddy's and Aunt Kiera's friend growing up. Now we are friends!" Lucy squealed happily.

Jazmín nodded, her teenage 'cool persona' back.

"Does Daddy know you are coming?" Tommy asked.

Sailor could see their father walking up behind the three kids. He looked mad. Sailor took a step back worriedly. She wasn't around dads much, especially angry ones.

"I knew," Quinn said, firmly taking Jazmín's hand. "You come with me. Tommy and Lucy, please stay outside and play more before I call you in for showers; Jazi and I are going to have a nice long talk. Excuse us." He was leading her away as she tried to talk her way out of being in trouble.

Sailor looked scared, but Tommy laughed, surprising Sailor. "She purposefully does stuff to get kicked out of school so she can stay here with us."

Sailor asked, "Why can't she stay?"

"She doesn't listen to Daddy..." Lucy said worriedly.

"It looked like she was listening now. She went with your dad." Sailor said curiously.

"She wants to stay; she'll listen until the house rules get too boring. Then she'll leave. Happens every time." Tommy shrugged.

She'll just leave? Sailor thought that was so strange.

QUINN RYAN
AGE 22

Quinn's life was hectic. He went to school in Florida and found a job listing in Miami for a firm he had been following. He still didn't know how he got the job as a Junior Architect.

He met Sofía, an up-and-coming Spanish actress from Colombia. Sofía hired Quinn's firm to alter her apartment for a larger closet.

The attraction between Sofía and Quinn was instant. Once they finished the job and Sofía was no longer a customer, Quinn asked her out. Three months later, she was pregnant. They decided to marry. Their relationship had been a whirlwind. Passion, sex, her career taking off, his indoor/outdoor loft design making the paper, and somehow, it had become the latest 'it' thing in Miami. All Quinn did was design a fully opening glass wall after he was asked for a way to add an office to an apartment. The apartment, though significant, had no place for an extra room. It did have super high ceilings, so Quinn added a loft. He also designed a terrace with a wall of windows to let light in. The windows recessed into the walls. It got him accolades. His firm gave him a raise and the new title of 'Head Architect.' They married at a Justice of the Peace and had a baby boy three months later. Life was perfect, or so he thought. Of course, life was not entirely perfect. He still dealt with his wild stepdaughter's antics. She was a whole lot at times. So troublesome that Sofía sent her to a private boarding school nearby; even though he disagreed with the decision, she was home once a month, so they saw each other often.

He was thinking about starting his own firm. Getting that business off the ground would be challenging, but Sofía was finally making real money. Luckily, his sister was about to join him after she graduated, so he hoped the business could take off once he took the leap of faith and left his current firm.

To add to the chaos, Sofía was pregnant again. It all happened while he was way too young. Sure, Sofía was a passionate Latina, fiery in bed but also in arguments. He found her hot, even pregnant. They did not see eye to eye on anything else lately other than sex, especially when it was regarding her giving attention to the kids, Jazmín specifically.

He stressed Jazmín needed to be home with two parents, structure, bedtimes, daily love, and consistency. Sofía focused only on finally being able to afford her daughter the best education. But he knew that meant Jazmín was also out of her hair so that she could work more. They had a baby nurse for

Tommy, who should have only stayed for three months but was still living with them.

"Quinn, do I need to go back to school? Tell Mami 'no'. I want to stay with the babies when the new one comes."

"I asked Jazi, but she wants you to go back to school. It's only for a few months then you will be back for Christmas break: you will stay with the baby for a whole three weeks. I will work on her for you, ok?"

Jazmín nodded sadly.

Quinn hugged her, "Sorry. She's very pregnant and easily upset these days. You know she loves you. She wants you to have the best education that she never had."

Jazmín smiled, "I know. You fought hard. I heard." Quinn felt awful hearing that. They purposely went out into the backyard to fight away from the kids. "The things I do for my kids." He laughed, "But her hormones are crazy." She laughed at the silly face he made when he said it. This might have been the most amicable conversation he ever had with Jazmín. Maybe she saw he cared.

BIRDIE BLUE

Shit, Birdie thought. She better clean up before Lupe had to heave herself up the stairs again. She finally set a reminder on her watch so she would be on time going forward.

As Birdie was coming down, she could tell Lupe was surprised not to have to go up and get her.

"Perfect, my doll." She said in Spanish and went back to her room.

Sailor was very talkative, telling a story of what she did today with Quinn's kids. But if truth be told, her mind was on the Nursery. She was in the middle of painting Captain Hook's ship and was debating if she should paint the characters as the Disney movie had so everyone would know it or how she had always seen it in her mind's eye. She kept debating back and forth but always came back to this being a mural and should be her work. Plus, she wanted to paint Sailor's face into Tinkerbell, the nickname she used when people mentioned how tiny she was. She would do it subtly. Maybe she would put Tommy's face on Peter Pan and Lucy's on Wendy! She was so excited by this idea her mind started racing.

"...then Quinn took her to their house. He was not happy."

Birdie felt bad she hadn't been listening as Sailor talked while she showered.

"Oh no," Birdie said dutifully, feeling bad she was pretending to have heard. She promised herself that she would be more present with Sailor.

"Tommy said it was about time. She can be naughty." Sailor said, shutting off the water.

"Well, that is their business," Birdie said, handing the white towel over to her. Lucy did not come across as naughty from what she saw, but every child had their moments, she guessed.

"Dry up. When dressed, call me, and I will blow dry your hair. Dinner should be ready shortly." Birdie looked at her watch; dinner was now. Shoots, Birdie thought. After a quick towel drying, she braided her daughter's wet hair, "We are late; I will dry it after dinner."

"I told you we did not have time to shower before dinner, Mommy." Birdie nodded; she wanted to get back to the pirate ship. She hoped she would have her showered and relaxed in bed after dinner reading so Sailor could fall asleep earlier, allowing her to go back to work. It just kept calling to her.

At dinner, she apologized for being late. Lupe's look was telling; she knew Birdie was trying to rush her time with Sailor to go back to work by seeing her showered already. Birdie felt horrible because she knew Lupe was right. On her first day back with the paintbrush in her hand, she was reverting to old habits. All she heard was one word in Spanish, "Priorities." Birdie could feel her face flush. Only Lupe could make her feel ashamed, like a child.

Cora tried to put food on their dishes, but Birdie stopped her, thankful for the distraction.

"Please sit with us, Ms. Casey and Mrs. Finnley, too. Just having someone cook for us is enough. We can eat together every night while we are here," Birdie said.

Cora looked taken back, "Are you sure?"

"Yes, please; we are not formal people. No need for formal china-"

"That is all we have here, I am afraid, Ms. Blythe." Mrs. Casey said, smiling.

"Alright, but please call me Birdie. Lupe, Birdie, and Sailor," Birdie said, smiling.

"If you call us Cora and Nancy. Nancy is just bringing in Beef Wellington. Let me get two more settings so we can join you." Cora smiled, going into the kitchen.

"Much better," Lupe said, nodding at Birdie.

"I miss my Sailor; shall we watch a movie in your bed tonight, Mamita?" Lupe asked. Sailor had nodded happily.

Birdie smiled. Lupe forgave her. She knew Birdie was anxious to get back to work. "We can watch it earlier since you have showered already. Though mom should blow out your hair first," Lupe said pointedly. Birdie smiled broadly. Lupe would still hold her feet to the fire but work with her. Balance.

Dinner was excellent, and Nancy was especially touched when they asked them to eat with them. "Just like when Sir Oliver was here. All sitting together for meals. Cooking for Sir Oliver had been my full-time job back in the day before I decided to be home more for the youngins."

"I missed Nancy when she left," Cora said sadly.

"I was a mile away." Nancy laughed, "And I cooked here on Saturdays and Sundays for the new cook's days off."

Nancy Finnley

"I missed her cooking more." Cora teased.

"Sisters." Nancy rolled her eyes, teasing. It was clear these two sisters were super close.

All laughed again.

QUINN RYAN

Taking away her credit cards had been an all-out fight. Quinn took the phone, too, as she had Apple Pay on it. Sofía had insisted he do it over the speakerphone.

"All are canceled anyway. Zero money for you; you do not appreciate it," Sofía said madly in Spanish.

"You are so stupid!" Jazmín yelled. Quinn gave her a firm look, and she looked away defiantly, arms crossed, tears held back, barely acknowledging what her mother was saying. Quinn heard Sofía shout at her assistant to have a courier pick up the phone as she was sure he would give it back—probably a dig at him being too lenient.

"School, Sofía. What are we doing about school? She needs to be registered somewhere," Quinn asked her, ignoring it.

"Expelled twice from the top two boarding schools! I may need to find another."

"NO!" Quinn saw the panic on Jazmín's face.

"You were expelled. I cannot send you back, Jazmín." Sofía sighed, defeated.

"Why were you expelled twice?" Quinn asked firmly. Jazmín looked away. Did Quinn see worry in her eyes, or was she just being obnoxious? He wasn't sure since she turned her face away fast.

"Shall I tell him, Jazmín, or will you?" Silence from Jazmín.

"The first school she left four times. FOUR!! They expelled her for it. This time, she left the new school and the country. She joined a friend and their family on their yacht to Cabo. The school frantically searched the property for three days and involved the police. Do you know what this could have done to my career if this had gotten out?! Luckily, the school hushed everyone. You don't deserve a good school, Jazmín. All that money and still no common sense. I should sue the parents; they hadn't even asked my permission!" Sofía said in Spanish angrily to Jazmín.

"You gave it." Jazmín shrugged, smirking now. Quinn noticed Jazmín only spoke in English, probably to annoy her mother, as Sofía now prefers conversations in Spanish.

"I did not!"

"I have it in writing. YOU signed the papers and emailed them." Jazmín laughed.

Quinn could see how it had probably played out in his mind. Jazmín probably said it was for a field trip to Cabo. Jazmín did not tell her mother the entire truth, but it was not a complete lie either. Her mother must have signed the electronic document in a rush, not even reading it between takes. Had the school not called Sofía, Jazmín could still be in Cabo with her friend's family right now. Her mother would not have had a clue she had left school at all. It made him wonder if she had done this before at school. Probably.

"You punish her, Quinn! Punish her good!"

"And how exactly am I to do that?" he all but laughed snidely. "Just taking away credit cards and Jazi's phone, she almost scratched my eyes out."

Quinn saw Jazmín smile.

"She comes to you because she wants you to parent her. This is the third time Jazmín has run away to you, Quinn. She loves you." Sofía said the last three words distinctly in English.

Jazmín looked away, probably not wanting to be caught being vulnerable to Quinn, he guessed.

"She does not listen to me," Quinn repeated.

"Yes, she does, and more importantly, she will. She could get her wish. She can go to the local school and live with her siblings. She can have a normal life if you grant her that. Only you offer what she wants." Sofía sighed, but he could hear her tears. Sofía was acknowledging her daughter's wishes over her own. This was new.

Quinn wanted to laugh. Jazmín never listens to him. She never had, but then he saw Jazmín peer at him from under her lashes. Jazmín had a hopeful face. She looked desperate for someone to keep her, want her, and maybe parent her. Then he thought of Tommy crying that Sofía hadn't cared about him, did not love him, didn't visit him, and Lucy too, more recently. Both kids sobbed in his arms many times. Her hopeful face broke him.

"We will try it for one school year. But there are rules. 'Barbaric' rules. I insist that both you and Jazmín need to sign off on every-" Jazmín had thrown herself at him, hugging him, "You'll let me stay?"

"Lord help me. I have two jobs, two other kids, and a famous artist here. You would need to toe the line, Jazi. I mean it," he all but begged.

"Do I get my phone back?" Jazmín asked instead, hopefully.

"No. You are grounded for being expelled; in your room only. If you break the rules, I will personally fly you back to your mom's set. Let's type up the rules, Sofía READ THEM this time before you sign." he said, aggravated. "Oh, and call a lawyer. I will be her guardian while she stays here, or no deal."

"Please Mami..." Jazmín asked softly.

"OK." Sofía sighed, "I will try to come soon to see the kids."

Quinn no longer believed that and by the look on Jazmín's face, neither did she.

BIRDIE BLUE

Birdie completed two walls already. It was magical and whimsical and precisely as she had imagined it. She was happy with how it was coming out. Perfect for a Nursery for the new owners.

She heard a noise. She turned, and from her angle, she could see two kids whispering, telling each other not to make a sound as they peeked.

Birdie stretched. She needed to take a break, and her right arm and back insisted she do so anyway. So she cleaned up and quietly tippy-toed to the inside of the doorway. She waited as she heard them shuffle closer. Everything echoed up here. It was why she usually wore earbuds; she wanted to tune out the noise around her. Only Birdie had forgotten to charge them last night in her exhaustion. She hadn't gone to bed until one a.m.

Just as they got closer, she jumped out, "Boo!" laughing.

Only Birdie was as startled as they were when she peeked at them. There was a teenage girl with them whom she had never met before. Who was this girl, Birdie thought to herself?

"Oh no, are you going to tell on me?" She demanded of Birdie.

"This is who I told you about, Mommy." Sailor, still laughing, used to her mother's silly jump scares.

"I told you this was a bad idea." Tommy sighed, looking at the older girl and shaking his head.

"She's supposed to be in her room," Lucy said worriedly. "Please don't tell Daddy, please, Birdie," Lucy begged, taking the older girl's hand worriedly.

Birdie had so many questions. Who was she? Why was she in her room? Where was that room? Why not tell Quinn? He had no nieces she knew of other than two-year-old Amanda, so why were they worried about Quinn? It didn't make sense.

"I just wanted to see you work. Don't tell, ok? I am in enough trouble." The girl said, biting her bottom lip worriedly.

"May I ask who I am speaking with?" Birdie smiled. After Lucy's little pleading, she would never tell.

"She's my sister. Jazmín." Lucy said, hugging her sister.

WHAT? Birdie thought, then noticed that Lucy and Jazmín looked very similar. Neither girl looked like Quinn. Only Tommy had. How could Quinn forget to mention there was another child? Had she been here all this time, in her room, being punished?

"I will rush back to my room, but please don't tell on me," Jazmín begged.

Birdie nodded, "Go on."

Jazmín smiled, "I always imagined you as cool as you are. Thanks! I can't wait to tell my friends I met you!" she rushed off.

"Thank you, Birdie, for not telling Daddy. He is very upset that she got A-spelled again." Lucy said sweetly.

"Expelled." Tommy rolled his eyes.

Lucy looked up at Birdie to confirm if her brother was right. Birdie nodded with a kind smile.

"Mommy! Tinkerbell! That looks like me!" Sailor said, peering into the room from the outside. "Peter Pan is Tommy?! Mommy, you made Wendy look like Lucy!" she hugged her mom excitedly.

"What will Jazmín be?" Lucy beamed excitedly.

"Captain Hook," Tommy teased, but he was quite pleased he was on the wall, too, especially as Peter Pan.

All laughed.

"I will need to think about that. Maybe a mermaid. But I need to get to know her better to draw her. When will she be allowed out of her room again?" Birdie whispered to them.

"She keeps getting caught, so never." Tommy laughed, and all giggled.

"Don't you both get along?" Birdie asked him gently.

"Yeah, except when she is mean to Daddy. Then I get mad. She was not nice last night." Tommy said in a huff.

"Maybe she is tired of being in her room. A touch cranky." Birdie suggested.

"She is Tommy. She doesn't like to be in the room all the time." Lucy defended angrily.

"I guess." He nodded. Birdie noticed Tommy was trying to keep an open mind.

At lunch, Birdie asked Cora why Quinn and the kids didn't eat with them. "You are guests. We used to do some dinners together when it was just us. He works hard to do both jobs and raise the kids alone. But when guests come, we do our own thing."

"Would it be too much trouble to cook for so many? I could pay the expenses-"

Cora laughed, "We cover all food expenses. Nancy always tries to cook for him, but he can be stubborn. He wants to do it himself."

"Really? Quinn can cook?!" Birdie asked, shocked. She had no idea how to cook. She had never tried nor needed to with Lupe or a cook around.

"If you call it that..." Nancy teased. "I'm kidding. He has improved a lot these last few months."

Cora laughed, "I can ask him, but he may feel funny about disturbing your dinners."

"Tell them we expect them at every meal." Lupe said, "Quinn is Birdie's friend, and now his children are Sailor's. Wouldn't you like that Sailor?" Lupe asked.

Sailor nodded happily.

"Maybe I can convince him to have dinners or lunches with us, but I know him. He won't accept both meals; trust me." Cora laughed. "I will let him know in the morning. He is helping me clean the dining room chandelier tomorrow."

Birdie smiled. She looked up at the massive crystal chandelier. It looked like a three-person job.

"Cora, he may not want to now," Nancy said enigmatically.

"Sailor told me all about Jazmín, all four of them please. Let him know." Cora and Nancy looked shocked that she knew about Jazmín, Birdie thought.

"...her behavior is sometimes an issue," Cora said delicately.

"In my day, we handled naughtiness differently." Nancy huffed. "All three of my youngins knew to toe the line or else."

"Now, Nancy, Quinn is too soft-hearted." Cora laughed.

Lupe looked at Birdie, smirking. "Maybe Quinn needs help with her too." Lupe offered.

"If you can unspoil me, you can unspoil anyone. I can think of two times Lupe wasn't so soft-hearted..." Birdie teased, and they all laughed.

SAILOR WREN

Sailor was so excited. Quinn invited her and Lupe to the Carriage House to play while Lupe watched the kids. Lupe explained that Quinn needed a sitter while he and Cora took down the hundreds of crystals on the chandelier. Lupe told Sailor how it took hours and hours to take down each one, wash them, make them shiny, and then put them up again.

Her mother was painting the next scene in the Nursery, so she was glad to be with the other kids. Lupe's phone rang, and Sailor heard her answer.

"Do you need anything, Mi hija?" Lupe asked. Sailor knew her mother was on the other end of the line.

"Sure, sure. Ok. How many? Alright, love." Sailor watched Lupe go to Tommy. "Birdie needs pictures of Jazmín."

Tommy led the way to the bedroom. Sailor followed curiously, and so did Lucy.

Sailor saw that Jazmín was lying in bed bored. Her feet were on the wall, and she was filing her fingernails.

"Jazmín? Birdie needs you to take many selfies. Different angles. Here, use my phone." Lupe said, offering the iPhone.

Jazmín's eyes lit up, "Why?" Sailor could see the excitement in Jazmín's eyes.

"Surprise." Lupe smiled. Birdie had asked Tommy, Lucy, and Sailor not to mention their faces on the mural to anyone. She wanted it to be a surprise at the reveal. All had agreed excitedly.

Like a teenager, Sailor saw Jazmín take many selfies, even some silly ones. After about twenty selfies, she gave back the phone.

"Come, kids, let's leave Jazmín now. Your father was very clear. I was to make sure she stayed in here the whole day. If she stayed like she was supposed to, maybe she could be released early." Lupe said, but more towards Jazmín, who huffed but nodded in a pout. She knew Lupe was right. Boy, Sailor thought, Jazmín must have been a very naughty girl because she had been in there two days now.

Lucy, Tommy, and Sailor played Old Maid with Lupe. Sailor was the old maid for the first time, and then Tommy. Lupe made a joke that she was an old maid in real life. At four o'clock, a filthy and tired-looking Quinn returned, thanking Lupe repeatedly. Quinn offered to pay her, which Lupe just laughed at. "What do I need money for? Besides, I enjoyed seeing the kids play together."

"And Jazmín, was she behaved? Did she stay in her room?" Quinn had asked, hopefully.

"Of course. Kids seem to know I do not tolerate nonsense." Lupe said, but Sailor couldn't agree more. As her mother always said, Lupe 'did not play.'

"I should learn your secrets," Quinn said, grumbling, making them smile.

"Say thank you to Ms. Lupe, please. After I shower, we are eating at the main house."

"Yay!!!!" Lucy squealed.

"Even me, Quinn?" Jazmín asked from the bedroom doorway.

"Yes, even you." He sighed.

Jazmín beamed, "Thank you." she said softly.

"Good girl." Lupe said in Spanish, nodding to Jazmín.

"When she wants to be," Quinn said in Spanish, making Jazmín laugh, agreeing. Lupe looked as shocked as Sailor did. Quinn spoke Spanish well, Sailor thought.

QUINN RYAN

After washing everything up, he showered, and they walked over to the main house. No amount of arguing had worked on Cora. He was to do dinners every night together with Birdie and her family. It would be rude to refuse, Cora had argued. To compromise, she also said if he needed to catch up on work, the kids would come some days, and they would give him a plate when he picked them up. If truth be told, he was so relieved. Feeding Lucy and Tommy was one thing, but Jazmín could be finicky.

Quinn smiled at Birdie, who looked freshly showered herself.

"Thank you for inviting us." Quinn had said to Birdie.

"We're just friends having dinner together. Help foster the newer relationships, too," Birdie said, adoringly wiping Sailor's bangs out of her eyes.

"How's the Nursery coming along?" Quinn asked awkwardly, sitting down and putting Lucy's cloth napkin on her lap.

"Great. One more wall, then touch-ups until satisfied. It's still too hot to think about doing the Solarium floors, so I must request the platforms to do the ballroom ceiling." Birdie had said.

"They are high up; how will you do it safely?" Lupe asked, concerned.

"Great question." Birdie laughed. "Especially as I need to step back to check perspective constantly."

"You will probably need to make the entire ballroom one level as if you brought the entire floor up," Quinn said.

"Is that doable?" Birdie asked.

"I've seen it done when they put up intricate ceilings. I even know who to call. Let me get you the number," Quinn offered. He did not want her hurting herself, and he could see her climbing on a ladder to try to paint.

"Yes, please, Quinn." Lupe answered for Birdie, "Safety first."

"Quinn. Please research it for us." Cora said.

Birdie gave him a conspiring look, and both smiled at being babied.

'I have my own Lupe,' he mouthed to her, and they shared a private laugh as everyone tried to figure out why.

"Jazmín, are you done with the naughtiness, Miss?" Cora asked firmly. Quinn wanted to groan. This meal had been the first relaxing one he had since she came. He did not want Jazmín to act out in front of everyone, especially since she had been shockingly behaved.

"Yes, Cora, I'm a good little girl," Jazmín said, bored.

Quinn looked at Jazmín hard, "Do better." He whispered.

"Sorry, but I was behaving, Quinn." Jazmín had pointed out.

BIRDIE BLUE

She called him 'Quinn'? Seemed disrespectful, Birdie thought.

Quinn looked at Birdie. She looked confused. "I am her ex-stepfather legally. But I agreed to guardianship for a year minimum if she behaved."

"Oh." Who would take on a teenager with behavior issues who has two full-time jobs and is a single parent of two small children? Quinn would... only Quinn, she thought.

"She needs a father," Cora said firmly.

"I have one, right Quinn? Like it or not." Jazmín laughed snidely.

Lupe put down her fork loudly and looked right at Jazmín. With a tirade in Spanish, she told Jazmín she was being disrespectful. Jazmín, shockingly, looked down. "Sorry, Quinn. I just... I just want you to want to be my dad sometimes. Not to say 'ex-stepdaughter'..." She said with air quotes, then got up and ran out of the room, about to cry.

All the adults looked at each other, feeling bad. Quinn took off after Jazmín with a quick, "Excuse me."

"I'm sorry, but I cannot tolerate how she speaks to him," Lupe said. Birdie noticed how bad she felt.

"Oh no, she deserved that," Nancy said, annoyed.

"Agreed, I think she needs to hear it from someone who doesn't have preconceived notions about her behavior, and she responds to you, Lupe." Cora said, then she got up and wiped Lucy's eyes, "It's alright; I think we are all starting to understand each other for the first time in a long time. Don't cry, Sweetness."

"She just wants to be with us," Lucy said softly, sniffling.

Birdie felt awful. Lucy was right. Jazmín wanted Quinn to treat her like he did the other kids. He needed to understand that. Birdie was sad for Jazmín, for all of them. If Birdie were honest, she even felt sad for an entirely different reason. She had been so excited he had said 'yes' to them eating dinners together. She wanted to be with her friend too, but both were so busy. This had been her only idea, to see him every day. Was it ruined now? Birdie now worried about whether he would change his mind about eating with them.

Birdie was shocked to see them both come back. Quinn's arm was around Jazmín's shoulder, leading her back to her seat. "Can't ruin this delicious meal with silly tears," he said to all, taking a seat. Then he looked at Jazmín, "Eat, daughter."

All the adults felt their eyes well when they heard that. Quinn was so sweet. He heard her, and Jazmín could not have hidden her smile if she had tried.

After dinner, they all helped carry dishes into the kitchen.

"Thank you for another lovely dinner," Birdie said to Nancy.

"Thank you, it was yummy," Sailor said. Suddenly, all the kids said it, too.

"My, the manners are improving." Cora laughed.

"We can learn a lot from Sailor, right kids? Even me." Quinn teased. Sailor smiled at him. It was the first time she hadn't been wary of him, and Birdie thought he looked relieved.

"Well, I will retire a bit early. I need to go through tomorrow's lesson plans." Lupe said, saying 'goodnight' to all.

"We should get out of everyone's hair, too," Quinn said.

"But Daddy, I need a new book. You said if Jazmín was going to stay, she needed to read too." Lucy pointed out. Jazmín did not look thrilled by that, but she didn't object.

"Shall we all go to the library? Cora, is it OK for them to read any book? Nothing signed, nothing rare they should stay away from?" Birdie asked.

"Not that I know of. But the kids know to treat Sir Oliver's things with care nonetheless, right kids?" Cora asked them.

"Yes, Cora," Sailor said.

"We will, Nana." Tommy and Lucy said.

"Go on then. Help yourself. Quinn, dear, thank you for helping me today. It is just too much work for me alone now."

"Any time, Cora." Birdie watched Quinn kiss Cora goodnight and followed the kids into the library.

As they searched through books excitedly talking amongst themselves, Birdie and Quinn sat next to each other on the small settee.

"Sorry for, uh, before," Birdie said, knowing Lupe probably should not have gotten involved even if she meant well.

"I'm not; that's the most progress we've made in years. I finally know why Jazmín acts as she does with me. And I was a total ass to have said 'ex-stepfather.' I thought that was how she saw me, why she never listened to me." Quinn said, running his hand through his hair. Birdie could see him beating himself up over it. He was a good dad, even if he didn't feel it at the moment.

"You will both come to an understanding. I thought dinner together would be ruined after all that work Nancy and Cora did. I am proud you both came back to the dinner table." Birdie smiled.

"It would have been more awkward any other time if we hadn't. It was best to rip the band-aid off," Quinn sighed.

"Well, I am glad you did." Birdie patted his hand before she realized it. Did she just feel a spark? Birdie panicked.

He looked up at her fast, Birdie thought. Did he feel it, too? She had heard about a spark in movies and thought it was utter bullshit in real life, but this very much happened. She had felt it. Birdie thought Quinn might have felt it, too. She wanted to touch him again to see if it would happen again but didn't dare.

"Daddy, I got two, alright? I promise to bring them back," Lucy said, coming over and climbing on his lap. She settled cozily on Quinn as she showed him her books. Birdie could feel his gaze as if it were burning into her.

"Is one book enough, Quinn?" Jazmín asked, checking out Birdie and Quinn sitting together. She was not sure if she liked how close they sat.

"Sure." Quinn cleared his throat, "Hurry up, kids, we need to take baths, then read a bit before lights out. I have a ton of work to do tonight." Quinn was rambling again, making Birdie smile. Quinn was nervous. Why did his being nervous make her want to smile? Did he like her? Did she like him?! Oh God, I think I like him, Birdie panicked. When had she gotten feelings for him other than as a friend? She needed to talk to Lupe right away. No, she had to stop liking him. Immediately. She did not want to lose her only real friend in years by messing things up by liking him. She had to stay friends only, Birdie thought. She had to NOT like him.

QUINN RYAN

Quinn's phone rang. It was Kiera.

"Hello."

"You're a jerk!" Kiera said to him.

"OK. Why now?" Quinn laughed.

"Not telling me Birdie is there! You always hogged her. We are coming. Jason can't come, but Amanda and I are. So make a place for us."

"House is over-stuffed. I am sure you heard about Jazmín too," Quinn said. Cora must have spoken to Kiera about Birdie being there and Jazmín moving into Lucy's small room. It was bad enough that both girls slept together in the same bed. Luckily both kid's cribs had been converted into full-size beds.

"I did. Stupid and a jerk. Why take that on Quinn? You are too nice to deal with her shit."

"Be quiet, Kiera."

"Tommy can sleep with you; we will take his bed. Ok? Please."

"Or sleep in one of the six spare bedrooms next door." Quinn rolled his eyes.

"No, Quinn, come on... Haven House is too formal; I would be afraid Amanda would ruin something. Also, I would need to constantly help Amanda up and down those massive marble stairs, please, Quinn. She could fall if she tries to do it on her own. I would be a nervous wreck the whole time."

Quinn sighed. She made a valid point and knew exactly how to get him to do what she wanted—as she always had. He knew he was being played; Amanda had visited Haven House to be with Cora many times, but he also knew she must miss him, too.

"Fine. How many days? You and Jazmín better be civil to each other. We are making progress."

"Two days, maybe three max. I can't leave the office that long. Oh, and Ramirez said he wants a vaulted living room ceiling now." She laughed.

"We discussed this many times. He wants an extra bedroom. Zoning laws do not allow for a basement since his house is too close to the canal. Also, he cannot build up, or it will block the neighbor's multi-million-dollar view. He already got a letter from their attorney threatening legal action if he went up anymore. I cannot change the tiny plot of land he purchased," Quinn said, annoyed.

"Then tell him no extra bedroom and a vaulted ceiling or an extra bedroom and no vaulted ceiling. Either way, you need to call him. And I need to know if I should stop designing this bedroom and ordering items."

"Yes, dear," Quinn said sarcastically.

"Coming Friday night. Let me know what he says." Kiera hung up.

With a huff, he dialed his customer. After fifteen minutes of arguing his point, they returned to no vaulted ceilings. He also managed to get a sign-off on the final plans so Kiera could get to work. Her visit was perfect timing because she was about to get busy, as this customer hired her to design it, too, Quinn thought.

Quinn was relieved that this problematic customer was happy and that his portion of this job was complete. He decided to get on to his next project: changing out all the exterior bulbs on Haven House. It sounded like a non-event, but the house was lit like Rockefeller Center. The two pallets had come in three days ago, but with all the Jazmín drama, he hadn't gotten to it yet.

The day had been a long one and it was only two p.m. Cora got permission to add cameras all over the property and to have security drive around the perimeter at night sporadically. The attorneys were already setting up both after a lengthy call with both Cora and Quinn on how they would handle this. He was relieved this was happening, another layer of safety for his kids, for Birdie and Sailor too.

Two hours after changing out the sconces on the first two floors of Haven House, he went to the third floor. Thank God for the balconies on every floor; otherwise, Quinn thought he would have needed to rent a cherry picker to accomplish it.

Quinn was about to go to the fourth floor when he saw a car drive to the gate. His phone buzzed. Anyone who rang the gate buzzer was directed to his phone first. If it was not picked up after a minute of constantly ringing, it went to Cora's phone.

"Can I help you?" Quinn asked.

"Yes, I am here for Birdie. Frank Altman, she is expecting me."

"Hold on, please, as I double-check-" Quinn started to say.

But then he looked down and saw Birdie running out the door towards the road, excitedly waving, "Frank! You made it!" Quinn could hear her shout happily from above. He buzzed Frank in, now irritated.

Frank Altman

'Nothing-worth-mentioning-Frank' looked like an asshole from here, Quinn decided. He was driving his pristine white convertible. It looked like it rolled right off the showroom floor; it was so shiny. Then Quinn thought of his three-year-old Denali, which could fit all of them and was perfect for all the errands he ran for Haven House. It was Black, which meant it was always dusty from driving on the gravel all the time. It sure lacked next to Frank's, Quinn thought to himself bitterly.

When the gate closed after Frank and he opened the car door, Birdie threw herself at him in a big hug. He was average height, though next to Birdie, he seemed tall. He seemed to have a bit of thinning hair but very tan, and dressed to the nines.

Quinn hated this man already.

He watched as Birdie happily pulled him into the house. Quinn angrily started to climb the stairs to the fourth floor—at least so high up he didn't have to run into them together.

BIRDIE BLUE

"Oh, thank you for bringing them, Frank!" Birdie hugged him again.

"Anything for you love. Why did you want these old letters anyway?"

"They are from Sir Oliver. I need inspiration for the Solariums. I have so many ideas. I want them cohesive but not the same design in all four."

"It is ninety-four degrees out there. I cannot imagine how hot it is in the Solariums right now. I hope you paint them at night," Frank said seriously.

"Even at night, it is hot. I need to do that after October, maybe November," Birdie said. Frank was forever worrying about her.

"Just keep rubbing in how long you plan on staying." Frank laughed.

"Please, Frank, don't start. I am working AND making my daughter a priority. Or I stop altogether and be with Sailor until she goes to college."

Frank laughed, "You? Not paint? It is more important than air to you, but fine." Frank agreed, laughing, "You are right; we work too hard. Jason and I are going to Italy anyway this week. That is why I personally rushed these to you—three weeks of seeing Tuscany, Milan, and Venice. I, too, had not had time off like this in years. It will do us both good, Birdie. You with your daughter painting at your leisure, me with my man."

"That explains the self-tanner." Birdie teased him, though Birdie thought he looked like a completely different person; he was too tan. "I am so happy for you both. Where are you staying? I will send you both-"

"Nice try, but I won't be reachable," Frank laughed jokingly. "Now, before I head back to the airport, show me what you have done and what you plan to do."

They toured the Nursery; Frank loved it. He spotted Sailor right away. Then Birdie showed him the bench, screen, and artwork she needed to touch up. Birdie laughed when he commented on the crabs. He said it looked as if the bench had an STD. Birdie roared, knowing she could never look at this bench again without laughing.

They left the art wing and went to the ballroom. He, too, had concerns about her working on the very high ceilings.

"The caretaker is right; the entire floor needs a giant scaffolding. Let me know by tomorrow if I need to order it," Frank said seriously.

"Quinn already has a company name. He is normally an architect from Miami. He works with people like this. He has contacts."

Frank looked at Birdie oddly.

"You know an awful lot about the caretaker, Birdie," Frank said slyly.

"We were friends when I was here as a child. He temporarily took over when his dad died," Birdie said, trying not to flush at the way Frank was knowingly looking at her.

"Well, this is new..." Frank teased, stepping back. He looked pretty pleased.

"What?"

"Birdie has a crush. In all these years working together, you had me believing you were actually asexual." Frank laughed. Birdie knew Frank was using a term she jokingly used all the time to describe herself, but that he could see it just from her saying his name had Birdie panicking; she could not let anyone else know, especially Quinn.

"Stop being a brat; we are only friends," Birdie said adamantly.

"Mmmm-hmmm, someone doth protest too much." Frank laughed and then finally got to work, which relieved Birdie.

"Tell me your ideas," Frank said.

They spoke for almost two hours. Birdie told him her suggestions for the Solariums.

"How about east, west, north, south? Or the four seasons? Do they have four seasons here?" Birdie asked him, chewing on her lip as she thought.

"Snippets of Haven House? Magnolia trees out front, gardens out back, the staircase, and..." She gave up; it would not look good on the floor, and Frank was not one to fake liking an idea. He hated it.

"Or... he was a lover of art. I could do famous artworks like Monet's Water Lilies in one Solarium and Van Gogh's Starry Night in another. Or Sunflower Fields? What do you think? Monet seems to go with this house. He doesn't own one in his collection but mentioned wanting to one day."

"I like it. Art for sure." Frank said, "But the right art. Starry Night might look weird on the floor. I like water lilies, and I like sunflower fields. Do not paint until we have the right four selected."

This was where Frank was brilliant and why he was her business partner. She was 'the talent,' but he was an art connoisseur. He had so many connections in the art world. He was also fantastic at handling the business manusia, legal contracts, protecting her work, managing her schedule, getting press, and so on—stuff Birdie couldn't do if she tried.

He got twenty-five percent of all her bookings, and sometimes she thought he deserved more. But when not focusing on Birdie, he also curated for an art gallery he and Jason bought with a friend a year ago. The gallery was his 'retirement plan,' as he always jokingly called it. It was starting to get recognition, too, and making some serious money. So, going away now while his partner ran the gallery was perfect timing.

"I need to go. Good luck with the ceiling. Be safe. I insist. If it feels shaky in any way, tell me. I will call it off. My two shih tzu's depend on you being alive to eat."

Birdie laughed; he was such a brat, she thought.

"Thank you for not mentioning the hair plugs. My scalp is red and killing me, so I may have added too much self-tanner to distract from the redness. Jason hasn't stopped laughing. He said I look like an Oompa Loompa, and it better scrub off before we leave, or he is taking someone else." Birdie cracked up. Only Frank!

Frank and Jason had been together for five years now. Frank was forever worrying about the age difference. Frank was fifty-five. Jason was thirty-nine. The sixteen-year age difference made him 'feel like a pedophile,' as he often joked. But Birdie always thought they were so perfect together. With a big kiss, he left.

QUINN RYAN

Kiera was coming tomorrow. He rushed around the Carriage House washing sheets, mop-steaming the floors, and doing laundry. She loved to give him shit for not always being neat, and he wasn't about to give her ammunition. Thankfully, Lupe stole the two little kids to go to a movie. Jazmín had been invited, but when she heard it was a cartoon, she declined somewhat rudely. However, one look at Lupe's face made her rephrase it quickly with a 'No thank you, Lupe.' Quinn hadn't needed to say a word. Thank God.

He needed to clean the bathroom, but Jazmín had been in there for forty minutes. After several minutes of debating, Quinn asked, "Jazi, I need to clean the bathroom. Will you be much longer?" He didn't want to embarrass her but thought it odd that she had been there so long.

He heard her sniffle.

"Everything, ok?" Quinn asked, now concerned.

"I need… um, I need to talk to a girl, not you. I need my phone."

"Jazmín, Mom had the courier pick up the phone until you apologized for calling her 'stupid,' remember? She knew I would give it back to you. Want my phone to call?"

A wail.

"Jazi, you can call Mom on my phone," he said through the door.

"I don't want to talk to her!!!" Jazmín screamed at the top of her lungs. Scaring Quinn, even through the door, it was so loud and abrupt.

"Want to talk to me?" Quinn groaned the moment the words left his mouth. Why would she want to talk to him, Quinn thought. He quickly said, "Call whoever. Open the door and take the phone."

"I can't; I don't have anyone's phone number memorized!" She screamed angrily.

He knew Cora and Nancy were food shopping. Lupe was out with the kids to the movies. He hated to do it, but he called Birdie as he heard Jazmín sob again, no longer conversing with him.

"Hello!" Birdie said, chipper as usual.

"Sorry to disturb you."

"I was taking a break, walking in the gardens for inspiration. What's up?"

Quinn told her Jazmín was locked in the bathroom crying but didn't know what to do to help her. He felt embarrassed as he was now guessing the issue. Birdie must think Quinn was a moron father, Quinn thought. But he was more worried about Jazmín to care.

"Quinn, do not talk to her from outside the bathroom door, ok? Leave her. I will be over in two minutes. I may be kicking you out of the house." She hung up.

Kicking me out of my own house- oh. It was confirmed. He had no idea how to teach her anything about her menstrual cycle. He knew females got them. Wore pads or tampons. He knew when Sofía had it, they didn't have sex—end of knowing anything on the subject. Even growing up, Kiera was very private about it.

Now his mind started to race; who would teach Lucy? Quinn was beginning to doubt his ability to be a single father at the moment. He thought he had been doing an alright job; the kids weren't little assholes. Quinn had handled no sleep, tantrums, kids bickering, and at times felt like he was drowning to do it all, like every other single parent. But when the girls needed a female, what would he do? Especially, Jazmín. She and Kiera did not always get along; Jazmín would never confide in her. Sofía, if he could get her on the line, would be useless as Jazmín and Sofía barely spoke these days. Quinn could feel himself all but panicking when Birdie knocked on the door while sticking her head in, "It's me."

Quinn never wanted to hug her more in his life. Birdie came in carrying a small toiletry bag. All he could do was point to the bathroom door as she laughed. "Breathe, Quinn. I see you finally got a clue. You are excused. Be ready to drive her to a drug store to get all the toiletries she needs. Have chocolate handy. If you don't have any, buy her that too. Trust me."

Quinn was confused. Why were they talking about chocolate at a time like this?

"That's not enough... stuff?" Quinn pointed to her bag.

Birdie lost it; she was all but bent over laughing so hard. She's having fun at my expense, Quinn thought, annoyed.

"Out, Dufus. Then you both are getting a course in menstrual cycles. Then I think I better take both of you shopping. In the immortal words of Quinn Ryan Callahan, we are 'ripping off the band-aid' today." Birdie laughed, going to the door as he took off fast.

How would he be able to look at both of them in the face without feeling awkward when he saw them again?

BIRDIE BLUE

Quinn was so damn cute in how uncomfortable he looked, Birdie laughed to herself. She went to the bathroom door, "It's Birdie. Sounds like you got your period, honey. Can I talk you through it?"

After ten minutes of speaking through the door, Jazmín asked her to get her clothes so she could shower. Going into the girl's room, which was super cute, she got her sweats, underwear, and socks. Jazmín was still showering. She put the clothes and pad on the pile in front of the door.

"I will be in the living room. I left your clothes here." Birdie called out loudly.

"Thank you," Jazmín called back.

Birdie looked around the clean Carriage House. It had a large kitchen with a table for them to eat and an even larger living room. Birdie thought he was pretty neat for a bachelor. She decided to call him.

"She's showering. Yes, she got her period. She's good. Get ready to go shopping." Birdie laughed into the phone.

"Thank you. I wasn't prepared for this. I will have a plan for Lucy."

"She will have Jazmín, Kiera, YOU as you will be taught everything today."

"I don't want to embarrass her."

"You are her everyday parent now, too bad. You will need to know what to buy in the future and what she likes. Take pictures of it and save it to your phone."

"Oh, yes, you are right. I just did not know what to do, you know? She wouldn't tell me why she was crying, but I had a feeling."

"Girls are usually excited for their first one and know what they will do when it finally comes. She was NOT prepared. She did not have pads, and she was worried you would not want to keep her if you got freaked out."

"She said that?" Quinn sounded shocked. Birdie wanted to kick herself for not using more couth.

"Um… yeah." Birdie and Jazmín had quite a long talk, some about Quinn. With the door closed, Jazmín felt free to say what was on her mind.

"I must tell her I am keeping my word about the year minimum. Unless she takes off, that was a deal breaker, and she knew it. We signed papers."

"How very formal of you. Have you tried talking to her?" Birdie asked sarcastically.

"Ouch."

"I'm sorry, but you deserve it. Talk to her. One thing I can see is that she loves you."

"Are we talking about the same girl-"

"Shut up." Birdie laughed, "She does. And you know it. So what's your next move? She wants you to be her father like she felt you were when Tommy was a baby."

Silence. Quinn must have been either taking it all in or shocked into silence again. After a long pause, he spoke, "She does?"

"I think so. Let's start with her calling you 'Quinn.' When we spoke, she accidentally said 'Dad' when speaking about you. She corrected herself fast, but I heard it."

"She stopped when we divorced." he all but whispered. Birdie noticed that Quinn sounded hurt over this.

Birdie heard the door open, and she looked up and saw Jazmín come out. Her cheeks flushed at seeing Birdie for the first time.

"Time to go shopping!" Birdie told both with a smile. Jazmín bashfully smiled broader.

"Get in here, Quinn," Birdie said into the phone. Then Birdie looked at Jazmín, "Before we shop, I need to educate Dad on how to have a female teenager here." Birdie smiled. "This is normal in life; you can teach him how to be ready for Lucy one day. Alright? Think of yourself as a teacher."

Jazmín giggled as she also heard Quinn groan.

"Smooth, Birdie, real smooth. I am coming back. But I will also pray the Earth opens up and swallows me whole first. Let's see if I am lucky." He rambled again nervously, then hung up. Birdie laughed. Jazmín looked intrigued.

"He's more nervous about doing something wrong than you are of him knowing. Be patient with him. He loves you." Birdie said softly.

Jazmín's eyes welled, "Alright." she whispered.

The door opened. With a big sigh, he went straight to Jazmín and hugged her, "Sorry, I did not know what to do. You seem to like Birdie, so I thought she could help." he said fast, into the top of her head.

"That was perfect, Quinn," Jazmín said shyly.

"About that..."

Later that day, Birdie and Sailor were washing up for dinner when a knock sounded on the door. "Come in."

It was Lupe, "Hello, my loves. I was wondering if you would mind if I skipped dinner. That movie was so loud I have a headache."

"Want anything? Tylenol? I can bring your food up."

"Nothing, just quiet."

"OK, I will bring up tea and toast later."

"No need. I will come down when ready." With kisses to both, she left them.

Sailor looked worried, "She gets a lot of headaches now, Mommy."

Then it hit her, Sailor was right. She needed to call Lupe's doctor tomorrow.

QUINN RYAN
AGE 24

The baby nurse was still there. Almost three years later. The baby nurse did not want to be chasing toddlers around. She wanted to leave and be with infants again. Kiera, who all but lived with them now, suggested daycare.

He bought a building and started a firm thanks to a Sir Oliver loan and was finally able to start paying him back sooner than he had imagined. Sofía was going to many award shows, film premieres, commercials, etc. Fights were happening too often about her not being home anymore. He didn't just want her around to help with the kids, though he always imagined they would do it together like normal couples; he wanted a partner, too. He missed her warm body next to him at night. He missed the sex if he were honest. Lately, he fell asleep too tired to even care about his needs.

When it came down to it, his kids needed a mother. Luckily, daycare and Kiera were of great help when he felt as if he were drowning. Starting a business was hard enough. Being a needlessly single parent when he was married to two, sometimes three kids, so young was overwhelming.

Her narcissism was getting worse and worse, as well, only thinking of her career and not of her family's needs at all. He didn't want her help at this point; he wanted his kids to know their mother. He wanted his wife, only the wife he first married.

It felt as if she barely came home.

Then, the final nail in the coffin, she bought a house in Spain without telling him. He found out accidentally by signing off on tax paperwork with his accountant. She was done. He called her about it and left a long, scathing voicemail. The next day, he got a text with one sentence. She wanted a divorce—a text.

SAILOR WREN
AGE 6

"Why do we keep coming here?" Sailor asked Lupe.

"Just a check-up, Mamita. Grown-ups do this all the time. Sorry, I have to keep bringing you every month. You can use your tablet, and I have fruit and snacks in the bag. Remember, these are our secret adventures." Lupe whispered to her with a wink.

Sailor giggled; she liked secret adventures. Lupe always got her ice cream afterward if she behaved. She wanted ice cream, so she was very quiet as the doctor spoke to Lupe.

He showed her some transparent black and white papers in front of a light. It looked like a raisin was stuck in the picture's head. What a silly doctor, Sailor giggled. Lupe didn't seem to find it funny, though; she just nodded quietly.

"How long?" is all she heard Lupe ask.

"We aren't at that point yet. There is a possibility it won't grow. Let's stay hopeful." The doctor said, staying positive.

Just as Sailor was about to open a snack, Lupe approached her. "Ice cream time!" Lupe announced with a big smile. Sailor noticed how much Lupe liked coming here; she always left smiling brightly, and her eyes shone a lot.

BIRDIE BLUE

Sailor was helping Nancy bake cookies for dessert in the kitchen. Nancy seemed to miss cooking with little kids as much as Sailor looked thrilled by the prospect. The excited squeal when Birdie said 'yes' to her making cookies made Birdie so happy. Note to self: Birdie thought, bake cookies with Sailor. Though Birdie had never been in charge of such a task, she had to learn how. She would YouTube how if she had to, whatever it took.

The Nursery was done. Birdie wanted to do a reveal after dinner tonight. She had hoped Quinn would be alright with using the three kid's likenesses. Should she have asked first? Birdie was suddenly nervous.

She could always paint over it if he were opposed to it, she thought. Not that she thought he really would ask that of her. After all, his kid's faces would be immortalized, and she was a sought-after artist and friend.

Nonetheless, she wanted to surprise them all, and she meant well. So, she locked the door, as she had been doing for the last two days, so no one could peek.

Perfect timing, too, as she needed to give her body a break; she knew she was getting stiff. When that happened, Birdie needed to stop painting for a day or two. Maybe a long soak in the tub tonight would help. She grabbed the envelopes Frank brought to her and took a walk.

She had treasured these letters and tucked them into a white silk bag she got in China from her father long ago. It was wrapped in a beautiful, soft red ribbon. Birdie had wanted these letters because she remembered him talking about his favorite artists in one of them. She remembered how she always asked a question or two in every letter, so he had to write back. Sometimes, she struggled to come up with some ideas for questions and begged Lupe for help. He had been so sweet and always made sure to answer everyone. She recalled he answered her once, naming artists and which works he wanted to add to his collection one day. That was the letter she was searching for specifically.

While in his office, she opened the bag and pulled out the treasured letters. She felt as if he was there with her somehow, sitting in his desk chair, knowing that this was most likely the spot where he wrote to her. She knew he used a fountain pen to communicate with her because every once in a while, there would be the slightest blot of ink on the letters.

She looked at the desk before her; right next to the bluebird picture she made long ago was a fountain pen in its holder next to an empty inkwell. She picked up the pen and felt a tear come down her face. She missed writing to him. More importantly, she missed getting letters back from him.

She read many letters until she found the one she was looking for.

Dearest Birdie,

What a great question! Too many artists immediately come to mind, as I studied Art History in Eton, where I went to school back in England.

I would have to say I love the Impressionists best. Claude Monet: I could just fall into a relaxing trance whenever I see his works. If you have not seen them for yourself, please do so post haste. You must tell me what you think of these works by him: Water Lilies, The Poppy Field near Argenteuil, The Parc Montceau, Bridge over a Pond of Water Lilies, to name a mere few. But I also love Edgar Degas. He used to paint dancers. Check out these fine art pieces and let me know if you like them too: The Ballet Class, Ballet Rehearsal, Three Dancers, etc.

Marie Bracquemond, Armand Guillaumin, and, oh, there are too many artists in this amazing Impressionist Movement for me to name. All of them! Please do write back to me and tell me which ones you like best. I am sure there are library books that can show you them. However, you live not too far from the greatest museums in this country. I do hope you visit them shortly.

Your second question was about whether I have received any new artwork lately. I have, but I am afraid I do not know if I like it or not. It is by an artist named Andy Warhol. I wanted a Marilyn Monroe painting, but instead, I could only bid on soup cans! Silly soup cans. Oh, thank God my former teachers could not see that in my collection. I haven't stopped laughing, just thinking of their reaction had they known.

Well, I hope you are still painting. Send my regards to your father and Lupe. I cannot wait to see your name in lights.

Birdie could barely read as her eyes were welling with tears. He had always said that her 'name would be in lights one day.' She hadn't understood the meaning at the time; she just knew he thought she was special.

Oh, how he loved art as she had, Birdie thought. She smiled, wiping at a stray tear that fell, thinking of how she made Lupe take her to The Metropolitan Museum of Art that week. Luckily, they lived in New York City and had access to the best museums, just as Sir Oliver had said. Birdie had excitedly made a list of artists and artwork to check off beforehand. Afraid to risk losing her precious letter. She wanted to find as many Sir Oliver recommendations as possible. Luckily, they had a large gallery on the Impressionist Movement, and Birdie was happy to see what Sir Oliver had talked about for herself.

Her favorite was a tie between two pictures by Monet: The Artist's Garden at Giverny due to all the colors and Woman with a Parasol. She too, loved his work best of all the Impressionists that were featured there. She hadn't much cared for the dancers by Degas for some reason, not that she had told him that.

Monet would be perfect, Birdie thought. They had both loved Monet. That was cohesive for all four Solariums. Different pictures by Monet, making sure that they were full of color and would match Haven House's elegance. And he never actually got a Monet, so it would be like she was finishing his collection. Could she replicate a Monet? That was a whole other question, Birdie wondered. But she used to copy famous artworks for fun with her father, so she probably could. Yes, it had to be Monet. She would tell Frank her idea. But somehow, it felt as if Sir Oliver was smiling down on her, pleased with her decision.

A sob escaped her after she thought of the irony that she was finally back at Haven House, but Sir Oliver was no longer there. Forever gone to her, never to have conversations again, Birdie wept. Sir Oliver was this incredibly kind man who thought so highly of her, and she missed him. To think they had zero blood relation had an enormous age difference, yet none of it mattered. They had a soul connection. He always made her feel special, like gold.

It was rare to find someone who always made you feel like gold. Who thinks the sun shines on you, the Earth revolves around you, and is now gone forever? Birdie put the papers down and finally let herself have a good cry. She hadn't allowed herself to mourn over losing him since she had first found out. A part of her would be missing forever.

She gathered herself, wiped her eyes, and packed her precious letters, leaving his office. She needed to find Sailor. Sailor was her gold. She needed to show it to Sailor daily, as Sir Oliver had shown it to her. She promised herself to do that.

QUINN RYAN
AGE 12

Quinn was stunned. He just found out Birdie would be leaving the next morning. Kiera ran off, sobbing as their mother chased after her. He just sat there numb as his father had his arm around his shoulder, trying to comfort him.

"Why so soon?" is all Quinn could get out huskily.

"An important person in the White House called her father for a job-"

"Sir Oliver is important. He's a knight! Don't you remember, Dad? He and two others saved the Queen's cousin at school when he was fifteen. Remember? The person rowing her was having a heart attack. Sir Oliver said he stood up and fell over, tipping the rowboat over. He and two friends swam out and saved the Queen's cousin and the man. He's important, too!" Quinn rambled. Quinn could feel his eyes start to water.

"Breathe, son. He is important too, I agree. But he has worked for Sir Oliver already, right? It is time for Mr. Blythe to go to the next job. Understand? I know you will miss her. You both had a special friendship. You will stay in touch."

Quinn nodded when his father suggested he get ready for dinner. He started to walk back to the Carriage House. He had so many thoughts going on in his head. How short the visit was. How fast they had become friends. Would she remember them? Him? In some weird way, it felt as if he had a beautiful butterfly finally land on his finger. He was gentle, gazing at it, interacting with it with joy and wonder, and watching everything the butterfly did. To see something so majestic and free up close is an opportunity not given to many. But then, when you got comfortable and trusted each other that no harm would come to the other, a wind came, and it flew away. Quinn thought he could feel his butterfly flying away; only maybe a bird was a better analogy. His bird was flying away, and he knew he could do nothing to stop it. South Carolina and New York were two different worlds, and he could not just get in a car to visit quickly. She was as good as gone.

He ran to the shed instead of going to the Carriage House as he should. He climbed the rafters and didn't leave until his father found him three hours later.

SAILOR WREN

"We can show everyone today?!" Sailor squealed.

"No. YOU can show everyone today." Her mother smiled.

Sailor threw herself at her mother, "I love you, Mommy! Thank you so much!" Sailor took off.

Before anyone could sit down, Sailor announced the unveiling of the Nursery to all.

"I meant after dinner, silly girl." Her mother laughed.

During the entire meal, everyone talked about rushing to see the Nursery.

"What about Lupe, Mommy? Wake her?"

"No, we will let her sleep. She can see it tomorrow." But her mother's eyes looked worried when she said it.

After dinner, Sailor was so excited that Cora insisted they leave the dishes on the table to see the Nursery. The kids rushed upstairs in their excitement. The adults took an extra minute to climb the many stairs. Sailor noticed that the door was still locked. It's a good thing, too; it looked like Jazmín tried to go into it first.

Birdie unlocked the door, turned on the light, and they all went in. Sailor could hear the adult's gasp. Then, excited squeals from Tommy and Lucy. Sailor wanted to hug her mother for making her new friends so happy.

"Peter Pan looks like Tommy!" Quinn said, shocked. Quinn looked at her mom with awe, smiling. "Thank you, Birdie. Your putting the kid's faces in the painting means a lot to us."

"Look at Wendy, Daddy, look!" Lucy squealed.

"You are Wendy!" Quinn laughed. Sailor was quite pleased by their reactions.

Then, full-on laughter from Tommy. Sailor saw him pointing at Captain Hook, laughing hard. It was Quinn's face. Her mother made Quinn be Captain Hook? Sailor was laughing, too.

"You are going to get it for that one, Birdie," Quinn laughed but honored just the same. Her mother giggled.

All were talking at the same time, looking at the three walls, backs to the wall with the door.

"Unbelievable. Truly a gift." Cora said, hugging her mother.

Nancy was wiping tears, "Whichever baby gets this room is the luckiest little kid in the world."

Then Sailor noticed Jazmín. She was quiet; she looked sad. Sailor went to her and took her hand, surprising Jazmín.

"Turn around," Sailor told her.

Jazmín turned slowly, as she hadn't realized the wall behind her was also painted; she was the leading mermaid. Her mermaid was the only one entirely out of the water. And the face looked exactly like the flirty selfie she did. Jazmín could feel her eyes well. Then Jazmín felt Quinn come over and put his arm around her shoulders. "How she captured the impish side of you so perfectly, I will never know." he teased into her ear.

"Yea, yea, Captain Hook." Sailor saw Jazmín try to tease him back but Sailor could see she was touched to be added.

"Daddy Hook to you, or I make you walk the plank."

"Nana! Auntie Nancy, look, you are mermaids too!" And then they all burst out laughing.

"I might have stayed up too late and got delirious." Her mother laughed."I can change it if you all hate it."

"No, it's great. Oh! There's Lupe as Mrs. Darling." Cora laughed.

"Smee is Sir Oliver!" Tommy said, having seen many pictures of him. Cora and Nancy's eyes watered.

"Masterpiece. Sir Oliver would have been so tickled by this." Cora said happily.

"And where are you?" Sailor saw her mother jump when Quinn said that into her ear.

"A mermaid, just under the water... that's my fin." her mother tried to tease, but she whispered it so softly, she wondered if she heard it correctly.

"Not fair, Birdie, not fair." Quinn laughed.

BIRDIE BLUE

Birdie went to sleep happy last night. They loved it. Even her adding Quinn as Captain Hook at the last second went well. Birdie just kept thinking of the kids laughing at it. She needed to take a break, though, as her arm hurt, and her back was spasming a lot now from overdoing it. She had a terrible time sleeping due to the pain. She also kept thinking about Lupe; she just didn't seem right.

She went to Lupe's room. She was folding laundry. She watched her; something looked off. Then she realized her left hand was bunched in a fist of sorts. She used it to smooth the clothes on the bed, but she mainly used her right hand to fold them. When did this start? How had she not noticed this before? Birdie could feel herself panicking.

"What's going on?"

"Just folding laundry. Good morning to you, too." Lupe laughed.

"Good morning. No, I mean, what is going on with you? Your headaches?"

"I am getting old. That is why I am asking you to step up with Sailor." Lupe laughed dismissively.

"Bullshit." It came out before Birdie even realized it. She never spoke that way to Lupe. Ever.

The Spanish dressing down came swiftly, but Birdie ignored it; it didn't even matter to her. She was worried.

"I want us to go to see your doctor today."

"I don't have a doctor in South Carolina," Lupe said quickly.

"I will rent a private jet, and we can see your doctor in New York today." Birdie rephrased back just as fast, annoyed.

"Aye, Mi hija, enough. It's just headaches." Lupe dismissed.

"I noticed you doing most of your stuff with your right hand. Is your left arm numb? Should we see a cardiologist? Maybe we should visit the local hospital for a check-up and run some tests."

"Birdie, ya! No more of this talk. Go work!"

"I can't, my back is spasming." Suddenly, Lupe looked concerned. She rushed over, "Let me put the liniment on you-"

"Oh, OK. So you can worry about me, but I cannot worry about you?" Birdie asked angrily. Lupe glared at her, "You are not too old, miss—enough of this subject. I am fine. Go soak in a tub and cool down before you get yourself in real trouble." Lupe pointed angrily to the door.

"I'm calling your doctor," Birdie said, pulling out her phone.

"Go ahead. You have never heard of HIPAA laws; even if I had a paper cut, they could not tell you without my consent," Lupe said angrily.

"Then I want to be your healthcare proxy."

"My sister is my healthcare proxy." Lupe dismissed.

"She is older than you, Lupe. It should be me." Birdie felt hurt over that. Didn't Lupe trust her? Hadn't she always referred to her as her daughter'? She loved Lupe. She couldn't be in better hands with all that Birdie could afford and not her elderly sister in Mexico. She was in MEXICO, for goodness sake! What good was she going to do so far away in case of an emergency?

"I will think about it. I will not discuss this subject further." Again, Lupe dismissed Birdie.

"Fine!" Birdie stormed out.

They did not fight often. She could only think of the occasional back-talking Birdie did while a tween and then, of course, the big fight—a real fight—much worse than this—the reason she had run away.

Birdie hated to think back to it but did. She had been sixteen, full of herself, thinking she knew all the answers to life as only a teenager could. She had been tired of being left behind by her father so much. She had been resentful. Birdie insisted on attending a New York Academy of Arts summer program. Birdie's portfolio alone would have gotten her in at an early age, but her name assured it. They were all but tripping over themselves to have her be a student. Looking back, what better advertising did the school have than to say she trained there? She got a free scholarship if she gave them the right to advertise her attendance. She agreed without asking permission.

Lupe fought it, saying she was not of age to attend or sign for herself. Birdie, not to be dissuaded, called her father in London. She sold him on the idea, and he agreed it would be a fantastic learning opportunity. He re-signed the letter, and she was accepted. Lupe was not happy; she worried she could not protect Birdie there, but she needed freedom from Lupe. It's not like she had friends to go to the mall with, go to each other's houses, and hang out like normal kids. She just had Lupe twenty-four hours a day. Lupe was extra strict during her teenage years, almost stifling. Constantly talking about college and S.A.T. when she knew her career already started. Her work under 'Birdie Blue' was already selling. Birdie, being the know-it-all teenager then, felt learning Math 101 and English Literature 101 would not help her paint, so why bother?

Birdie had been tired of not having friends, too. Why didn't Lupe or her father insist she do things to make some? Birdie missed Quinn and Kiera so badly. It was like she finally had a taste of something, and it was ripped away from her, and she craved it. Needed it. She had often asked to return to Haven House and was told 'not now' or 'We'll see.' She was tired of waiting. Why couldn't she and Lupe visit alone without her father? She was tired of listening to 'not now.' She decided to start making decisions for herself. After all, she was all but an adult, Birdie thought.

New York Academy of Arts was filled with many interesting, artsy people trying to outdo each other. Birdie was so happy to be amongst the other artists. She imagined art sessions together, sharing techniques. She had visions of making friends, but her talent somehow segregated her.

They hated that their work was under par next to hers. The teachers fawned over her, using her work as an example even when she begged them not to. She just wanted to be a normal student. Be unrecognizable. She didn't even put much effort into some assignments, yet the teachers still loved them. The students shunned her. She learned a valuable lesson. One that Lupe had been trying to shield her from. Kids could be cruel. The other students were jealous of her. The staff wanted from her. Sign this, sign that, take a picture, etc. It was not fun.

Not until one day when someone came over and sat by her. The only person who would talk to her as a human, not as a famous person. Just someone who wanted to be her friend. That person's name was Steve Richards.

They partnered on a project and worked many hours together. Steve was amazing at shading in any media they used but loved charcoal best, so they worked well together. They started eating together every day, and Birdie was happy. He wasn't Quinn, but he was a friend. Then he came over to finish a project. Lupe hovered but saw they were working and went about her business.

Steve

Birdie never saw the kiss coming. And she liked it. She liked it enough to keep doing it whenever Lupe left the room. That was the start of many 'project sessions.'

QUINN RYAN

He saw Birdie storm out the back door as he edged the garden walls. He stopped. She was furious. Has he ever seen her mad before? Quinn wondered. She paced, then she went where she would be alone. Quinn decided she needed a friend. He followed her.

He caught up and took her hand, and she stopped, startled. She had tears in her eyes and looked panicked. What was going on, Quinn wondered. She looked equally mad and sad. Why?

He pulled her into a hug, dirty and all, and held her tight. He continued to do so until the sobbing stopped. They were alone under the trees, away from being seen, so he felt comfortable doing so until she managed to mutter "Thanks.", wiping her eyes.

"What's going on?" Quinn asked gently, wiping another tear that had just fallen.

"Lupe..." She sobbed.

"What? What happened to Lupe?" Quinn asked, now concerned himself.

Birdie told all. He listened quietly.

"She can't leave me, too. First, my mother, whom I don't even have a single memory of, then Sir Oliver, then my father months later... I cannot lose her, too." Birdie started to cry again.

"Maybe you are assuming a bit...?" Quinn asked gently.

"No. I know something is wrong. I just know."

"She spends every Saturday with Nancy. Let me find out if she knows anything. Alright?"

A big hug; Quinn knew by her response he had said the right thing.

"Thank you, Quinn. You have always been my best friend— you and Kiera." she sniffed. Her eyes looked extra blue, her nose red, and her cheeks pink. Quinn thought she looked as beautiful as ever.

Quinn guessed she could tell he was looking at her because she tried to laugh, "I must be a mess."

"Beautiful as ever." He just thought those words. Thought. They were not supposed to come out of his mouth! Quinn could feel his face flush. He was all but panicked.

"Only you, Quinn. You always saw beauty in everything." With that, she reached up and went to kiss his cheek, but without thinking, he turned his head, and they kissed on the lips.

Both pulled away, shocked. Quinn was mortified; he could not control himself. Birdie looked confused and intrigued, as if her lips wanted more, but she was surprised, too.

"I... I'm sorry." Quinn said, fumbling over his words.

After a moment's pause, she finally said, "I'm not." With a slow smile, she took a deep breath.

She's not?! Quinn could not comprehend the words she was saying.

"You aren't?" Quinn whispered.

"Nope. It got me to stop worrying about Lupe for a moment. Got me to stop panicking and clear my head a bit." she smiled at him. She then sobered. "I know she is older than me. I know she will most likely die before me. I am a grown-up who must deal with it when it happens." She paused before looking up, "I just do not know what I will do. She has always been there; Lupe always helped me parent Sailor. Lupe still parents me.

Please, Quinn, get Nancy to find out. I beg of you. I need to be mentally ready, not like with the others."

With that, she turned and walked back to the house.

As she walked away, Quinn exhaled. He had kissed Birdie, and every childhood fantasy became a reality. Then he looked down. He still held the trimmer in one hand. He looked at his clothes, covered in stems, weeds, and dirt. He probably smelled of sweat and lawn. Quinn groaned. He finally kissed her, and he was a hot, stinky mess. Great.

SAILER WREN

Jazmín was sitting in the children's room's reading nook. She lazily drew something in a sketchbook while Lucy and Tommy played Legos. When Sailor got bored of Legos, she went over to Jazmín.

"You like to draw too?" Sailor asked excitedly.

Jazmín smiled up at her. "I like to design dresses and stuff. Nothing like your mother. Or even half as good as you, but I like it."

"Can I see?" Sailor asked. Jazmín looked conflicted. "Only if you don't make fun of me, okay? I am still new to this."

Sailor nodded, shocked that a girl as big as Jazmín would worry about her opinion.

Sailor looked at the red dress with its high slit on one side, ruffled along the slit with one shoulder. Though the drawing could be better, the design was super straightforward. "Wow. I love the dress. When you get older, can you make me one?"

Jazmín, already defensive, was ready to snap back but was stunned into silence.

"Do you like to sew it too, or will you have someone create your designs for you?" Sailor asked.

"I want to learn how to sew, but I don't know how to."

"Yet." Sailor said, "You learn, practice, and keep practicing until you are comfortable. I did that with drawing." Sailor said, sitting next to her.

"You... really like it? I think I draw badly." Jazmín pouted.

Sailor thought it wasn't that bad. She knew what Jazmín wanted to portray. "Drawings get better with practice, too. But I knew what you designed. I like it. Can you make me one when I am older?" Sailor re-asked her sincerely.

Jazmín, biting her bottom lip nervously, "Sure."

"Goodie!"

Then she went over to Lupe, sitting by the door, eyes closed, hands in prayer.

"Lupe, are you ok?"

"Just praying, love, just praying. God always hears your prayers; remember that." With a kiss to Sailor's head, "Go play with your friends."

Sailor thought that was the nicest sentence she ever heard. She had friends now.

BIRDIE BLUE

Birdie had to force herself to walk normally back to the house, but she secretly was freaked out. Quinn kissed her. Or she kissed him just as he moved his head. It didn't matter which, THEY KISSED! And it was everything she hoped it would be. When had she hoped that Birdie wondered?

Once inside, she rushed up the two flights of stairs to the children's room, where she got Sailor each day. As she walked in, she saw Lupe sitting by the door. Birdie stopped, now feeling ashamed. She had been rude and disrespectful earlier. She had been so mad, so scared, so-

"Come here," Lupe said to her, standing up. Birdie hesitantly did so, feeling truly bad now.

Lupe pulled her into a hug, "It will be ok. Alright? Trust in God in all matters. You can talk to my doctor. I will add your name."

Birdie nodded, feeling tears come again. Relief. She hugged Lupe hard.

"No, Mi hija, no crying," Lupe said in Spanish, wiping her tears before looking up and seeing all four kids look concerned.

"We are ok," Lupe assured them, smiling brightly. Eyes shining.

"I'm sorry, Lupe. Please do not shield me. I will go through anything with you. But I need to know. I need to prepare myself if anything were to happen to you. No secrets. Promise me." Birdie begged, still crying.

Lupe nodded resigned.

Dinner that night was quiet. Lupe had her mind on things; Quinn hadn't uttered a word. Birdie was overwhelmed by the highs and lows of the day. Jazmín was trying hard to keep the conversation going. She was talking about maybe taking a sewing class when the kids went to their swimming class. Quinn nodded, "We can look into it." he said quietly.

"Dessert, anyone?" Cora asked, trying to break the unusual silence.

"I need to do work at home. Can the kids take it to go?" Quinn asked.

QUINN RYAN

Quinn had felt so happy, then he walked into dinner and saw her looking... what? Not happy, that was what! Was she regretting kissing him—well, lips bumping into each other? Whatever it was, could she be regretful now? Probably. Quinn berated himself. He knew better. What was wrong with him even to hope she felt the same thing he had?

He had to leave. Quinn needed space away from her to think clearly. When he got overwhelmed, he needed to be alone to process things. All he kept hearing over and over in his mind was that he lost her. He had lost her twice. There would be no third time.

BIRDIE BLUE

He left early. Why? He hadn't meant to kiss her on the lips; she knew that. Not that Birdie would consider that fact when it felt so right, like finding the perfect set of lips to match hers.

She didn't know what to do. It was nine-fifteen at night, and she wanted to see him for some reason. Talk to him. See for herself his rejection clearly, not flushed from a kiss. Not awkwardly in front of their families. But alone.

She decided to call him. Only, what would she say? That she had enjoyed the kiss? Let's do it again sometime. Birdie laughed at the thought. And again. And again. She giggled to herself.

No, she had to be serious. Their kids were friends now. They needed to be respectful now that they worked together, too. If Birdie and Quinn had not been careful, Cora, Nancy, and Lupe would have seen the tension. She had to call him. They needed to act normal in front of others. She needed to tell Quinn that before she lost her nerve. So she called him.

It rang three times before he answered. Did he not want to speak to her?

"Hello?" he sounded winded.

"Everything ok?" Birdie asked, completely thrown for a loop.

"Uh, yes. I was washing the bathrooms. I have company coming tomorrow, staying with me for a few days."

"Oh."

"Did you, uh, need me?"

Did Birdie need him? Yes, very much. But she couldn't say it out loud.

"I ... you left in a rush. I wanted to see if you were alright." Birdie could not remember the reason she finally decided on when she called. His answering like that made her mind go blank.

"I needed to do a lot of work and clean." He said quietly.

"Sure... alright. Goodnight." Birdie chickened out.

"Goodnight."

She hung up. That was an utter disaster; Birdie shook her head.

Birdie couldn't fall asleep. Who was coming? A girlfriend? Staying with his kids? No way. Had to be the ex-wife. Sofía had to be coming. Oh my God, maybe he wanted a relationship with her again for the kids. Jazmín was here now. Maybe they want to be a family again.

Birdie felt sick. She had never actually googled Sofía before, as she did not know Quinn's real last name or about her at all before she came. So Birdie, suddenly curious, picked up her phone. Birdie felt ridiculous. It was midnight, and she was lying in bed in the dark like a psycho, reading everything there was on the internet about Sofía like a stalker. Two hours later, if she trusted the press, she got a very different picture of her. She was portrayed as a selfless mother who gave her kids everything. She put their needs first, getting them the best education and having them out of the limelight with Quinn for their safety.

Then she looked at the pictures of them. She and Quinn are in front of step-and-repeats, holding hands. Thousands of pictures of her alone, posing. She looked up 'Sofía and family' next. Right away, a picture of her, Quinn, and Tommy as a newborn on the cover of People Magazine en Español. She and Tommy on the cover of Latina Magazine with her adoringly looking at Tommy as if he were her greatest joy ever. A kissing picture between Quinn and her on the cover of Luxury Latin America Magazine. She threw her phone onto the bed. They had once loved each other. By looking at the pictures, he had loved her. Did he still have feelings for her?

QUINN RYAN

Quinn was relieved Kiera was coming. It would be a good distraction from the kiss. After Kiera's call, he decided to surprise Birdie with the news of Kiera coming, his kids too. Only Cora and Nancy knew. They promised not to say a word.

So when Kiera texted, saying, 'Two minutes away,' Quinn smiled. He missed her. They got along well for most of their lives. They both went through so much by each other's side, such as mourning Birdie's leaving and then their mother's death. They relied on each other a lot as kids. Their relationship improved more as adults while working and living together in the same building in Miami.

Quinn walked over to the gate and waited. Then he had an idea. He called Birdie.

"Hey," she answered with a smile. "Do you need the kids? We are just playing by the pond in the back." Quinn smiled. She had told him earlier that she needed a few days' break for her back and arm. Birdie had pushed herself too hard without taking breaks as she normally did. So, she asked the kids to hang out with her that day. They even planned a picnic earlier. He would have joined them if he hadn't had a deadline for a client.

"Someone is here to see you. Can you come to the gate? Sorry, I need to take this important call." He hung up, chuckling. He owed her for making him Captain Hook, he laughed. Then Quinn cursed; Kiera would never let him live that down. He groaned that he would have to bribe Birdie to paint her and Amanda somewhere, or she would be relentless.

He could see a car coming. It was a rental and not her usual crossover vehicle. This car was gray. She could see him and beeped, excitedly waving her hand out of the window. They have missed each other since he moved back. He called her as he stood there. "Stay in the car once inside the gate. Birdie, nor the kids know. We are surprising all of them. I will open the gate now. Ok, I see them. Pull in and stop."

"Who's here, Dad?" Tommy called out, coming closer.

"Someone for Birdie," Quinn called back.

Birdie looked confused as she came walking over. However, she stopped several feet away. Quinn could tell she did not recognize the car. Then it dawned on him: she probably assumed the paparazzi had found her. Quinn saw Birdie grabbing Sailor's hand, standing in front of her protectively.

"Quinn, I need a name, and we should never open the gate until we know-" Kiera stepped out of the car, opening the back seat.

Kiera Callahan Summers

"Quinn, this could be dangerous. Please get a name—" Quinn felt bad. He hadn't realized how she would panic. Being married to Sofía, he understood the worry. He was so mad that he hadn't considered it before surprising her.

Kiera pulled Amanda out and set her on the ground.

"UNC!" she called out and ran to Quinn as fast as her little legs could. But Quinn watched Birdie, and realization crept over her face. Birdie fell to her knees, tears forming. "Kiera?" she asked.

Kiera ran over and hugged her, both crying like dummies. Quinn, though, was so happy to see them together again as he scooped up Amanda.

Kiera wiped Birdie's eyes, "I missed you!" she exclaimed, "Come meet Amanda. I need to meet Sailor."

Quinn was so happy to see everyone hugging each other. Kiera even went over to a quiet Jazmín, "Come here, niece. This time, stay, please."

Jazmín smiled broadly, her face showed her relief. "I'm trying to." She said. Quinn smiled. Kiera was not one to normally hold her tongue, but she was giving Jazmín another chance.

Then Kiera came over and hugged Quinn. "I may stay longer," she laughed. Then she took Birdie's hand, and they did not stop talking as they walked to the house. Old friends back together again.

"There's my girl!" Cora called out, happily hugging Kiera before lifting Amanda and kissing her face. "My little doll. Nana missed you. Come, everyone. I already have a room for you next to Birdie so that you can catch up. I put child gates on it. I took out everything fragile," Cora said.

Kiera looked at Quinn, even though he looked shocked himself.

"Um, Cora, she was going to stay with me…" Quinn said, feeling bad that she had gone to so much trouble.

"Where? Jazmín doesn't even have her own bed now." Cora stated with a dismissive laugh.

"Tommy was going to sleep with Quinn, but sure, I will stay here." Kiera smiled. Both Quinn and Kiera usually just did what Cora wanted, he thought. It was a respect thing for them. Even when their mother was alive, she played a big role in their growing up. Their mom was sick a lot before she finally died of heart disease, so Cora watched them often at the main house. Neither Quinn nor Kiera would purposely upset her.

"I even put a pack-n-play for her like last time. She is safe." Cora beamed, happy to have them all at Haven House again.

"I was just worried about the stairs."

"You just wanted to bug your brother, miss." Cora laughed knowingly.

"That too," Kiera laughed. "She will be okay. Thank you, Cora." Kiera kissed her. Cora looked beyond happy to have them there again.

Quinn saw Nancy run in. "Are they here? I made her favorite-Kiera! Mandy-girl!" Nancy hugged them both so tight. "All the babes where they belong. Sir Oliver would be so happy. The house is full again." Nancy teared up a bit.

SAILOR WREN

Sailor saw so many people. They all sat around the table, every seat was taken at the large table, laughing, telling story after story about when her mother was there last.

"How about when you handed me a frog? You made me close my eyes and open my hands. I never jumped so high!" Her mother laughed.

"You mean, you never screamed so much. You all but jumped into my arms." Quinn laughed.

"I told you I would get you to hold a frog one day." Kiera laughed. Sailor liked Kiera instantly. She was fun, silly, and very expressive when she spoke. Amanda liked Sailor, though. The two-year-old kept reaching for her hair, "Pe-teee." Sailor looked at Kiera for an idea of what she was saying.

"She likes your blonde hair," Kiera said, smiling. "No more touching Sailor's hair now. Should we move her away?" Kiera asked Sailor worriedly, pulling the highchair closer to her.

"It's ok." Sailor smiled. The toddler was sweet. Now, she was offering her a half-eaten cookie.

"Oh boy. She really likes you, Sailor. She never shares desserts." Kiera laughed, "She takes after her mother."

Quinn lost it, nodding as everyone else laughed.

With dinner and dessert done and all the dishes taken into the kitchen, the kids helped bring Kiera's stuff upstairs, and Quinn took up the heavy luggage. Quinn said it was Lucy's bath time, and Birdie looked at Sailor, too. With kisses and promises to spend the whole day tomorrow, they all left.

BIRDIE BLUE

After Sailor was put to bed at nine p.m., she showered, put on pajamas, and left her room. She walked next door to Kiera's room. She felt weird about entering someone's room without an invitation, but she kept telling herself friends did that. And she needed to talk to a friend—about life, maybe about Quinn. However, she kept reminding herself that this was Quinn's sister, so she probably wouldn't touch on that topic.

"Knock, knock," she whispered.

"Come in. You can tap dance on her bed; she won't wake," Kiera said, smiling while unpacking the toddler's items. She looked freshly showered in a long t-shirt-style pajama, and Kiera looked as if she could feel her awkwardness." Sit," she pointed to the bed.

"Need help?"

"Nope. I do, however, need you to relax. Alright? Just me, Kiera, 'the tag-along' who always followed you both on every one of your adventures." Kiera laughed.

"You were never a tag-along friend," Birdie said softly. Birdie felt sad she might have felt like that for even a second. "You were my friend, my only female friend."

Kiera laughed, "How could that be? We orbited you like you were the sun itself. I am sure every other friend did the same."

Birdie looked up at her, shocked.

"Birdie, you always had this… something. Not just being a famous kid. Or a highly admired artist. We just all wanted to be with you. We cried for weeks when you left."

Birdie sat there in shock. Had they missed her too?

"We had to search the whole estate to find Quinn the night we found out. It was sprung on us that you were leaving early the next morning. An urgent job came up for your father or something." Kiera came over and sat next to her. Kiera grabbed her hand. "We didn't even get to say 'goodbye' to each other properly. Get your address. Finally, a year later, we thought of asking Sir Oliver for your father's information, and when we told him why, he gave us your address. We were so stupid." Kiera laughed. "Though we weren't always the best at writing to you or doing it faithfully, so sorry for that. Then, one day, they just started being returned."

Birdie looked surprised. She had gotten a few post cards, mainly saying they missed her or asking when she was coming back. Oh, her father was commissioned in California to paint the main wall of a movie studio with all the famous actors the studio filmed over the decades. It had taken months and months as they kept adding other artists they forgot about and did not want to insult. In total, it had taken nine months. But they had come back. Maybe the mail was not forwarded when they sent it. Birdie wasn't sure.

Silence. Birdie just looked at their hands. Comfortable. Kiera's was tanner and daintier, while her strong-looking, drier hands from years of paint remover both clutched together. A thing Birdie always did was notice the subtle details in things so that she could paint them. She looked up at Kiera, smiling. All Birdie could think was how much she missed holding a friend's hand. Confiding in someone.

"I need you to tell me everything." Kiera laughed, "And I will, too."

Birdie and Kiera spoke on every subject, even topics she was uncomfortable discussing.

"But what happened to make you leave?" Kiera finally asked. At her insistence, both were now under Kiera's covers. It felt nice; they hadn't done that before.

"We got caught kissing outside of school by Lupe, like kissing-kissing. His hands roaming, seriously kissing. She forbade us to see each other. Wanted to pull me out of the school, saying I was learning so many fresh things and that I was talking back a lot. She desperately wanted to blame it on the school. I think she missed me, and I had always confided in her before; I think I hurt her by not telling her. You know?"

Kiera nodded sadly. "She always loved you."

"I know. I was just rebellious."

"Then?"

"She told me I was done there. That Steve was out of my life effective immediately." Birdie said, looking down. "So I called him and told him what she said. We agreed to meet that night at three am. We thought we were in love. I packed some of my things, too stupid to pack money or food. And I left."

"It was all over the papers," Kiera said.

"I know. We were already in Oklahoma by the time my father allowed it to be released. And they only used "B.B." as my name. Steve told me. We had taken a Greyhound bus with the money he had. We stayed at his parent's cousin's summer house. It was small but a safe place for us. Only they had no idea we were there. It was their hunting house. They had food stocked there in the cupboards and a ton of fish and meat in the freezer. We felt like Romeo and Juliet. There was no television, no radio even. We just drew and hung out and never left for two months. I lost my virginity there. I did not know that I got pregnant at first. After another month, we ran out of food. He went to get some. He was worried because he only had $107 left. It wouldn't last long. He came back saying my face was on every tabloid, newspaper, etc. He brought food and a pregnancy test after I wouldn't stop throwing up. He panicked when it was positive. I don't think it hit me for days, you know, the gravity of the situation we put ourselves in at such a young age. I wasn't seventeen yet." Birdie looked away.

"Then he started to act odd; he would start fighting with me for days over nothing. I couldn't understand why he was cranky. We had our world there. Safe, away from everyone, we could do as we pleased. It was strange how he changed overnight. Three weeks later, he went to get more food. He barely looked me in the eye as he left. Told me he would call me at noon to ask what lunch I wanted from fast food. He did not call or come back. I was in a sheer panic that he had been caught, arrested, or worse, hurt. Afraid to leave knowing my face was on every paper. I had to stay hiding... Two days later, he called me at the house and told me he couldn't do it anymore. He wasn't ready to be a father. He was home, back at school. That he would find a way to pay for an abortion, but to get one. I cried incessantly. I stayed, not sure what to do. Finally, I called Lupe." Birdie could feel her eyes welling.

Kiera hugged her tightly.

"I wanted to be independent, an adult making my own decisions. I wanted to decide my life alone, but I never needed her more. I did not think of Lupe's or my father's feelings even once. They had been needlessly worried for months, wondering if I was alive and all because I was a stupid kid who thought I knew everything. Who thought I was an adult? And still... They took me back. My dad was not happy with me and did not talk to me for days until Lupe realized I looked different. I had been wearing this big bulky sweater, hiding the pregnancy at first like a dummy. She surprised me one day by demanding to see my stomach. Asking if I was pregnant. Then I confessed, sobbing."

Birdie wiped at her eyes.

Kiera hugged her again, "Must have been so scary."

"They loved me even through that. They accepted the pregnancy, which was too late to abort, not that I ever wanted to, but I overheard the doctor talking to both my father and Lupe outside my examination room about 'options,' as he called it. Lupe said she would raise the baby if I did not want to. I heard her tell my father and the doctor. So I opened the door and said, 'This is my baby, and I am raising it.' All nodded. Never questioned it once. He didn't ask more than who the father was and if he wanted a role in the baby's life. I told them he wanted me to abort it and left me there alone without food or money. They looked ready to murder him, but then my father looked at me. Deeply. 'This is your baby now and only your baby. We will help in any way, but he lost all his rights to it.' And I felt the same way. It was my baby and only my baby. They knew I was serious. Though they were probably panicking, I would run away again if they didn't concede. Regardless, they were there for me every step of the way once they found out. Father canceled shows and commissions, and Lupe was in the delivery room with me. Keeping Sailor was the best decision I ever made."

Kiera wiped at her tears; Birdie noticed.

"You always did things big Birdie." Kiera laughed, trying to lighten the moment.

"And you? You are twenty-three with a two-year-old. You did things young, too."

"Quinn, too." Kiera laughed. "But I have been dating Jason since tenth grade. He went to med school to be an orthopedist. We got married at twenty, but I was already pregnant too." Kiera whispered. "I was two months pregnant when we went to Las Vegas and got married by Elvis."

"Only you, Kiera. You are bigger than me any day of the week." Birdie laughed.

"I never told Cora or Quinn, but they suspected. Quinn couldn't talk. They got pregnant before marriage, too. And Jason had been part of my life for so long that no one made a big deal of it. They like him, too. I can't wait for you both to meet. He wants to move up here. Miami is getting so expensive; he wants Amanda to have a more relaxed upbringing like we did."

"Will you move?"

"If Quinn stays, yes. I want Amanda to grow up around family, and Jason's family is here too. I can do my work from anywhere. Have stylists be my eyes, or just work from here. I will miss the restaurants, though." Kiera laughed.

"Only you, Kiera. Maybe go back and forth?"

"Once she starts preschool, she needs to be settled. I don't want to break it to Quinn, though."

"Do you run the business now?"

"No, he runs it. He has staff that are there every day. I tend to do more interior design than he does; he is amazing at structural design. We found our niches, though I got trained to do both." Kiera yawned sleepily. "I can see he is so happy here. The kids are safe behind these gates. Sofía's fans can be a lot. So as soon as you are done painting and Sir Oliver's estate settled, he will need to think about the next steps."

Birdie nodded. It did feel safe here. She hadn't realized it. She felt free.

SAILOR WREN

Amanda was so cute, Sailor thought. She followed Sailor everywhere. Lucy seemed jealous at first, but Cora assured her she just liked to meet new people. The wink Cora gave Sailor made her want to giggle. Cora's look agreed that Amanda was enamored with her.

"Swim lessons today, kids, get changed, please," Quinn said.

Sailor looked up sadly.

"Just one hour. I think Lupe said you had work to do." Quinn said, seeing Sailor's face.

"I don't want to work today." Sailor pouted.

"They will be back. Want to draw instead?" Sailor's mother asked.

Sailor nodded.

"Let's break the news to Lupe."

Sailor and her mom both got sketchbooks and colored pencils and went to Sailor's room. Her mother opened the French Doors next to the desk and they walked onto the porch as she said, "I have been dying to sketch this view." Sailor beamed; she had too.

It was fun to have both look at the same image and see what they produced. Sailor looked at her mother, busy shading using a dark green colored pencil. Sailor smiled to herself; she really loved her mom. She knew her mom should be resting and yet here she was with her.

"I love you, Mommy," Sailor said.

She saw her mother put down the pencil. She leaned over, shoulder touching Sailor's head, "And I love you. You were the best thing that ever happened to me."

Sailor felt her eyes well a bit as she smiled broadly.

Sailor felt a tear escaping. Her mother put down the sketchbook, pulling Sailor into a hug, "Why the tears?"

"I'm just happy." Sailor shrugged.

"Because we are together more?"

Sailor could only nod.

"I'm sorry, Sailor. I didn't mean to not be around so much. I am trying to fix it. If I am doing it again, please tell me you want to spend time with me." Her mother said it so seriously she nodded again.

"Never doubt my love or your importance in my life. You are the most precious thing I have in my life."

"More than Lupe?"

"She's very precious to me, too, but yes. You are more important than anyone in my life."

Sailor beamed, she leaned back into her mom's chest happily. That's all she ever wanted to hear. Her mom was right; Haven House was magical.

BIRDIE BLUE

It was four in the morning. Birdie could not sleep. She had been tossing and turning for hours. The gardens were lit up so beautifully at night that she washed her face, brushed her teeth, and decided to take a walk.

Birdie could only think of wanting to get back to painting, but Kiera was here, and her back still needed a day or two more. It was just as well; Birdie thought she needed to wait for the platform to come anyway.

It was warm out. Cicadas were making their usual noise, the flowers casting weird shapes from the lighting on the floor.

"Birdie?"

Birdie gasped and turned around. Quinn.

"Why are you up?" He smiled. He, too, looked tired.

She felt funny; she was in her pajamas. Luckily, nothing too scanty.

"Couldn't sleep. You?"

He shrugged. Why, Birdie wondered.

"Quinn...?"

"I sometimes wake up too early." He said and she knew instantly it was a lie. Something was on his mind.

"How about I make us some coffee?" Quinn asked instead.

Birdie smiled, "Sounds great." She followed him to the Carriage House.

"Fair warning, I left work all over the table." He said.

"Good. I need to see what you do." Birdie laughed.

As he tried to clean up, Birdie stopped him. "Show me your work, Quinn."

She hadn't meant to whisper his name like that. Or touch his hand. However, she was enjoying feeling the warm skin on hers. She asked many questions, made suggestions that he seemed to like and she kept staring as he made coffee. He excused himself and knew he went to wash up; she smiled. Glad she did so before going out, she laughed to herself. It was bad enough to still be in pajamas, no bra.

He came out and poured them both coffee. "Milk, cream, sugar?"

"A touch of cream, one sugar, please." She smiled up at him, "You are talented, Quinn." She meant every word, too. He truly had an eye for design. She was proud that he was so good at his job.

He smiled bashfully and rolled up the plans he had been working on. Putting it aside.

"Walk the grounds often in the middle of the night?" She teased him.

"Sometimes, but only in summer." He smiled.

"What's worrying you?" She asked knowingly.

He shrugged.

"Talk, Quinn," Birdie said softly.

"Thinking about the business back in Miami. How I should handle that. I might want to stay a bit longer. The kids like it here. I love it here. I should have made a decision last year." Quinn finally admitted. He exhaled. It was as if he said it out loud for the first time.

"Have you spoken to Kiera?"

The look of dread on his face made her sad. He looked petrified to tell her.

"She is thinking of moving here too... but I never said anything. Jason's family is here, and you are here now. She wants a home base for Amanda."

"Why didn't she tell me?" Quinn asked, stunned. "She loves Miami, the restaurants, the entertainment... Are you sure you heard her correctly?"

"Like I first asked, have you spoken to Kiera?" Birdie smiled.

Quinn took her hand and squeezed, "Thanks. I will. I think I want to sell the business or move it. But... What if I cannot make a living here? Miami has money. Like crazy money."

"We are surrounded by mansions. I think there is money here, too." She laughed, stating the obvious.

He smiled broadly. "I never thought of that." He laughed.

Birdie could still feel his hand holding hers, neither pulling apart.

"Please don't tell Kiera that I told you, Quinn."

"I would never. Either I sell it, or I staff it and manage it from here. But I think I want to stay here. Thank you for helping me realize that. I can even rent out my two-floor home. It's beautiful; it should get a great price. Maybe Kiera can, too. Instead of me taking the third floor and her taking the second, we cut it in half and have two floors each. Both have views of the city; neither of us will disturb the other that way. My kids would not bother her if Lucy decided to tap dance..." Birdie wanted to laugh. He was rambling. He was nervous. Maybe he realized they were still holding hands.

"Quinn?"

He gulped, "Yes?"

"What about a relationship? Would you be leaving anyone in Miami?"

He pulled away, sitting up, taking a sip of coffee.

Why did he pull away? Birdie was so mad at herself for asking that last question. Why did she ask? She berated herself.

...Because she had to know.

QUINN RYAN

It was like she threw cold water on his face. She had Frank, so she was asking if he had someone, too. He did not. Wanted nothing to do with the female population after Sofía. The peace had been so nice; it was addicting. Then Birdie came, and it all changed. He wanted her. Wanted to kiss her, hold her; he wanted her in every way. In ways that have been dormant in his body for way too long. The wanting was keeping him up at night.

"Quinn, talk."

"There is no one." He said quietly.

Birdie looked at him. She didn't believe him; he could tell by her face.

"Quinn, you miss Sofía?"

Quinn burst out laughing, startled by that question. "No."

"You must miss intimacy."

He blushed as she did, "Yes. But it has to be with someone I want to be with. Not just anyone."

"And who is that?" She leaned in, curious.

"Someone I can't have." Then he got up and brought both empty mugs to the sink if only to gather himself. Mask what he was feeling. Thinking it was one thing, saying the words out loud gutted him. He could never have Birdie, and he loved her forever.

"Fight for her." Birdie came over, "If you love her, don't stop fighting for her."

Did she know she was talking about herself? Quinn wondered. She had her hand on his arm, and he turned, and they were face to face.

"She's taken." He whispered, looking down into her eyes. He looked at her lips, wanting to kiss them again. He couldn't; those lips were for someone else, Quinn had to remind himself. They were Frank's.

"Oh." Birdie stepped away, "Sorry."

"Not as much as I am," he murmured so quietly he hadn't known if he said it out loud.

"I better get back. Sailor will wake soon." Birdie said, though it probably was still too early. "Talk to Kiera today, alright? Settle that once and for all. I'll hang with the kids. Lupe is off." With a squeeze of his hand, she left quietly.

BIRDIE BLUE

Birdie felt her eyes sting with tears and made it out of his house fast. Luckily, he hadn't seen them. He loved someone. He could not move on, even though she was taken. She felt sad for him. She felt sadder for herself. She never thought of loving someone again. Trusting that that person wouldn't shatter her heart again, this time for good. But Quinn... she would have tried it again with someone like Quinn. No, that wasn't correct, not like Quinn, with only Quinn. She would have tried love again with Quinn. Birdie could have trusted him with her, her daughter, Lupe, her art, her everything. She knew this with all her heart. But the timing was just not right. And there was a good chance it never would be.

SAILER WREN

Sailor was in her glory. Her mother and all the kids were going on a walk to see how many bluebirds they could find. Her mother was trying to keep them busy as Quinn and Kiera spoke alone about 'something important.' They found seven bluebirds before they could even leave the porch. The other kids were arguing, trying to find the next one.

"There's one." Lucy giggled. She pointed to a wooden carved picture of a bluebird on the porch.

"Real birds dummy," Tommy said, rolling his eyes.

"Daddy said no calling names!" Lucy said, "Right, Jazmín?"

Jazmín nodded, "Apologize or I'll tell." Jazmín said, carrying Amanda.

"You think you are so cool because Daddy said to listen to you while he and Aunt Kiera talked." Tommy accused mad.

Jazmín smiled, "Yes, I do."

"Hey, now. Let's get back to counting birds." Her mother said fast.

"I don't want to now!" Lucy pouted. Arms crossed, mad at her brother.

"Me neither then," Tommy said, though Sailor could see his eyes well up. He looked worried, Sailor thought. She liked Tommy best. He was always sweet, but since Jazmín came, he has been a bit cranky towards Lucy.

"I'm telling," Jazmín said, laughing. "You are going to be in big trouble."

"No!" Tommy said, panicked now.

Sailor looked from one to another. Poor Tommy.

Sailor noticed her mother looked nervous, as if she didn't know what to do.

"Please, everyone, calm-" Her mother tried to say, but Quinn and Kiera were walking over. Both had smiles on their faces, and Quinn had his arm over Kiera's shoulder.

"UNC!" Amanda tried hard to get out of Jazmín's hands, who was trying hard not to drop her as she set her down fast. Amanda took off towards Quinn, running as fast as she could. She was screaming, "Unc, hold!" Over and over.

Now, all three kids were fighting as Sailor just watched, a bit fascinated. Did they fight a lot? She hadn't seen them argue in all these days.

"Daddy, Tommy called me a 'dummy'!" Lucy said angrily.

All turned around, Sailor saw Quinn's smile fade. He handed Amanda over to Kiera after kissing the toddler's cheek.

Sailor looked up at her mom and saw her apologize to the adults. "Sorry, Quinn, things went south fast," Her mother said; she looked embarrassed.

He shook his head, "No, I'm sorry."

Then he looked at the kids. "Go to your rooms. I will be there soon. You, too, Jazmín, sit on the couch. We will talk first."

Did Sailor need to go to her room, too? She was worried. Kiera winked at her, and Sailor smiled. She felt relieved. Sailor grabbed her mother's hand anyway for confirmation that she didn't need to go too. Her mother pulled her close even if her face looked worried.

Jazmín argued with Quinn. She was not happy. "Why me? I was in charge. Tommy was-"

"But I didn't-" Tommy started to say.

"Now." Quinn cut all off. He said it quietly, but they stopped bickering instantly, and all three went. Lucy was pouting, Tommy sniffling, and Jazmín stomping mad, leading the way.

Quinn looked at her mother, "Sorry they didn't listen to you. I thought if I gave her responsibility it would help. So much for that idea." He sighed.

"Please don't be mad at them," Her mother said awkwardly.

"Please, Quinn," Sailor said before she realized she had spoken to him. Kiera smiled at her. "Tommy didn't mean to say it," Sailor said worriedly.

Quinn looked down at Sailor, smiling, "It's alright, Sailor. Tommy and Lucy rarely fight, but when Jazmín comes, they fight a bit more than usual. Lucy loves Tommy until her big sister comes. Then, he feels lonely because Lucy always wants to be with her and not him. The girls have a special relationship, but sometimes he misses her and feels forgotten." He said patiently. He then added, "But they have to listen to adults. That is non-negotiable. Mom looked like she wasn't being listened to. It was not acceptable since she was doing me a favor. Understand? So now they have a time out."

Sailor nodded. It made sense what he said. Tommy and Lucy were always together until Jazmín came. Then, the girls were always together. Sailor hadn't noticed it before, but Quinn was right.

"Quinn, I'm really sorry..." her mother said again.

"Don't be. Let me go." Quinn took off towards his house.

Kiera and her mom looked at each other.

"We are thinking of moving the business headquarters here. We will turn our bottom floor into three offices, and rent them out. Airbnb the two apartments or rent them too. Bring in crazy income that way. I need to call Jason. Can she stay with you and Sailor for five more minutes?" Kiera asked her mom.

"You trust me?! Even after that?"

Kiera laughed, "Birdie, stop worrying. We are all winging this parenting job. And it takes a good month for those three to find a groove. Jazmín normally comes in like a wrecking ball, but I noticed she matured a lot this time." Kiera beamed, Amanda had kicked and kicked until she was set down and was smiling up at Sailor, holding her hands up.

"Sorry, she wants you to carry her, Sailor. No, Mandy, you are too heavy." Kiera said fast.

Amanda pouted, holding her arms up insistently.

"Can I try?" Sailor asked curiously. She never held a baby before. Sailor saw her mother and Kiera smile. "Sure! But if she is too heavy, just set her down."

Sailor lifted her. She was a little heavy, but the wet kiss Amanda gave her made her so happy. This is what having a little sister would be like, she thought.

Kiera pulled her phone out of her back pocket and excitedly went to the garden.

"She's sweet, right?" Her mother asked, looking at the cute toddler leaning her face on Sailor's cheek.

Sailor nodded at her mother, "I always wanted a little sister."

BIRDIE BLUE

Such a simple statement. Something Birdie could never give her daughter. Birdie felt awful. Luckily, Nancy and Lupe came back from their outing. Birdie took the baby, placed her on her right hip, then took Sailor's hand, stepping back onto the porch steps.

"Hello. How was shopping?" Birdie could see the approval in Lupe's eyes, proud she was caring for the girls. Birdie felt as if she had passed a test by the look on Lupe's face.

Later that day Sailor was playing with Kiera and Amanda in their room. She wanted to sketch somewhere private. She was about to go to Sir Oliver's office when she overheard Lupe, Nancy, and Cora talking.

"You need to tell her now. Everything." Nancy insisted in a whisper.

"I will," Lupe said hesitantly, "But I need to be ready first."

"Nancy, really, let her do as she pleases." Cora scolded her sister.

"Nancy is right. Thank you for befriending me and letting me talk my feelings out before I tell her. These Saturdays have been hard, but when we go to the diner afterward and talk, I feel less panicked."

Lupe felt panicked? Over what? What was she doing on Saturdays before eating at the diner?

"Let me rest. I will pick a day this week. Please, not a word. You both promised." Lupe said, talking closer.

Birdie had to move. She could be seen from the hallway if she didn't hide. As she went to lean up against a wall in his office, just out of view, she heard a click and fell backward. Falling before she could stop it. The wall wasn't there anymore.

Birdie was caught between confusion and pain as her shoulder hit something hard.

Birdie didn't dare move off the floor; somehow, she was in a stairwell. It must have motion-sensitive lighting because a light came on.

"Hello?" Lupe called out. She must have heard Birdie fall, she thought. She quickly got up, closed the door lightly, and hit the light switch, shutting the light. She was in the dark, but she heard footsteps come into the office. She didn't dare move an inch, afraid the light would automatically come on again. Then she heard footsteps leaving the room. She rushed upstairs, the light going on once again. It must be a servant's passage from back in the day. Upstairs, she saw another door. She pushed it open fast. It was her room. Her room?! Birdie was confused.

Two minutes later, "Birdie? You up here?" She heard Lupe call out. She closed the door quickly. The door seamlessly blended in with the wallpaper striping so well that she had no idea it was there earlier.

"Yes, Lupe?" She rushed to where she left her phone earlier. She picked it up as if scrolling through emails.

Lupe gave a huge sigh of relief before schooling her face, "There you are, Darling. Where is Sailor?" She looked around.

"With Kiera and Amanda, where else?" Birdie tried to joke. Birdie hoped she pulled it off.

"Such sweet girls. They play so nicely together. I am tired. We just ate, and I am so full I plan to nap. See you later." Lupe took off fast, shutting her door.

Birdie stood there stunned. What health issue was she hiding? She needed to know already. She needed to broach the healthcare proxy subject again. Birdie needed access to Lupe's doctor. She needed to know what was going on.

QUINN RYAN

Quinn noticed that Sofía was on Facetime again with them. She has been better lately, Quinn acknowledged. Sometimes twice a week.

"How is Papi?" He heard her ask them in Spanish.

"Good. Aunt Kiera is here with baby Amanda." Tommy said back in Spanish. Quinn noticed they only spoke Spanish to her.

"Oh, fun. Enjoy them. I am coming very soon, ok? Tell Papi. I may be moving to America soon, so we can see each other more often."

What? Was she really moving? Quinn wondered, confused. They talked for another five minutes, well Tommy and Lucy did. Jazmín only answered direct questions if she wanted to. Had he not been there, she probably wouldn't even be on the call at all. But he would point to the tablet every time she was being rude. She got the hint fast. He expected good behavior. Fortunately, she was listening. Maybe Kiera was right; she was maturing a bit.

As they were talking, he researched Sofía's latest doings on his phone. He used to look at the pictures the paparazzi took daily. Finally, Cora pointed it out, and he rarely does it anymore. It was easier this way. Seeing her at restaurants and clubs, mingling with famous people while he was home dealing with stomach viruses, tantrums, and bickering made him angry. Cora was right to point it out, he thought.

This time, though, he needed to know what was going on. Could she be moving? He read all he could find. Her show had killed off her character. Wow, she called it. It was the highest-rated Fuego episode ever. Per the papers, many people were not happy. Then he saw an interview link. He stepped into the other room and listened. She thanked her fans for supporting her throughout the years, as well as the writers and producers.

She said it was time to put her family first. Then she went into a speech about the paparazzi and some laws she had passed. What laws? She really passed laws?? As Quinn was going to look it up, Lucy came in.

"Daddy, Mami wants you."

He put his phone away. "Coming."

Sofía told him of her plans. She was moving to Florida for a bit. Then maybe Los Angeles if she got bored, but she was ready to slow down a bit. Maybe even retire. Quinn rolled his eyes. Retire? Yeah right.

"Sofía, we are staying in South Carolina. I finally decided."

"Oh. Alright, um… I'm engaged. No one knows yet. I wanted to tell you first. Sorry to spring it on you. His name is Jorge. He owns a house on Star Island in Miami. He owns several marinas and also sells custom-built yachts. I want to tell the kids in person unless you want to tell them first. I defer to your judgment. You know what is best."

Jazmín came over as Quinn's mind went blank. She's engaged?! Is she moving to Miami right as he decided to leave Miami for good? When he had Kiera's buy-in, all were excited and now she moves there? Should Quinn second-guess his decision? The kids could have a relationship with her now if he stayed. But Kiera. His wants. Maybe he could do both…

Jazmín stuck her face in the room, "I am not going with her. You promised." she whispered nervously. He pointed to the door. He mouthed, 'Give me a minute.' He locked his bedroom door. Went into his bathroom and shut that door, too. This was as private a spot as he had.

"Sofía. I am staying. Jazmín is staying, too." Quinn said quietly. Quinn was shocked at what came out of his mouth so fast.

"I figured. Quinn, please let me back into the kid's lives. Please. I probably don't deserve it, but I need your forgiveness.

Theirs too. I have always loved them. Please never question that."

"I know you love them." He said, trying to forgive her.

"Quinn, I told Jorge all about you. How important you are to me. How you will be my family forever, and that will never change. He, too, has an ex-wife. I have met her. She raises their son, though he's twenty now. They get along. Can we? Please, Quinn? I need to fix things, starting with you. I am sorry I cheated on you. I am sorry that I chose fame over family. I am sorry I left it all to you. I will forever be grateful for all you have done for them, Quinn. For me, too. I will never try to take the kids away from you. Even Jazmín wants to stay; if you are willing to still be her father. I just want to be let back in." Her voice broke. Was she starting to cry?

Quinn was numb. So many admissions, so many things he wanted to hear over the years, and all in one phone call. Her tone sounded sincere, too.

"Quinn, you there? I'm sorry. Jorge has been showing me a lot. Is it too late?" He heard Sofía softly cry.

"No," Quinn said softly.

"Please accept my apology, Quinn. Please forgive me."

Quinn felt a lump in his throat. Can he truly forgive her for hurting their kids? For hurting him?

"You do not need to answer that yet. Let me prove it. OK, Papito? I will prove it. Let me go." With a "siempre te querré" saying she always would love him, she hung up.

Shock. Quinn was feeling shocked right now. He stood there for two whole minutes, processing. Then he thought of the kids. He had to tell them. He knew how to say it to each of them separately. In a way that makes them feel secure. He needed to check on the kids. He rushed out of there.

Tommy looked hopeful, Lucy ecstatic, and poor Jazmín looked panicked. He pulled Jazmín into a hug, "You stay with us. She agreed." Then a sob escaped Jazmín as she hugged him super tight, crying now.

"No more crying. Let's go out to dinner." He said, "But first, I need to talk to Aunt Kiera. Can you watch them this time? Amanda too? I need your help, Jazi. I need you to be patient with both siblings." he looked at her, wiping her tears.

Jazmín smiled up at him, "Of course. And Tommy and I will be fine. I love my little brother, and he should know this." She said to Tommy, "I really do, you know. You just get mad at me all the time when Lucy wants to spend alone time with me. That's not my fault. Sometimes, little girls like to be with big girls."

Tommy nodded, cheeks tinged pink, but his smile was broad.

"We will do stuff all together," Jazmín said to Quinn, assuring the kids too.

Quinn was shocked; she truly had matured.

He found Kiera packing and Amanda napping in the Pack-n-Play. He knocked softly. Kiera looked up, smiling, waving him in, then stopped. Her face fell. "What? Sofía again?"

He told her all. She looked just as stunned. She even sat at one point shocked. "I had an idea about the business as I walked over here. Please hear it all out."

Quinn told her that Chase, their Finance employee, wanted more responsibility and was one of his eyes now. Maybe he could offer Chase a partnership, say twenty-five percent of all the Miami jobs, as long as he runs the place successfully. He was already in charge of all financial responsibilities for jobs and office, so he would just oversee the staff and networking, too. Quinn or Kiera could do spot checks here and there. Quinn obviously would need to have a contract protecting them and can terminate at any time; this would include dissolving the partnership if things went wrong, but he sort of loved this idea. Their headquarters would still be here in South Carolina, but they would have two offices. Growth. They could rent out one apartment and keep the other for them to share when in Miami.

Silence.

"No good? I was hoping I could have the kids go there often to see her. If she tries, I am willing to try." Again silence.

"Kiera, talk." Quinn all but begged.

"Where do I sign? I will miss the food." She laughed, eyes welled.

He hugged her, relieved.

"I told you she would just wake up one day and realize she missed it all," Kiera said, wiping her eyes. She was proud of her ex-sister-in-law.

He nodded.

"Quinn, I trust Chase, but he can't manage the billing, too. We need to bring that here. Things can get missed there. Maybe hire a Junior Financial Associate there to bill, but give it to a senior person here to have checks and balances."

"True, OK, makes sense. It was a thought. I need to get legal involved. I need a month or two to really plan this out."

"And if he says he isn't interested?"

"I will reach out to our competition. Merge. Carlos has contacted me many times over the years. I would rather not go that way, though; he is shady. But there are a ton of others."

"Hell no to Carlos," Kiera said. Neither liked how he didn't do things correctly.

BIRDIE BLUE

"Lupe?" She knocked. It was nine-fifteen, and Sailor was asleep. Kiera was at her in-laws for the night with Amanda.

Lupe was lying in bed. She patted the bed, and Birdie came over worriedly.

"I see it's time. Come lie in bed with me." Lupe said.

Lupe told her of the mass growing in her head. They found it years ago, but recently, it grew a little. She told Birdie that she started radiation every Saturday when they came to South Carolina. She's had three treatments but now she is so tired she is worried about caring for Sailor.

"Do not worry about Sailor!" Birdie cried, hugging her, "Why did you go through this alone?"

"I wanted to protect you and Sailor. I always want to protect you both," Lupe said tearfully, "You are my world."

"And you are ours. But I want to go with you from now on. I will hire-"

"Cora agreed to watch Sailor as Nancy takes me."

"No, I will go with you each time. I will get a nanny. She will go to school with the other kids. It starts in three weeks. You just focus on getting better. Alright? You need to beat this. I need you, Lupe." Birdie sobbed.

Lupe just hugged her, unable to talk, then finally said, "I am not here forever, Mi hija. I am sorry, but I have no say in this. You are doing so well with Sailor now. You look more comfortable. My stepping back should have happened long ago. I am sorry I did not push it sooner."

"No, I am sorry. I relied on you too much."

"Well, we will fix this. You are so smart and loving. Sailor will need you a lot more as I am stepping back. Can you do it?"

"I will pay Cora to help while here. In the meantime, when Frank gets back, I will ask him for help finding someone when we leave here."

"Good, Mi hija," Lupe said softly.

"..Does radiation hurt?" Birdie broke out into fresh tears. How had she not realized Lupe had done three radiation treatments?

"No. Not at all. For that, I am thankful. But I am too tired to be on my feet afterwards. Radiation exhausts me."

"You just rest all day if you need to. I will bring you food and -"

"Breathe, my girl. I am fine. I am only a little tired; I get headaches sometimes but otherwise good."

"Need anything now? You did not come to dinner."

"Just sleep. Remember sleep heals the body. Don't work so hard, either. You have a year to do all this. God gave you this job at the perfect time." Then Lupe started to say a prayer in Spanish, thanking God. Birdie started to cry again.

"Sailor and I will be ok, Lupe. So if it ever gets too much, just tell me. I will understand. I love you too much to see you suffer. Promise me you will tell me if it ever gets too much." Birdie begged tearfully.

"I promise, Mi hija, I promise."

"You only go once a week?"

"They want me to go three times. I said no."

"Lupe!"

"So they can kill me another way? No."

"Two times a week? Can I call your doctor? Please, Lupe, I need to talk to your doctor."

"I have an envelope all ready for you in my top drawer. Let me sleep now." With a big kiss on Birdie's cheek, she pointed to the drawer.

Birdie got out the white envelope with one word written on it, 'Birdie.'

She shut Lupe's light and left the room. Tears were still streaming down. Her hands shook as she held the envelope. Once in her room, she wiped at her tears and read the letter.

Birdie,

I am sorry I kept this from you. Know that it is because I want to shield you from every bad thing in life. Sailor too. I have a tumor in my brain. I found it a couple of years ago. We monitored it, and it stayed the same size, so I chose to tell no one. It recently grew. Last month, I tried to tell my sister, but she is suffering from dementia now. She cannot understand anything, and as you can imagine, she cannot be here for me in the way I need right now. I am so torn telling you.

You are my executor. My will is updated and given to Stephen Conway, your attorney, with strict instructions not to say anything until my death. I do not know how many days God will grant me, but if I were to die at this very moment, I would have lived the most glorious life imagined because of you.

Having you as my surrogate daughter has been a gift that I am so very grateful for. I am so proud of you in every way. You are beautiful, smart, talented, loving, funny, spunky, and my best friend. I hope you know that. How much I love you. How much I love Sailor, my beautiful surrogate granddaughter. You are a great mom, Birdie; do not question your abilities. Cling to each other when I am gone. She will need you more than ever.

My doctor's card is in this envelope. I let her know you may call one day, once I decide to tell you. At this point, we will try radiation; if it works and grants me more time with you both, great. But if it doesn't, I am alright with that, too. It's been a wonderful life.

One last thing: find love. Don't be alone, Sailor will grow up one day. She will spread her wings. PLEASE find a partner to go through life's ups and downs with, for there will be many of both. Don't overwork yourself. Make having a new family your priority.

I am not scared of death. I never have been. What is there to be scared of? Going to God sounds beautiful. So I expect you to be happy when I finally get there. And trust me, I will be watching from above. You will not be free of me so easily.

I love you more than you will ever know, Mi hija. Thank you for making me a mother.

Lupe

Birdie sobbed so much she thought someone would come running in to see what was wrong. She couldn't breathe. She needed air. She ran out of the room, down the stairs, and went outside to her favorite spot, frantically trying to breathe. Once in the gardens, she just wailed, still clutching the letter.

Then she felt arms around her, but she was crying so hard she had no idea whose arms they were. It took almost two minutes of trying to get her breath to even look up and see she was in Quinn's arms. He just kept rubbing her back, not saying a word.

After gathering herself, she finally said, "Lupe is sick." Then she rushed out of his hands and dry heaved over a bush. Again, she felt his hands rubbing her back as she tried to push him away.

"I'm not leaving you. Single dad of three here, nothing scares me." He tried to tease. Birdie felt a handkerchief put into her hands, and she held it over her mouth even though she had not been sick as she thought she would be. She was too devastated to even be embarrassed.

"Tell me more," Quinn said, and suddenly, Birdie was depleted of energy. She handed the letter to him and just sat on the ground, unable to move.

QUINN RYAN

He took out a handkerchief from his pocket, compliments of Sir Oliver. He had given them to Quinn with his initials stitched into them long ago. Sir Oliver taught him a gentleman always had one in his pocket. He always took it to heart and always had one on him. Even if it was just out of respect for a man who had always been so kind and generous with him, why he thought of that at this moment was odd, but he was glad he had it for her.

When she fell straight to the ground, he rushed to her. Letter in one hand, about to lift her but she said, "Let me sit, please." He nodded and sat next to her.

He read the letter. When he finished he looked up at her, pulled her onto his lap, and just hugged her as she cried all over again. After a minute, he said, "Come, let's get you to bed."

She got up, and he did, too. He held her hand as they walked back to the house in silence.

Why would Lupe say for her to find a partner? She had Frank, or was he a secret too, like the first guy? Why didn't Birdie tell Lupe about relationships? He had so many questions.

BIRDIE BLUE

As she realized she was going to the stairs, she stopped. "I can't go up there yet. Please."

Quinn nodded; instead, he led her to Sir Oliver's office. One of her favorite rooms in Haven House. She breathed a sigh of relief when she got there. They sat on the settee. He took her hand again, "She will need you to be strong for her. She is probably scared herself."

Birdie nodded. She felt numb.

"You cry it out with me. Any time. When with Lupe, always have a positive attitude. My father did that with my mom. Only I saw him cry when we were alone." Quinn said. Birdie looked up at him, shocked. She hadn't known.

"The look of relief that he was being strong around her, for her, showed on her face. It was one less thing for her to worry about. Sickness was enough for her to deal with. She couldn't see him break down, too."

Birdie hugged him, "I am so sorry Quinn."

Quinn could only nod. She needed her partner now. Lupe was right.

"Maybe you should call Frank. Tell him."

Birdie looked up, confused, but then nodded, "I should. Tomorrow. I can't handle anything tonight."

Quinn looked confused but nodded.

"Why were you out in the garden again?"

"Thinking. A lot of decisions need to be made."

"Why?"

"Not important, I am here for you."

"And I am here for you too, Quinn. I could also use the distraction, so tell me, please." Birdie begged.

He updated her on the business about Sofía moving to Florida. Before he could finish, Cora came in. "Oh. Excuse me, I thought I left the light on."

But her face looked quite intrigued to see them both together, holding hands. Then she saw Birdie's blotchy face still tear-filled. "What on Earth?"

"I know about Lupe," Birdie said.

"Oh." Cora's face showed her sorrow.

"You knew," Birdie said flatly.

Cora nodded, "She made me promise, love. It was hard to do, but she was adamant."

Birdie nodded. She knew Lupe well enough to know, she would not tolerate anything other than keeping their word. Cora came over and hugged her.

"Can I pay you to watch Sailor when I paint until I find someone? I want Lupe to rest."

"Of course, any time. Would I be out of place if I made a suggestion? Don't make her obsolete. She needs to be needed. I will fill it in any time, whether it's Nancy or me, Sailor will be taken cared of. Even my niece would be great as she just graduated college."

Birdie nodded.

"I need to enroll Sailor into the local school until I know what I plan to do. I do not know anything about the home-schooling lessons Lupe did, so I want her in a real school. Can you guide me?" Birdie looked at Quinn.

"We can go together when I enroll Jazmín. Lucy was enrolled two months ago during kindergarten registration already."

"Thank you. I will be sure to stay the entire school year as that ceiling alone is a lot."

"We will solve this together, love. Don't worry about anything. Lupe is strong. And you have all of us." Cora said.

"Thank you."

"Alright, I am off. Quinn, the lights when done, please."

"I will, Cora." he kissed her goodnight.

They both looked at each other.

"The scaffolding comes next week; I will need to make a childcare schedule-"

"If you are alright with it, the children can just be watched together from now on. Alright? You can paint, and we all will manage and help the other out."

Birdie nodded but knew she would need a plan. Maybe Cora's niece could help watch all the kids if needed, but she could not think it through yet. She needed to gather her thoughts. Her head could not think of anything now.

He pulled her into the crook of his arm, and they just sat there. Both overthinking. Birdie felt cozy and safe in his arms. It felt like a lifetime, but it must have been only a few minutes.

"Let's get you to bed. You need to rest. Sleep will give you insight." He said.

She nodded. She got up, and Quinn did, too.

"I'll come back to shut everything." He led her to the wall.

"Shortcut. You are staying in Sir Oliver's room. He had this passage made." He pushed the door, the light went on, and he led her up.

"You can lock the wall if you want, but only Cora ever uses it. Less walking for her."

Birdie was shocked; she was staying in Sir Oliver's room?

"Eloise moved across the hall with the nurse next door when she got very sick and needed twenty-four-hour care." So Sailor's room was Eloise's and Lupe's the nurses. It made sense.

"Cora did not want to split you all up or make you take the third floor. The stairs are crazy long per floor due to the high ceilings." He said.

Birdie almost smiled. She knew he was nervous.

"Quinn?"

"Yes?"

"Thank you. I needed a friend, and you were there. I appreciate it."

"Yes, of course. I need to get back to the kids in case one wakes up." With a curt nod, he went back down through the wall door.

Did she hurt his feelings? Maybe she didn't help him enough with his issue? Birdie was mad at herself for being selfish. Now, she thought about hurting Quinn as much as she thought about Lupe. It was going to be a long restless night.

QUINN RYAN

He had to get out of there. Birdie only thinks of him as a friend. Maybe Miami right now was the answer.

Kiera came into the Carriage house without knocking. "Cora told me, how is she?"

Amanda was on her left hip, so she set her down and ran into the living room to watch TV with the kids.

"Heartbroken."

"I am sure. I thought it was odd how often Lupe did not come to dinner; I would have never guessed."

"Are you still leaving today? Maybe she needs a friend." He hadn't meant to say it like that, but that was how it came out.

"Whoa! Hold it right there. What did I miss?" Kiera narrowed her eyes at Quinn.

"Nothing. I'm tired. I didn't sleep much." He said fast.

"Don't give me that crap."

He pointed to the kids with a glare. They all looked up curiously.

"Business issue, Kiera." He stressed her name.

"Yes, we need to be on a conference call right now. Jazmín, can you watch the crew?"

She nodded quickly. Amanda was already climbing on her lap.

Quinn walked outside with Kiera following. "Again???"

"Speak in full sentences, Kiera." Quinn wouldn't admit it, but he knew what she was saying, as they always understood each other.

"You have feelings for her. Not just a crush anymore, but REAL feelings." Kiera said, both shocked and excited.

He shrugged; there was no sense in lying to her; she knew all his tells.

"And...?"

"She thanked me for being her friend."

"What else would you call it at a time like that? She is finding out that the only other 'parent' in her life is dying. She will just have Sailor. She is scared."

Quinn felt stupid. Kiera was right. They had a small family, but Birdie only had Lupe and Sailor. He was an idiot; he berated himself.

"Ask her out."

"Are you crazy?! She is seeing a guy named Frank."

Kiera looked confused. Then maybe she was hurt that she did not hear about Frank from Birdie herself. He could tell by the look on her face.

"Are you sure?" Kiera asked, disbelieving.

"I heard them with my own two ears. Birdie has a man."

"Damn. I need to investigate this some more."

"Kiera, I swear to God if you say anything-"

Kiera laughed, "What? You'll give me a nuggie? Please." She laughed, went back inside, and then came out with Amanda. "I am leaving today. I may come back. You will need me." she laughed, like the bratty little sister she always was.

"Oh, and I caught Jazmín on your phone earlier. Change your password."

With that, she left.

Quinn shook his head. Jazmín was getting comfortable again.

SAILOR WREN

Sailor was being measured by her mother. She wasn't sure why. She said the measurements outloud as she told them to a lady on speakerphone.

"She's a 4/6 now, but I may get 6x too. They may be a bit big at first, but she will outgrow 4/6 fast." the voice said.

"Yes, please, both sizes. Wait, not just for her. I have a stylish thirteen-year-old, another girl around the same size as Sailor, and a tall boy who is seven or eight. Bring a ton of stuff for all of them. I need it here next week. They can try it on to see what they like."

"Done. Text me the address. I love styling kids."

"Thanks." Her mother said, hanging up.

"Clothes for all of us?"

"Yep. It's a surprise, so please don't tell the kids," her mother smiled.

Sailor nodded happily.

"Mommy, did you know Jazmín wants to be a fashion designer? But she doesn't know how to sew. I told her when I get big, I will buy a dress from her."

"That is sweet, Sailor. I will, too. Now, what else do we need for school?"

"A school bag and a lunch box, I always wanted one." Sailor squealed.

"Why didn't you tell me?" Her mother frowned.

"I never went to a real school before."

They searched for almost thirty-five minutes until she found the perfect one. Then, Sailor selected three lunch box and school bag sets for each of the other kids based on their likes. Then her mother ordered several more sets so they could pick just in case.

Sailor was all but jumping up and down. She was so happy. She couldn't wait for a real school, a lunch box, a school bag, and new clothes.

Though... Sailor wondered what would happen after she moved again.

BIRDIE BLUE

It was raining. The newscaster said it would rain for three days. She had already touched up the crab bench, two areas of the ballroom wall, and her circus-themed screen needed quite a bit of work as she did not know how to protect it so young. Also, the platforms were stalled again as the prior job needed another two weeks. She went to the children's room. Lupe was there supervising like normal, as she often brought them up to play between lunch and dinner. Today though, they were leaving the children's room.

"I suggested a movie as I figured you would want to come up with ideas for this room." Lupe smiled.

"Thank you. Actually, before you all go, I need opinions. I was thinking of making each wall a different story. Pete's Dragon, Sound of Music, Hansel and Gretal, and maybe Alice in Wonderland. Do you like this idea?" Birdie asked all the kids.

All nodded.

"I love Pete's Dragon." Tommy nodded enthusiastically.

"I like the Cheshire Cat from Alice in Wonderland. Can you please make sure the cat is in the picture?" Lucy asked, all but jumping up and down at her feet with her sweet face looking up at Birdie.

"I can." Birdie smiled, touching her nose.

"I guess I like the Sound of Music," Jazmín added, shrugging.

"Name movies older kids would like," Birdie asked her.

Jazmín thought about it, "I like Wonder Woman, or Descendants from Disney, or Harry Potter."

"Plan forming," Birdie said. "Different ages need to love this room. So, a wall for toddlers, another for elementary age, then tweens, and finally teens. Perfect!"

Jazmín blushed proudly.

"Thank you all so much," Birdie said, mind already thinking up ideas.

As they went to the theater one room over, she sat down at the art table and started sketching.

One wall had Hansel and Gretal as the main scene. She specifically showed the house with colorful candy all over it. Then decided to add other nursery rhymes like Jack and Jill, Humpty Dumpty, Jack who jumped over the candlestick, Red Riding Hood, and Peter Piper. Only those would need to be found in the scene like little easter eggs. The house would be in the middle of a forest, so it would be easy to do and it would also give the forest some interest. For the elementary wall, she would do Alice in Wonderland. The Cheshire Cat is prominent in the scene for Lucy. Then, for the tween wall, Pete's Dragon. She did this before for a former client in Dubai. Only they wanted the Disney live-action version and she planned to do her vision using the cartoon Elliot for inspiration. The final wall would be twenty or so superheroes. Wonder Woman was taking the lead role. Then she realized she needed to do the alcoves. Birdie needed to think about that. The reading nook would look awesome with Starry, Starry Night on all three walls. The other alcove had the dollhouse. It mimicked Haven House. Maybe behind that wall, the gardens? It wouldn't look right, she realized. Maybe a fairy village? After all, the fairies' painting was the first thing she ever did for Sir Oliver. The more she thought about it, the more she liked the idea.

She sketched a bit more, then she realized she could not stall calling Lupe's doctor anymore. In her bedroom, she shut her door and called. The nurse said she was with a patient but would call back shortly.

Looking at her sketches, she made some tweaks. The superheroes' sketch was completely redone, so they weren't all just standing there. Spiderman was upside hanging from a web. Hulk was smashing a wall. Wonder Woman was lasso-ing Iron Man from flying up and Batman's signal in the sky, to name a few tweaks she made to the sketch. It looked so much better, but she would get the kids' feedback on which they liked better later.

Then her phone rang, and she instantly felt sick. She nervously answered. The nurse told her the doctor would call her after eight p.m. once all appointments were complete; she did not want to rush this conversation. Birdie thanked the nurse. Scared once again by the conversation requiring time.

After dinner and tucking Sailor into bed, she stole up to her bedroom. It was eight-forty at night when her phone finally rang. She grabbed it nervously.

After pleasantries, Dr. Lee gave a full rundown of Lupe's tumor diagnosis and treatment.

"Is this fatal?"

"I must prepare you. If it continues to grow, then yes." the doctor said as kindly as possible.

Shock. Birdie felt the tears welling up, and she gulped.

"Is the radiation helping?"

"Too soon to tell. She is not allowing us to do as many treatments as I would suggest."

"Does this hurt her?"

"Radiation? The treatment itself, no, but after a while, she may get swollen, red, or raw feeling. She can use Aquaphor if her skin is affected. Mainly, it will exhaust her. It may also affect motor functions and cause headaches and memory issues. We just won't know as each case is different."

"Can we operate?"

"Not advisable. Not where it is located."

"How long does she have? Please be blunt." Birdie all but begged.

"Depends on the speed of growth."

"How long?" Birdie insisted.

"Somewhere in the range of six months to two years if it continues to grow. Sorry, I am unable to give exact times right now. It could stop growing. It could double in size in a month. It depends on how often she goes for treatment, if the tumor responds to it, too many factors to give exact timing."

Birdie felt a panic attack coming on. She had two other panic attacks before; she knew what it felt like. The first one was when she realized she had to call home at sixteen; the other was when her father died, and she thought she was alone in this world, but then Lupe reminded her she would be with her. She couldn't lose Lupe, as well. She just couldn't. She needed to stop the panic attack. She remembered what her doctor told her years ago, to do the 5-4-3-2-1 trick. Birdie looked around to notice five things: a bed, chair, mirror, curtains, and sneakers. She counted each on one hand. Touch four things: comforter, jeans, tears as she wiped them away, a tissue as she grabbed the box close. Listen for three things: the doctor's quiet breathing, the ticking of the clock, and the rain beating outside the window angrily.

"I'm sorry. I am just glad she told someone." Birdie was brought back to the conversation by the doctor speaking. Birdie managed to stop the panic attack as she was finally able to take a deep breath. She was calmer now, thankfully. She took another deep breath.

"This is hard, I know." The doctor was still talking, but Birdie couldn't quite speak yet. She tried to take another breath. Then, a sob came out before she could muffle it.

"I'm sorry." The kind doctor said.

"Ok... Thank you for talking with me." She barely whispered before saying 'goodbye' and hanging up.

She sat there numb. So many thoughts suddenly flooded her mind. Mainly, had she known immediately, they could have done treatment sooner and brought her anywhere in the world to the best specialists. Then, in a fit of anger, she threw her phone across the room. Somehow, it crashed into a decorative pillow on a couch across the room. Birdie just allowed herself to sob. She lay on her bed in a fetal position for what felt like a lifetime, just crying nonstop. Finally, her throat hurt so much that she tried to sit up. She needed to do something. She would talk to Lupe, but not now, not like this. Not scared. Not sobbing. She had to get herself together first. Ready to reason with Lupe to do all the treatments her doctor suggested.

She looked at the clock. It was a quarter to eleven. She could not sleep. She took a shower, brushed her teeth, put her wet hair up in a claw clip, padded barefooted to the secret door, and went downstairs to Sir Oliver's office with her sketch pad and a box of colored pencils. Why she grabbed them, she wasn't sure, but when upset, they were her source of comfort. Birdie turned on the desk lamp and then went to the window. It was still pouring out. The rain was lashing against the large window pane as if trying to get in. She wished she could go to the gardens tonight. She needed to think. Walking out there always seemed to clear her mind and helped her decide her next steps, whether for work or personal issues. At best she only had Lupe for two years. Two. She would be twenty-seven in two years. She did not feel knowledgeable enough to parent Sailor alone or ready to be parentless herself. Two years was too short. Did Lupe know the timing? Had she accepted it? Could Birdie make a lifetime of memories with Lupe in that short time frame? If Lupe lived that long...

She tried to sketch but couldn't. She needed comfort. Sir Oliver was always a source of comfort to her. She just wanted to sit amongst his things and distract her mind from thinking. No television, so maybe a book? She went to a bookshelf to the left of his desk and saw a whole bunch of books. One grouping of books bound in leather caught her attention. Birdie noticed some books did not have names on the spines. How odd, Birdie thought; they just had Roman Numerals on them instead. She pulled out XI just because it caught her fancy and went to the settee. She turned on that lamp next to the seat, took the throw draped gently over the armrest, and laid it over her as she opened the book. Only it wasn't a book. It was a journal in Sir Oliver's penmanship. She should put it back. This was personal. Oh how she missed seeing his writing. She longed to hear anything from him just one more time.

As she was about to close the book, one word caught her attention and made her read. 'Eloise'. Someone that she did not speak to him about other than her love of flowers. Birdie was curious about her.

"Forgive me, Sir Oliver, but I need you right now. Please show me something to let me know if it will be okay." And a peace came over her, as if granted permission by him.

Tuesday - May 8th

Eloise, oh my Darling, Eloise. How do I get you back? It's been a year since you were gone and still, I wake up wondering why I am alone in bed as if I forget, or probably more accurately, refuse to believe. Then, as I rush across the hall and see that your bed is empty as well, the realization hits yet again, and I want to crumble to my knees. A nightmare that I cannot escape. I can hardly bear it. Soon, Eloise, we shall be together again.

Birdie closed the book. Would she feel this way, too? This was too sad to read at a time like this. She put Volume XI back, then took out Volume V. Hopefully, this will be happier times. She got cozy again, praying this one was happier. Then she felt a bit of guilt again.

"May I?" she asked out loud. Birdie could not hear a sound, and she listened, yet nothing but rain. "Please have a branch, or something hit the window hard if I cannot look. Any noise." She waited, just steady rain. With a 'thank you'. She opened it.

The gardens are starting to take shape. Eloise has such a lovely vision. She even asked if we could have rose trellises installed. So that shall be the next project after the last Solarium is built. The artist who does the stained glass roofing is the same as the one who changed out the front windows two years ago. Such talent! Sarah's bluebirds and Eloise's roses adorn everything. Why not? I want my girls happy, even if Sarah sees it from heaven. It's a token of love for them both.

Eloise and I will be traveling to New York next month. I plan to buy more artwork, but first, I must see the Metropolitan Museum of Art. I heard that Frank Lloyd Wright will soon build a new museum for Guggenheim to hold his entire collection. I cannot wait to see it. Maybe I should consider having my own one day. What else am I to do with all this money I have inherited when I have no one to pass it on to? At least I can surround myself with beautiful art, gardens, and homes. Eloise and I hope to share it with others one day.

Birdie smiled, "Thank you for sharing it with me, Sir Oliver." She closed the journal and put it back. She planned to leave her mind on that note for the night—happiness. She promised herself to one day read more. Sir Oliver was always so expressive with his feelings; maybe that is what she loved about him, too.

As she was about to shut the light, she heard a noise. She went to investigate. Quinn was lying under the kitchen sink with tools all around. Quinn's head could not be seen under the cabinet, but she knew it was his body. If Birdie were truthful, she had studied every bit of his body before now. She couldn't help herself, Birdie told herself; she was an artist, so noticing details was customary to her. But she was also curious about him; Birdie had to admit to herself. Tonight, he wore faded jeans that were molded to his thighs when in that position. He had one knee up as he was tightening something. She could see his plain white t-shirt, a touch wet from the rain, most likely molded to his abs. He had abs?! Birdie guessed that gardening and working around Haven House got his body in shape.

"Shit!" Birdie could see him pull his body out from under the sink a bit and was holding his finger, trying to stop the bleeding.

"Let me get you a-," Birdie rushed over. In shock at not being alone as he thought, he went to sit up and cracked his head on the cabinet above him.

"OW!" His good hand flew to his head.

"Oh my God, I am sorry. I was about to say 'hi'" then both looked at each other and burst out laughing. She handed him a paper towel and helped him up.

"Need ice?"

QUINN RYAN

Quinn needed something much stronger than ice. This day was already too much with Jazmín's antics, and he couldn't sleep. At least with Jazmín there, he could quickly slip over and fix the sink before Nancy needed it. It saved him from waking at six in the morning to come to do it before she started her breakfast routine.

They cleaned his cut and put a band-aid on his finger. Then, Birdie grabbed a frozen bag of peas from the freezer and gently stuck it on his head.

"I think I am alright." He laughed but let her hold it there when she growled at him.

"It's the least I can do," Birdie said. She looked like she felt awful.

"I am fine. I get hurt all the time doing this job."

"Why are you here so late?" Birdie asked.

He shrugged.

"Kids? Work? Sofía- Alright, what's new with Sofía?" Quinn was shocked; was he so readable?

"She is no longer working. They killed off her character. She is moving to Miami." He said, head pounding.

"Miami. As in, where you just decided not to move back to?"

"Mmm-hmmm." He took the peas away and put them into the freezer.

"Shit." Birdie breathed out slowly.

"Yep. Sofía's timing is always surprising." He said sarcastically.

"Any booze around here? We need a drink. We are both having a seriously shitty day."

"Give me five minutes. I need to fix this, and I will meet you in Sir Oliver's office. I know where he keeps his alcohol in a hidden compartment. Don't tell Cora. She caught me once at seventeen, and I have never had a sip around her since." Thinking of her chasing after him with her feather brush made him think twice. Especially after she cornered him and got him good, then she told his father. After that conversation, he worked for a month straight with no friends or plans. No thanks. Adult or not, he didn't mess with Cora at all.

BIRDIE BLUE

Birdie laughed but nodded. The way he said it, she knew he had gotten a lot of flack because of it. Going into the office, she looked around. She eyed every bit of the room, looking for the secret compartment. Where was it? She peeked behind pictures, but nothing could be found. She knew about the door to the stairwell that led to her room. Maybe there was another one? She pressed all the empty walls; where was this compartment? All she saw was a bookcase and a side table up against a wall. It had to be one of them. Suddenly, Birdie thought of old movies where bookcases opened or maybe it was more like the wardrobe from Narnia. She tugged on many shelves, but nothing. She was about to check out the side table when Quinn came in, all washed up, looking like the world's weight was on his shoulders.

QUINN RYAN

"Do you drink a lot?" he asked before he showed her. Short of a beer on the weekend, he only had a drink when he was beyond stressed. Today was beyond stressful. But maybe she had an issue with alcohol. She was an artist, after all, and went to many fancy shindigs. He wouldn't assist her in harming herself.

"I do not drink at all, short of a Mojito or an occasional Bloody Mary when on vacation, which rarely happens as I am always trying to catch up on jobs. But... I spoke to Lupe's doctor today. I need something. No judgment."

Man, that did not sound good, Quinn thought. He was glad to be there for her then. He walked to the bookshelf and tilted a book towards the back of the bookshelf. The book was called, 'The Hazards of Libations'. He saw Birdie actually laugh when she read it, and he pushed it back again until it was horizontal, then there was a click. It was a double push to keep it secret from people. The book even pulled out and was a normal book. Quinn's Dad had told him how much fun Sir Oliver had creating this compartment with his Dad and a carpenter.

The entire bookshelf opened inside a small room. There is a bar to the right and two easy chairs to the left. He pointed to the bottles, "Which one?"

Birdie shrugged. He saw her look at the many whiskey, bourbon, scotch, brandy, and other bottles confused. She clearly had no idea what to pick, as she had not tasted any of them before unless mixed in the two drinks she mentioned.

"Sir Oliver always liked cognac, especially as he got older and was always cold. Let's have one and say cheers to him." He pulled out a bottle of Courvoisier XO, not daring to touch the Louis XIII by Remy Martin. Quinn poured a small amount into each brandy snifter. Then they sat in the overstuffed chairs.

"Cheers to Sir Oliver and the end of a shitty day," Quinn said, holding out his glass.

"Cheers." Birdie smiled, if sadly, clinking the glasses.

He watched her take the tiniest sip. She made a face. He smiled. She was so cute, he thought. He took a sip himself. The warmth hit him immediately. He felt his shoulders relaxing a bit.

Jazmín had been too much tonight before bed; he found her talking to someone on Lucy's tablet. She thought he was working. She was in Lucy's closet on the floor laughing when he came in to check on the girls. It was ten o'clock when he went in. As he listened, and yes, Quinn could admit he eavesdropped, he heard the voice. It sounded like an older guy. College-aged. Quinn freaked. He told the guy she was thirteen, and the guy panicked, hanging up before he could go off on the little shit. He gave her such a dressing down.

She acted as if she had no idea talking to such an older guy was a big deal. Quinn had so much to teach her. She 'felt safe behind a computer screen,' she had said, 'no one could touch her.' Quinn explained how guys started innocently, then asked to meet up, etc. He tried to explain the concept of grooming young people. He spent almost half an hour talking with her until she looked like she got it. She cried, apologizing, saying she just missed friends and talking to someone older than eight. He got it, and hopefully, so did she. So now he had to find Jazmín an extracurricular activity with kids her age as she wasn't into swimming. Another thing to do, Quinn thought. But clearly, this one was important. However, next to the Sofía drama, that was nothing. He felt he was doing the kids a disservice if he stayed. Though, would Sofía really stay in Miami? Would she not travel, do interviews, and maybe move to California anyway? His mind was just at a loss as to what he should do. He needed Birdie's opinion. He trusted her.

"So am I an ass if I stay? Their mother will finally live in the same town as ours, and I want to move here. Well, not here. I would love to live here forever, but I know this house is going to someone soon. I will miss it." Quinn said sadly, sighing deeply.

Now, he felt worse. The Carriage House had been his home for most of Quinn's life. Once sold, he wouldn't be able to come back. He wished he knew who the house was being given to. If it were to someone he knew, he would stay in South Carolina. Maybe get a chance to visit it sometime. Cora once said there was a sealed envelope with the new owner's name at the attorney's office. Maybe he should hold off deciding for a few more months. Then Quinn kicked himself; he was selfishly thinking of his problems when poor Birdie looked gutted.

"Sorry! Tell me," Quinn said.

"Tumor in her brain. She has six months to two years to live, but we cannot tell for sure, it depends on how fast the tumor grows. She is only going to one treatment a week. They want more. I need to talk her into it." Birdie had said that flatly, defeated, looking like she was a dam about to break.

Quinn put his glass down, took her glass out of her hand, and put it down, too, then pulled her onto his lap to hug her. It didn't feel weird; it felt oddly right. She curled into his lap, needing the hug, as she softly started to cry again. He just held her.

Quinn thought of what to say to her and couldn't find anything to fix it.

"I'll be alone, Quinn. Aside from Sailor, though she is getting bigger and will want to do her own things soon; I will be alone." She sobbed.

"You will never be alone again, Birdie. Kiera and I are your family now. I promise." And Quinn meant it.

"But we won't be near each other when I leave. I will be alone. Who will help me with Sailor when I work? I can travel anywhere." She pulled away from him to look into his eyes. Her tear-filled eyes broke him.

He thought.

"There are options," Quinn finally said, already knowing she wouldn't like some of them.

"Like?"

"You can find a nanny, now, one that Lupe and you approve of together." He put his finger on her lips to silence the immediate rebuttal.

"Please let me tell you all your options. You could stop doing jobs until she is off to college. It may even make the demand for your work skyrocket. Or you could paint on canvas, whatever, just not at their locations but from home or a studio with her there."

Her mouth dropped open. Maybe realizing that there were options she hadn't thought about.

"Or maybe we help each other out. Find a common town to live in. She stays with my kids when you need to go away for a couple of days or at Kiera's. I don't even know where you call home." Quinn realized.

"Manhattan, I guess. I have homes in many places, including Los Angeles and London, though I basically live on the road."

"Sailor should be in a real school. Before, it might have been fine when she was young, but now she will want friends and extracurricular activities like sports or drama. She will want to go to prom, all the things YOU longed for but didn't do as you traveled from place to place. Or did you forget telling me that long ago?"

Why was Quinn selling this so hard? He was way off base, making her feel bad about Sailor's needs, rubbing in her face her own childhood. He just wanted her in his life, Quinn thought. He'd do anything to make that happen.

"I need to think about it," Birdie said, again devoid of emotion. She looked done. He shouldn't have added any more pressure. He was so mad at himself.

He handed Birdie her drink, "Take another sip." She did. She went to get up, but he held her there, and she looked up at him, confused. Like she realized that she was sitting on a man's lap, Quinn couldn't help but feel aroused by her, but he shifted earlier so she wouldn't realize it. The need was getting too strong, yet he did not want to let her up.

"Quinn?" Birdie looked up, eyes searching his.

Quinn leaned in softly, and he noticed she did, too. He kissed her. He hadn't planned it, but he did. This time, the kiss was deep. Tongues probing, hands exploring, both just lost in the moment. Then Quinn felt his brain start to work again. What was he doing? He was taking advantage of her in this state. He pulled away from her lips just enough. Her eyes, still filled with passion, started to slowly change to questioning, then confusion.

"Sorry, you are not in a good place for advances like that. I am sorry. I just..."

Quinn could not finish the sentence.

She looked up at him, hers searching his, "What, Quinn?"

"I'm not being fair.", is all Quinn could think to say.

"Life isn't fair." She whispered.

"It's the second time I kissed you without asking first. That's not right."

Birdie actually smiled, "Quinn Callahan, always doing what's right."

"I try." He said, unsure what she was saying.

"Don't try so hard," she said, pulling him into a kiss.

Quinn could not think. Was she kissing him now? Did she not know how much he was trying to hide his attraction to her, to not ravage her?

BIRDIE BLUE

So this was what sexual attraction felt like? Birdie had not gotten the big deal before this moment. To want someone to want you the way you wanted them. To want to kiss, hug, and touch all over. She wanted him in her. She needed to be with him. Her hands were pulling off his clothes.

QUINN RYAN

Shit, Quinn thought as he realized they were undressing. Why couldn't he stop himself? Why was he suddenly over her body and about to enter her?

BIRDIE BLUE

She had never felt longing like this. Never wanted to rip off someone's clothes, never wanted to be taken like this. She was the aggressor for once. She was being insistent every time he tried to cool down. She just wanted Quinn. She was about to lose everything again. She was not allowing anything to take this moment away from her too. She needed Quinn; she needed to feel him at her very core. And she did.

"Birdie..." he gasped as they lay in each other's arms, physically exhausted. Both were trying to catch their breath.

Birdie just lay her head on his shoulder contently, no need for words.

"I- I didn't use a condom, Birdie," Quinn said panicked.

She just nuzzled closer. So what? What was the worst thing that could happen, she would get pregnant? Who cares? She needed all the family she could get. And it would be Quinn's, too... the thought warmed her heart, and now praying she did, in fact, get pregnant.

She knew Quinn, though. He was very by the book. Things normally came in order for him. However, Tommy hadn't been planned. Then another thought... Maybe he thought she just slept with everyone so fast?

"Quinn?"

"Yes?" He asked, confused looking.

"You are my second. I don't just sleep around."

Now Quinn looked even more guilty. Why, Birdie wondered.

"I'm sorry, Birdie."

Sorry for what? Having sex with her?

"For?" Birdie felt a bit annoyed now.

"I took advantage of a weak moment. I just... I can't help myself with you." he whispered, looking away.

Birdie turned his face to look at her, "Why?"

He shrugged.

"Tell me, Quinn."

With another shrug, "I love you. Always have."

He loved her? He always had? Quinn loved her. She needed a second to process this.

"You don't have to say it back. I've always known it was one-sided," he said, sitting up, hiding his face from her. Protecting himself, most likely.

Birdie took his hand and squeezed it, "It was never one-sided, Quinn. You were always special to me. Lately, I look at you differently. It's stronger now. There is attraction, yes, but also love."

He looked shocked.

"Let's go to sleep. We both have a lot on our plates right now. But I hope we can get through it together, Quinn." She said softly, hopefully.

He nodded, face still surprised. He helped her up, helped her dress then buttoned his pants.

They washed the glasses in the bar sink, shut everything, and looked at each other.

"It's late. Let's put you to bed," Quinn said, leading her toward the wall door. Once upstairs, he leaned in for a kiss, a soft gentle kiss. Then went back out the same way he came in.

QUINN RYAN

Did that just happen? He thought as he walked back to the Carriage House. He checked in on all three kids, all asleep. Thankfully, even Jazmín, who was always bucking him, saying ten p.m. was too early a bedtime for a teenager. It was the fact that she shared a bed with Lucy, who had an eight p.m. bedtime, that helped him hold firm. He showered and fell into a deep sleep before his head hit the pillow. Content.

"Daddy, Jazi won't let me in the bathroom!"

Lucy woke Quinn with her complaint. What time was it? He looked at his clock, a quarter after eight a.m. What? He never overslept. He jumped out of bed, "Use my bathroom, but hurry up. I am late."

"I don't need to use the bathroom, Daddy. I already did that long ago. I just left my headband in there, and she won't let me in to get-"

"Lucía, way too much for the first minute I am awake. Wait patiently for her to get out or use another headband. You have plenty."

Lucy crossed her arms, mad.

Quinn sighed. Lucy was a mini-Sofía when she didn't get her way.

"Sit on your bed for five minutes or wait patiently." He said evenly, opening draws to get clothing.

"I'll wait." She pouted.

"Good decision. Let me get ready, please." He ushered her out, shut the door, and rushed to get ready. He had his first restful sleep in forever. It was nice.

He poured everyone cereal as he was late getting outside to mow.

"Cereal, ill. Peasant food." Jazmín said crankily.

"Eat peasant." He teased her.

Jazmín glared at him.

"Cereal, daughter, please. I overslept." He said, trying another approach. She smiled. She couldn't help it even if she tried to stay angry about the scolding from yesterday.

"Fine. I am going for a walk with Tommy and Lucy, ok?"

"Stay on the grounds, not by the pond."

With a sigh, she agreed.

"Dad? Can I get my phone back? Can you ask Mami?"

He nodded, "I'll call her today. But you must promise that you remember our talk yesterday."

Jazmín nodded, beaming, "I won't do it again."

Quinn nodded.

After he rushed out, he jumped on the mower, put headphones on, and started to mow the many acres. Unfortunately, it would take most of the day. When mowing, all he could do was think. Fortunately, he could think about Birdie and what they did last night.

Should he call her? Maybe see her in person? Would that be awkward? What if she was having second thoughts? Quinn was overthinking again.

He felt his phone buzzing. He stopped the mower.

'Don't avoid me. We are adults. I do not regret anything. You should not either.' It was a text from Birdie. Quinn's eyes widened.

'Not avoiding you. Can't get you out of my mind. Woke late. Need to mow before landscapers come to clean trimmings and shape the garden bushes.' He pressed send but then shook his head. He was nervously rambling again.

'Good.'

Quinn smiled.

'I can't wait to see you tonight at dinner.' Quinn texted back. All she sent back was a smiley face emoji. He got back to mowing.

An hour later, Lupe called him. He stopped the machine again.

"Hi, Lupe."

"Will Jazmín be coming to the children's room today, or is she too old? I do not want to assume."

Quinn frowned. All three kids should be together. She also didn't have a phone for him to call her and ask where she was. Could she be talking to that guy again while everyone was out of the house?

"She was supposed to be with everyone." He all but growled.

"Maybe you can talk to a certain guilty-looking little sister?" Lupe whispered. Quinn could hear the smile in her tone.

"Put her on, please."

After a brief conversation, Lucy confessed that she knew where Jazmín was. She was going to suntan by the pond. Alone.

"Don't tell her I told, Daddy. She'll get mad at me." Lucy worried.

"I won't. Tell Lupe thank you."

He mowed all the way to the pond. He was getting angrier the closer he got due to how long it was taking to get there. He saw her lying out on a towel in a bikini. A tiny red bikini. Her eyes were closed with headphones on, no idea he was staring at her. How loud was the music that she hadn't heard the mower?

Quinn was cross between being mad that she did not listen to him again and scared that she didn't know better than to be on guard at all times. She was Sofía's daughter. She needed to know to always be aware of her surroundings to be smart. It's been ingrained in his children since birth.

He went closer, his shadow covering her face. She looked startled, "Oh shit." Then covered her mouth fast. Quinn fumed.

"Where did I ask you not to go today?" Quinn asked firmly.

She got up, taking off her headphones.

"I thought you meant with the kids." She said fast, looking away briefly.

"Are you lying, too, now?"

Jazmín bit her bottom lip guilty-looking, cheeks blushing. She was never a good liar, and he knew when she did, for the most part.

"Lying and disobeying. Not a good start, Jazmín. Go to your room. You step out of it other than us going to dinner at the main house-"

Jazmín pouted, "Sorry, Daddy."

Quinn stopped, 'Daddy' like the old days, not 'Dad.' Not a snarky, bored 'Daddy Dearest' to taunt him. She said it sincerely, which was refreshing. It stopped him from going off on her.

"Get going." Then he pointed in the direction of the Carriage House.

She went to leave, but he stopped her. "Jazi, I catch you alone again, not watching your surroundings. You are in serious trouble, and I mean it. Fans are nuts."

"I will. I just felt safe here. I never feel safe anywhere..." eyes welling now.

Quinn softened, then nodded, "Go on."

She rushed off.

"And wear a cover-up!" He said, hating that she was developing. Her body was going to be an exact clone of her mother's. Sofía was known for her curves. The thought that men would be drooling over Jazmín soon made him sick to his stomach. To him, she was an impossible eight-year-old and always will be. She stopped to wrap the towel around her, then looked over her shoulder. "Sorry."

He pointed again, and she took off.

He called Birdie before he realized it.

"Hi." He heard her smile.

"Busy?"

"Just rough sketching a wall of the children's room."

"Jazmín was in a tiny red bikini." He blurted.

Birdie's laugh calmed him.

"I'll add bathing suits to my stylist's list."

Quinn was confused.

"Um... I don't do stores or shopping. Had a few scary experiences."

He could relate to that. He had to do school shopping and stressed it every year. However, last year hadn't been too bad here in South Carolina. Miami was a whole other situation.

"I understand more than you know. I will take her shopping. I just do one kid at a time so I can keep them safe."

"So I sort of have clothes coming. Just a fun day of trying things on." Birdie said worriedly.

"Let me know when to expect them, along with their name for the gate."

"... For all four kids."

All four kids? Quinn did not know how he felt about that. Sure, she had a ton of money, but he proudly paid for everything for his kids. Every cent Sofía sent was in the bank for the kids. Even if it meant they went without sometimes.

"I should have asked, sorry. Lupe scolded me already. She said I should have asked first. So I am asking. She comes tomorrow."

Quinn smiled. Sometimes, Birdie acted like a kid herself. Maybe not last night, he thought before re-focusing fast. He'd thought about last night enough.

"If I pay," Quinn said.

"Alright, I'll cancel their stuff," Birdie said snarkily.

"Birdie." He sighed.

"It's just a few outfits, a school bag, and a lunchbox. Five each. Ok?"

"I will pay, Birdie. I have money. I am not just a caretaker-"

"Are we fighting? I don't want us to fight." She asked so innocently he stopped.

"No." He sighed. He did not want them to fight either.

"Please? A gift for being so great to Sailor and I."

"You've been even greater. The kid's faces on the Nursery walls."

"Quinn, please? Can I spoil them a little? I promise not to do it a lot."

"Can we split the costs?"

"You can pay for the school bags and lunch boxes. OK?" She grumbled.

"Sailor's too."

"Fine. Now, I don't want to kiss you." Birdie pouted, and Quinn laughed. "I bet I can change your mind."

"Time will tell." She laughed back.

"Seriously, though, I do not spoil them. I do not do Gucci, Prada, or whatever the newer names are. I want my kids to have a normal life. Be happy with simple things." Quinn said.

"Same. But I really do not feel safe at malls. I even have hired security a couple of times and it still felt overwhelming. I could afford to spend a fortune daily if I wanted to. I don't. Only where it pertains to assuring we are safe."

Quinn understood that, and he realized she did not dress up; she was not covered in jewels, nor did she have Amazon packages arriving every day.

"I understand."

"So, can I let them have a few outfits each? Please, Quinn? I just want to do something fun for them."

"Your just being here is fun for them."

"Quinn! No kisses!"

He laughed again.

"Three kisses and then a one-time yes."

"Deal. I would have settled for five. You need to work on your negotiation skills, Quinn." Birdie teased.

He laughed, "Let me get back to mowing. I am so behind."

"Ok." she hung up.

Quinn checked on Jazmín three times. He couldn't help it. She was alone. She could have easily not listened. But she was in the girl's room. Headphones on, bikini replaced by a shorts set.

The gate rang as he was getting a glass of water.

"Can I help you?"

"Surprise!" The accented voice said and Quinn thought he would be sick. What the fuck was she doing here?!

SAILOR WREN

Tommy and Sailor were busy building a Lego castle, but Lucy kept knocking it over or stealing pieces that were put aside for it. Sailor scowled. Lucy was annoying them!

"Stop, Lucy!" Tommy scolded.

"But I want some, too!" Lucy shouted, mad.

Lupe looked up from her book. "What's going on?"

"No one will play with me." Lucy cried, running to Lupe's waist. "Jazi is not here, and they won't play with me or share pieces."

Sailor felt terrible. Lucy missed her sister. Also, Tommy and Sailor did not include her. Lucy had a point. Being with other kids was complicated, Sailor realized.

"Sorry, Lucy," Sailor said, coming over to them.

"Much better. Three is hard. Someone can easily feel left out. Right Tommy?" Lupe asked Tommy knowingly, who looked torn between enjoying himself and being guilty.

"Yes, Lupe. Sorry, Lucy, you can help us build it too."

"Good children," Lupe said in Spanish.

Sailor heard arguing in the hall. Lupe got up and crashed into Quinn and a lady. She looked familiar.

"Mami? Mami, you came!!!!" Lucy all but threw herself at her as Tommy chose to stay back.

Lucy glared at Tommy, "I told you she would come. Tommy said you wouldn't."

Quinn spoke up fast, "Lucía Isabella Callahan." as he went in. Lucy got very quiet. Tommy's eyes welled up. Sofía looked hurt. Quinn went to Tommy, "It's ok, buddy. Mami understands why you would be surprised." Then he glared at Sofía angrily.

Lupe came and hugged Sailor. She must have known that she felt scared. The big lady looked exactly like Jazmín, maybe even Lucy too, Sailor thought. Tommy just looked like Quinn with dark coloring.

"Besito, Tomás," Sofía said, still hugging Lucy. He came over after Quinn rubbed his back encouragingly. He hugged her, then burst into tears and ran out of the room. Quinn followed as Lupe took Lucy's hand, "I have her, go on." Lupe told Sofía in Spanish. With a nod, she tried to follow after them.

Lupe took Sailor and Lucy downstairs to get a snack if only to keep them busy.

BIRDIE BLUE

Birdie was in Sir Oliver's office talking to someone on the phone.

"Yes, we will be ready. Please remember the floors are delicate. They need to be protected from the scaffolding. It's a historical home; treat it as you would a museum."

Birdie nodded, "Good. Thank you. See you in two days." She hung up and went upstairs to her room through the shortcut. Birdie put her phone away and then went up to the children's room. Only no one was there. Did they go for a walk? She checked her phone. No text from Lupe. That was odd. She decided maybe they went to the kitchen, and she came down the landing to hear Quinn and a woman shouting outside. From midway on the staircase, she could see out the window over the door. Sofía.

"You don't just show up. Tommy needed to be prepared." Quinn was saying loudly.

"You are poisoning my kids from me. And where is Jazmín? You promised to treat her as the others!" Sofía shouted back.

"Poisoning your kids?! I have never done any such thing. I never talk negatively about you to them, and you know it. Not a single word of your selfish behavior was ever mentioned. And what exactly do you mean by where's Jazmín? You have no idea where any of your kids are at any point-" Sofía slapped him. SHE SLAPPED HIM?!

"Too close to the truth?" He asked, deadly quiet. The slap didn't even look like it affected him. Birdie flew down the stairs and opened the door wildly.

"Where do you get off hitting him? Get out now!" Birdie said angrily.

One look at who was talking shocked Sofía, and then she started to laugh as it dawned on her who was shouting at her.

"Still Quinn? Go to hell, pendejo!" Sofía turned and rushed to her car.

Quinn looked stunned, then gathered himself. He locked the gate from his phone fast. Sofía saw what he did. "Open it, Quinn, or I'll ram it open." She said it in English.

"Say 'goodbye' to your children first. This isn't about your ego anymore. Then I will open the gate."

Birdie looked shocked. Quinn was no joke.

Sofía screamed loudly in a fit of anger, scaring all the birds.

"I'll wait," he said as if speaking to Lucy and not his ex-wife.

"You want to play, Quinn? I am staying." She went to the trunk and took out an overnight bag. "You can stay with the Puta, I will be with the kids."

Quinn was in front of Sofía before Birdie had a chance to even realize the 'Puta' was her. She knew what that meant even though Lupe never taught her curses.

He got in her face angrily but lowly had words with her. Words Birdie could not hear. Then he took her arm and turned, "Apologize now."

"Fine. Where are the kids?"

"When I hear 'I am sorry, Birdie,' I will let you know."

More curses in Spanish, but then nodded, "Sorry, Birdie. I am mad at him, not you." She rushed, then glared at Quinn, "My kids. Jazmín, too."

With a sarcastic bow, he led the way to the Carriage House.

Holy shit! Birdie thought. No wonder why he wanted peace from females.

QUINN RYAN

He gave Sofía Tommy's room and put Tommy in bed with him. He did not need any late-night visits from her, her usual way to make up with him... though there was a Jorge now, so maybe not.

Against his better judgment, Sofía begged to tell them all together. The five were sitting on the couch as Sofía told them she was getting married again.

"To Daddy?" Lucy asked excitedly in a loud squeal.

"No," Quinn said fast.

"No, my love, to a man named Jorge. He's nice. He has a son, too. I am moving to Miami."

"Yay! I get to see Mami every day now." Lucy clapped innocently.

Before Quinn could say anything, Sofía spoke."No, my beautiful Lucía, you will stay in South Carolina. But we will visit each other a lot. Not like before. I decided to stop acting. I will stay in America now."

Whoa, he hadn't told the kids his decision yet. And bullshit on the stopping acting, Quinn fumed. "Sofía, when I fully decide the next step in MY life, with MY kids, I will tell them, not you." He growled.

"I want to stay here, Dad," Tommy said, coming over and sitting on his lap.

"I like this house, too," Jazmín said worriedly.

"If this house is sold, we may not be able to stay here. I am not sure of anything yet and Mami should not be speaking out of turn. Nothing to worry about until we know more. For now, we stay here. Mami can visit IF everyone is getting along happily." He said that to Sofía. She knew that he was serious, too.

"But… but if we all live in Miami, we can be together a lot." Lucy started to cry. He pulled her into his arms, next to Tommy, heartbroken for her. She could only see it through a child's eyes, and he was now second-guessing his decision to move to South Carolina with her reaction.

"We'll see, my girl. Right now we are visiting each other. We all must get along." He said, putting her down again.

Jazmín, still not near her mother, went up to Quinn with a sarcastic look on her face, "So if we all don't get along, she leaves? Bye Sofía, don't let the door hit you on the ass-" She laughed at her mother's expense but was shocked by the "Hey!" Quinn said loudly, startling her. He gave her a firm look making her look ashamed.

"Sorry, Dad, I shouldn't have said that," Jazmín said to him, completely ignoring her mother. He kissed the top of her head forgivingly.

Sofía looked jealous.

"Say sorry to Mom." Quinn said to Jazmín, "I know you are mad, but she let you stay. Be respectful."

"Sorry, Mami," Jazmín said in a whisper. She looked up at Quinn to see if that was good enough, and he nodded.

Quinn saw the look of sadness in Sofía's eyes. All three kids were all but on him, even if he hadn't encouraged it.

"You can stay one night. Spend time with the kids. I will order food. Let me tell Cora."

Quinn knew there was no way in hell Cora or Nancy would allow her to sit at the table. Both despised her lack of mothering.

"I will stay next door so you four can spend time together. Tommy will be in my bed." He said, shocking all.

"I'll sleep with Tommy," Jazmín said fast.

"Yay! I will sleep with Mami!" Lucy clapped.

Sofía looked at Quinn. "Thank you, Papi." Quinn noticed she said it sincerely.

Quinn nodded, packing a bag for himself. He ordered food for them and kissed each kid. Taking care to give Tommy and Jazmín reassuring looks. With a 'You know what behavior I expect.' He left.

He walked into the main house to see an annoyed Cora, "You left my babies with her? All night?"

"I left them with their mother." He sighed.

Cora gave a humph.

"Can I stay upstairs?"

"Of course, don't be silly. Third floor bedroom was made up already in case she stayed." However, she rolled her eyes when she said it.

He kissed her cheek, "Thank you, Cora."

He went up.

BIRDIE BLUE

Birdie was sketching the second wall of the children's room. She was trying to keep her mind busy. She had so many erratic thoughts running through her mind, from anger that Sofía slapped Quinn to embarrassment. She yelled at her to leave when the kids would naturally want to see their mother. Would they get back together? Birdie knew she was panicking.

She looked at Sailor and took a deep breath. Birdie would just need to wait and see. She smiled when she saw that Sailor was trying to copy what she was drawing onto a piece of paper.

"Good job, Sailor." Birdie smiled. Her drawings were getting better and better each year.

"What's that going to be, Mommy?"

Birdie had been drawing Captain America's shield as it spun through the scene. Birdie explained her plan.

"Knock, knock," Quinn said softly.

Birdie saw him, dropped the pencil, and rushed over, "Sorry, I yelled at her." She hugged him, "Are you alright?"

He nodded but then looked at a worried Sailor. Birdie understood he would not talk in front of Sailor. Lupe went to lie down earlier, so she would need to wait to find out what happened.

"Cora asked if you would like to bake cookies with Nancy?" Quinn said to Sailor. Her face lit up.

"Can I, Mommy?"

"I'll just take her down. Please sit." Birdie took Sailor down and was out of breath by the time she did the two massive stairs up again.

"This place needs an elevator." She tried to tease, but he just looked so conflicted.

He updated her on everything that she missed. They were sitting in the reading nook next to each other. He leaned in and kissed her, "Sorry, I had to do that." He smiled. She leaned into his chest.

"So, what are you going to do?"

"Stay until all projects are complete. Yours and a list of things I have to do around the property, like build a deck by the pond with a few Adirondack chairs."

"I wonder if he will sell this place. I could buy it. We could keep it for us... all of us to use, I mean. Kiera, Cora, Nancy too." Then she blushed. Sex and kisses were one thing, but they have not defined their relationship yet, let alone the future. Here she was stupidly buying them a house, Birdie thought. Talk about jumping ahead!

"That would be nice. It needs someone who can afford the upkeep of the place unless the house comes with money, too. If given to someone who doesn't have the amount required, they would have no choice but to sell it. The grounds alone cost money to maintain." He was rambling; she leaned over and kissed him, "Breathe, Quinn." She could tell he was all over the place.

He looked at her, "So much of my life is a mess right now, and I am so far behind on my architectural work. I literally pulled myself off of a project. I never do that. And Jazmín is here, and you-"

"And me what?"

"I want to spend time with you." He said into her ear as she leaned back against his chest cozily.

"And I want to spend time with you, too."

Quinn's phone rang. He got it fast, thinking it was his kids.

"Hello?"

He mouthed 'Kiera' to Birdie.

Of all the times for Kiera to call, Birdie thought. Birdie needed to know what they were doing.

"Just talking to Birdie", he put it on speakerphone, then he told most of the story until Birdie interjected with the slapping part and her reaction. Then apologized again, knowing the kids would want to see their mom. Quinn looked like he wished she hadn't mentioned it because Kiera was furious. She mentioned she had done that once before. What? She slapped him another time? Quinn looked mad at his sister.

"Should I come?" Kiera demanded.

"That would be a no. You start fights with her. And stop telling Birdie stuff." He growled.

"Oh, be quiet. Birdie needs a full picture. And don't give me that 'highly passionate Latina' bullshit. She's half-Italian. Her real last name is Rossellini. Did you tell her that? She was born in Italy and then moved to Colombia when she was six. Her father is Italian, and her mother is Colombian. She is just hot-tempered, no matter what her nationality is. And you make excuses for her." Kiera pointed out, annoyed, then sighed. Kiera then added, "But I know you are a good guy Quinn, always seeing the good in people. Right Birdie?"

"Yes." Birdie smiled.

"So... what's going on with you two?" Kiera laughed, "Just the two of you alone?" She teased. "Fill me in, please." She added laughing.

Quinn and Birdie both blushed a bit.

"Be quiet, Kiera," Quinn said instead.

Kiera burst out laughing, "Yeah, I thought so."

"Kiera..." Quinn growled.

"Quinn..." Kiera teased back, "Out with it. You both like each other. Do not lie. I saw it with my own eyes. Am I right?"

Both Quinn and Birdie looked at the other.

"Yes, " Quinn said, honestly. Birdie was shocked. He admitted it to his sister.

"Date!"

"Hanging up, Kiera," Quinn said, and then he did.

Was he embarrassed? Having second thoughts?

"Sorry, she's full of mischief today. I would love to just date you, but..."

"But what?" She asked fast. Was he worried about Sofía? Would he try to get her back for the kids? What?

"But I am unsure what this is. Are we friends? Dating? Friends with benefits?"

"Yes."

"Friends with benefits?!" He looked shocked. He looked repulsed by that and Birdie had to hold in a giggle. She tried, but his face made it impossible.

"Gross, no. We are friends, seeing each other, and there are benefits." Birdie grinned.

Quinn smiled, relieved, happy.

"Do we tell anyone?" Birdie asked.

"What do you want?"

She shrugged. Her track record with men, or rather 'man,' was not good. Lupe liked Quinn, though. She trusted Lupe's opinion.

"Wait, what about Frank?" Quinn asked as if he had just woken up.

"What about him? He won't mind."

"He won't mind?"

"He's my manager, not my Dad."

"I thought you were dating."

Birdie lost it, full-on belly laugh. Tears were coming out of her eyes she was laughing so hard.

Quinn looked crossed between, annoyed and confused.

"He is married to a man. Frank is gay. I am not. He's also double my age or close enough."

Quinn processed that.

"He has access to your house?"

"What does that mean? Oh! Were you eavesdropping?" Birdie laughed, in a sing-song voice, "Bad, Quinn." She shook her finger at him teasingly.

"I couldn't help but hear it. The hallway echoes." He muttered.

"And what about the girl you can't have? You moved on?" Birdie asked, feeling awkward.

He looked at her like she was purposely being obtuse. Oh. OH! She was that girl?! He thought she was with Frank! Birdie slowly grinned, realizing that both were very single and loved each other.

"So... what are we doing?" she asked, trying to contain the huge smile that was threatening to overtake her face.

"Dating. Can we, uh, be casual at first in front of the kids? I want them to see us together and see it progress naturally."

She nodded, loving how sweet he was to worry about them.

"You can tell Lupe, we told Kiera already. I would rather not tell Sofía anything."

Birdie looked down. Was he afraid to tell her? "No, Birdie, nothing like that. She's an 'I don't want him, but I also don't want anyone else to have him' type of woman. Especially you." It was cute when he blushed, Birdie thought.

"What did she mean by 'again'?" Birdie asked; it had been on her mind.

He really blushed, "I would be caught following your career if you were on TMZ or a special. She was jealous even then, even though I told her we were childhood friends. I was always happy to see an update on you." Quinn admitted.

"As I would have been with you both. I get it."

"Have you talked to Lupe about your talk with her doctor?"

"Yes. She is optimistic for one second. Then, in the next, she is telling me stuff about her will, how to deal with things that may come up with Sailor as she gets older... she's preparing me."

He pulled her close, "I will be here for you in any capacity. Either as a partner or a friend. You won't be alone."

"Friend?"

"If you decide you do not want to date in the future."

"Quinn, what did she do to you to make you so jaded? We both were hurt. We both will be gentle to each other. Who better understands the pain than us?"

Quinn's eyes clouded, but nodded, "Just promise to tell me before moving on to someone else. A Birdie promise."

"I promise, Quinn, and you know how I feel about promises."

He nodded.

"Same for you, promise me."

"I don't need to."

"Quinn, I need you to."

He nodded, "I promise."

SAILOR WREN

Sailor missed her new friends. She hadn't seen them since yesterday. Today, Lupe and her mother were taking her for a walk by the pond for some reason. Sailor heard them talking earlier about telling her something important.

Lupe started the conversation but suddenly could not talk anymore. Her eyes were watery. Why? They didn't seem like happy, shiny tears this time.

"Sailor honey, Lupe is very sick. She has a tumor in a bad place that they cannot take out without hurting her." Her mother said, her own eyes tearing.

Sailor glanced up at Lupe worriedly and hugged her tightly, as all three were crying now.

"Are you going to be ok?"

"No, Mamita, probably not. One day it will be too big." Lupe said softly while hugging her tight.

Sailor looked up at Lupe, who was openly crying. She had never seen Lupe cry before. She was always so tough. It scared Sailor.

"Sailor, honey, Lupe is here now. We will enjoy her while she is here. Then she will go be with Grandpa and Grandma." Her mother said as a sob escaped, looking like she was trying to gather herself fast. Her mother wiped her eyes and continued.

"We will miss her when the time comes like we missed Grandpa. She will always be watching over us."

Sailor hugged her mom now. Sailor saw how sad she was; she pulled Lupe in, too. All three just cried together. It would be so strange not to have Lupe around. Where would she go if her mother worked? She was suddenly scared again. She wanted to ask, but she knew this was not the time. It would sound selfish, Sailor thought. She would ask her mom alone.

After a minute or two, "Enough of this. God can't have me yet. I still have things to teach my girls." Lupe wiped away her tears, annoyed with them. "I may rest more, but it's not because I do not want to be with you. Understand, Mamita? Never think I do not want to be with you. Resting helps the body fix itself, and I need a lot of fixing. As I get sicker, I will need more and more rest. But never doubt my desire to WANT to be with you. Understand? You and Mommy are my entire world."

Lupe kissed Sailor and her mother as her mother wept again.

"No more crying. And no more secrets, alright? You have each other. You will also have Quinn, Tommy, Lucy, Jazmín, Kiera, Amanda, and so many others."

"Until we move," Sailor said before she realized it came out. Sailor covered her mouth fast. That was not the right thing to say. Sailor thought, embarrassed now. She felt bad.

"No. Quinn and I decided we needed each other. Our families need each other. We want you all to grow up together in some format. Live near each other or something."

"And Quinn and Mommy like each other, tell her Mi hija. Tell her all. No secrets." Lupe encouraged.

Sailor looked up at her mother, shocked.

"We do like each other, but Quinn does not want the kids or Sofía, their mom, to know just yet. He wants them to slowly get used to the idea of him dating. Understand? This is one secret we will keep, just us three."

Sailor beamed, nodding.

"Do you like him, Sailor?" Her mother asked tentatively.

Sailor nodded, smiling, "He's nice."

"Are you ok with Mommy and Quinn dating?" Lupe asked.

Sailor nodded again.

"Good. See Mi hija, I told you she is mature enough to hear this. She would understand and want you to be happy, too. This is life, some bad news and some good news. Always focus on the positive in life. Alright, my girls? Even if it's overwhelming, always find the silver lining." Then, Lupe explained the saying to Sailor, and she understood.

"I need to rest. You got Sailor?" Lupe asked her mother.

"Always." Her mother hugged Sailor, and she felt happy. If her mom worked, there was a plan so she wouldn't be alone. Relief, even if she would rather keep Lupe forever.

BIRDIE BLUE

She had been concerned to tell Sailor about her and Quinn but she took it so well. Birdie was so proud of her. Birdie watched her paint a giant rose on the easel. She was looking at a fresh-cut rose that Quinn had brought Birdie earlier and was standing in a vase.

"Notice the lighting. Which way is the sun coming in? Where is the shadow?" Birdie explained.

Sailor was a fast learner.

"I even made a white spot like you do." Sailor giggled.

"Great job. It's dinner time soon. Quinn said he'll eat with us after he checks on the kids. You are still good with him, right?"

Sailor nodded, smiling. Then looked up at her, "Do you kiss?" She asked, giggling.

Birdie laughed, "Yes. But not in front of anyone until everyone knows."

Again, another giggle.

Birdie's phone rang; it was Quinn.

"Shawna Weber is here to see you." Quinn then asked, "Let her in?"

"Oh! The clothes. Yes. Will your kids still be able to come? You said they could pick."

She heard his sigh, "Let me call Sofía. I don't expect it to go well."

"Then I will keep the stuff for when she leaves."

"It's alright. I'll call her." He hung up.

Birdie and Sailor went down to Shawna, hugging her.

"Sailor, you got so big!"

Sailor beamed at her.

Shawna looked at Birdie, "Maybe still 4/6." Implying Sailor was still tiny, despite what she just said.

Birdie laughed, "Where do you want to set up?"

"I finally did the mobile closet idea. Everything is ready."

They walked outside to a giant touring bus wrapped in a 'Styled by Shawna' design. When they went in, Birdie gasped.

It was beautiful—racks along one side, dressing rooms, couches, desk, and lighted full-body mirror.

"Champagne?" Shawna asked.

"No, thank you; you know me, Shawna." Birdie laughed.

"I know, my easiest customer. I just wanted you to see the full treatment my customers get." She laughed. Birdie was with Shawna when she started her business. She even loaned her $100,000 to get the business going. So, with each clothing session, she is closer to paying off the debt—a win-win for both.

"Ok, Miss Sailor, come look at each outfit."

"Shawna, school clothes. I think some of these are too fancy for that." Birdie wasn't sure, but some looked too nice to send to school. Don't they climb jungle gyms and stuff?

"School picture days. Let the professional work." Shawna teased her.

After measuring her, she pulled out half of her clothes in 4/6 and the other half in 6x, "To grow into."

Birdie nodded; it sounded logical. Lupe usually handled this. She wanted to do it all herself to show Lupe they would be okay, even if she wasn't truly sure herself.

Ten shorts, eight pants, seven dresses, a coat, underwear, tee-shirts, dozens of socks, a raincoat, boots for fall and rain boots, two dress shoes, and three pairs of sneakers were selected. All were tried on, "Sorry Pammy couldn't come to tailor it. She had a bad cold."

"Hug your sister for me." Birdie smiled.

While Shawna packed up the many bags, she also totaled the items. The total came to $2,088.00.

Suddenly, there was a knock on the door, but it wasn't Quinn and the kids, as Birdie thought; it was Sofía alone.

"May I?" She asked Birdie as she awkwardly came in. Sofía was seriously stunning in her clothes. Maybe Quinn was attracted to that, more than Birdie's comfortable wardrobe.

Birdie had to stop herself from spiraling. He loved her, not Sofía. Get it together, Birdie thought to herself.

"Shawna Weber, this is Sofía Colon, the mother of the other three kids coming."

"Not coming unless I approve and pay," Sofía said haughtily.

"Wonderful!" Shawna said smiling, ushering her inside with a face to Birdie telling her to shush. "Champagne?" Again, the smile back on her face. Of course, Sofía said 'yes'. Birdie wanted to laugh; Shawna was a pro at these rich prima donnas.

"I need the children, please," Shawna said.

Sofía dialed, "Tell them to come." She hung up, probably on Quinn. Ugh, she did not like this lady. Or was this attitude just a front for her? She wondered.

Lucy came running up the stairs, "Me first."

"Come." She was measured by Shawna.

"Is this all the clothes you have to try?" Sofía asked incredulously.

Quinn walked in holding Tommy's hand, "Yes, because they are school clothes, and I only agreed to five outfits, Sofía. Be polite or leave." Quinn said, annoyed.

Shawna's eyes widened. Sofía's mouth shut. Birdie was surprised. Sweet Quinn had a tough side.

"Lawyer is sending paperwork now. You sign, or you leave. That was the deal." Quinn added.

Sign what? Birdie was confused. Shawna pretended to be busy with Lucy, but Birdie could see her listening to every word.

Another outburst in Spanish from Sofia, which he gave back in Spanish. Then said, 'You are in America now; please speak English. People will think you are talking about them.'" That last sentence said in English.

"I said yes!" She said in English.

He took his phone, opened an email, zoomed in, "Sign."

With a frustrated look, she did.

"There? Happy! Jazi can stay with you until college. BUT... the visitation stands." Sofía said as if she needed to have the last word.

"Glad Jorge was able to talk sense into you during our talk," Quinn said.

"Pendejo!"

Quinn, Sofía, and Jorge spoke about Jazmín? When?

"And she gets her phone back, but it is given to me. I will give it to her when school starts."

Sofía shrugged, "It is still in the p.o. box my assistant opened here. Go get it. The key was sent to you."

"That is what that key was for?" Quinn shook his head. He thought it was to a vault box. There were no markings on it other than the number '918'.

Quinn shook his head.

Birdie looked at him. He looked relieved, he gave her a look that said 'I will update you later'.

"If I pay, per our agreement, Quinn, they can have more than five. Ok? Be reasonable." He nodded, forwarding his signature to his lawyer. Then he looked up at Jazmín and winked. She beamed. She looked ready to do a backflip.

"I'm strict, but it's too late now." Quinn teased her.

She laughed, "Do I ever get my own room?"

"When we move out of the Carriage House." He smiled.

"Ok… oooo, that's pretty, Lucy!" Jazmín helped her sister pick out eleven outfits: a coat, a raincoat, two pairs of boots, rain boots, and sneakers.

"Tommy, your turn." Sofía said as Shawna tallied the items.

"I want Daddy to help me pick." He said, unsure.

"Of course, men only for this selection," Shawna said, smiling.

Tommy chose six pairs of jeans, seven pairs of shorts, ten shirts, a coat, and two pairs of sneakers. He did not want a raincoat or boots. He absolutely refused. Quinn let it be.

"Jazmín, your turn," Shawna said, tallying everything.

"I had the most fun pulling your stuff," Shawna said.

Jazmín was giddy, "I've only worn uniforms for years!!!!"

"Not true, Jazmín," Sofía argued.

"Yes, it is!" But one look at Quinn and she stopped. "I mostly wore uniforms." She amended.

"Fair. Let me help-"

Sofía was shot down, "No. I will pick the clothes I want alone." Jazmín said firmly.

Sofía sat dejectedly.

Quinn looked at Jazmín, "You promised. I'll shred this document right now."

"No…. Ok, you can say if you like it, Mami. Ok, Dad?" Jazmín asked fast. He nodded.

Birdie took Sailor and their bags to Sailor's room. She hung up most of it and put the rest in the drawers.

An hour later, Shawna called her.

"They left. They bought almost everything. Jazmín got almost twenty outfits! Come say bye."

Sailor and Jazmín went down. The racks were literally empty.

"Sofía asked that I bring clothes to her in Miami next week. I love dressing Miami ladies, but only if you are OK with it. You didn't seem to like her."

"Business is business. You better have said 'yes.'" Birdie hugged her.

"Can I do your wardrobe one day?"

"Yes, once I know where I live." Both laughed.

Shawna pulled out two bags from the back, "My gift to you."

"Shawna! Thank you."

"Thank you, you made this possible. And you got me so many customers. So thank you." With a hug, they got off the bus and watched the driver back out carefully once Quinn was called to open the gate and guide them out.

Upstairs, in Birdie's room, they opened the bags. Three pairs of jeans, one pair of slacks, two boots, four tops and a coat. All her size, all understated, relaxed clothing Birdie normally loved when not painting. All for fall. She texted a 'thank you' to Shawna and met everyone for dinner. Sofía too. Yikes, she felt the tension between Cora and Sofía from the hallway.

"Thank you for inviting us," Sofía said stiffly. As if prompted by Quinn. Cora nodded curtly, "Dinner is coming out now."

Sofía was across from Birdie, next to Quinn.

"Cora, Sofía is staying for two more days. So I will use the upstairs room until then if it's ok."

"Anything for you, my boy." The stress on 'you' almost made Birdie laugh out loud.

Sofía sighed, "Thank you, Cora."

Again, another nod.

They all ate. Nancy was not as polite as Cora. She didn't even acknowledge Sofía.

"Birdie, thank you for helping poor Quinn. He gets so nervous taking them to the stores. That must be a big relief." Cora said sweetly.

"Why? This isn't Spain." Sofía asked, confused.

"It was worse in Miami, but I am still relieved. I just need to get them a few things, but they can stay home." Quinn said.

"Like?" Sofía asked curtly.

"Underwear, socks, t-shirts, pajamas, toiletries for Jazmín -"

"Can I take her for that? Please, Jazmín, let me?" Sofía asked, all but begging.

Quinn nodded at Jazmín, and she reluctantly agreed.

"Thank you." Sofía's eyes looked like they welled, happy her daughter was being kind to her.

"See, we can co-parent successfully," Quinn said, trying to appease everyone.

"Yes, I am agreeing to everything. I just want to be involved again." Sofía said.

Nancy snorted. Birdie wanted to laugh. Nancy was not buying it.

"Nancy Ann!" Cora scolded.

Nancy nodded, "Fine. But I need to see things with my own eyes to believe it."

"Fair," Cora said, probably agreeing.

Quinn sighed loudly. Birdie felt terrible as the kids quietly ate, just watching them all.

"Did you all like the clothes Shawna brought?" Birdie asked the kids, then suddenly all were excitely talking and the awkward start to dinner was gone.

"Oh, the school bags and lunch boxes are coming tomorrow. If you don't like any, we can find more online," Birdie said.

Sofía looked up, "I will get them that."

"But I picked them for my friends. I even selected soccer for Tommy, pink unicorns for Lucy, and some in Jazmín's favorite color." Sailor said sadly.

"I want what Sailor picked," Tommy said, defending her.

"Me too, Mami. I love pink unicorns." Lucy smiled.

"Well, of course, that was sweet of you, Sailor. I mean, I can pay for everything..." Sofía said, again looking down. That she wouldn't hurt Sailor's or her children's feelings made Birdie soften towards her. She finally realized what she missed, Birdie thought and was trying desperately to get it back. She still could not forgive the slap, but she could be kinder.

"They may not like what we chose. I have no idea about school bags or lunch boxes. My daughter has been home-schooled. So if they prefer others, that is perfectly fine. They come tomorrow and can decide." Birdie said. Quinn looked up at her and smiled a 'thank you' smile. Even Sofía looked confused, but she nodded.

After dinner, the kids wanted to show Sofía both the Nursery and the children's room, even though there were only rough sketches on the walls. The Nursery was one thing, but the uncompleted rough sketch was another. She was afraid she would open herself up to criticism; however Birdie agreed when seeing the kid's excitement.

Sofía looked surprisingly impressed by the Nursery, even complimenting Birdie on the beautiful room.

"Is this where the crib would go?" Sofía asked Birdie directly. Birdie had purposely made one little section a little less busy for that very purpose. Birdie nodded.

"I would have done the same. This will be one very lucky baby." Sofía said as Lucy tugged her hand out to lead her upstairs.

Quinn held Birdie back as they all went up, "Thank you. She is in my life no matter what; I need peace with her for the kid's sake."

Birdie nodded.

He took his chance and kissed her, but Jazmín must have come back for them, and she gasped. Both broke apart guiltily.

Then Jazmín shocked Birdie by clapping while jumping up and down, "I knew it!" She smiled happily.

"Sh!" Quinn said fast, cheeks pink. "Mom won't like it. When she left, we were telling you all."

"I feel a phone coming sooner than I thought..." Jazmín grinned, eyebrows going up and down mischievously.

Birdie laughed as Quinn shook his head, "I feel a phone not coming before you are sixteen if it gets out earlier than I am ready." he said teasingly back to her. Jazmín laughed.

Sofía came back, "Jazmín? Are you coming, Mama?" But she looked at all three, accessing the scene before her.

All looked guilty. They just froze there, wondering if she heard.

"I already knew. It's all over their faces. I am engaged, Dad is dating, and we are moving on. Alright, everyone?" Sofía said in English, shocking them all. And in that moment, the tension between the three dissipated.

"Tommy and Lucy do not know," Quinn said, "Jazmín accidentally found out just now."

"So tell them. Or don't, your business. But I know you, Quinn. I can read your body language. Jazmín, let me speak to Papi, please." Jazmín left and Birdie was going to leave also, "Please stay." Sofía said softly.

Birdie nodded cautiously.

"You will be in my kid's life more than me. I know I have anger issues, and I need to work on it. Jorge is good, Quinn. Good for me, he will be good as a stepfather to our kids. He is a great father, like you." She took a deep breath, then looked squarely at Birdie and then Quinn. "I need the three of us to get along. I apologized three times now, Quinn. Old habits are hard to break. I am mostly at fault but you also need to stop rubbing my mistakes in my face all the time. It keeps me from wanting to come back, scared of hearing it every time. It is hard to keep having a spotlight on your failures as a mother… as a wife. To keep having to relive your mistakes. Please, Quinn, we need to be civil." Sofía all but begged.

Quinn nodded.

"I love the kids. Always have. I wish you had seen all the changes I promoted with the paparazzi, with laws adopted in Spain. I wished you brought them more as my time was limited. If I am out, a hundred and sixty other people do not work. My job was contracted. I had hoped you understood that. You also had more flexibility than I did. The kids were not in school yet. Your career was just starting, whereas mine took off. I was older than you. I put more time into it. I thought it was a jealousy thing at first; I thought me making more money may have bothered you. If only we spoke more to see it from the other's perspective. But more importantly, I wish I tried harder to get you to come. I felt rejected by you. I was angry and stayed away because you wouldn't see how hard I tried to fix it. The bodyguards, the gated villa, the laws… I tried to fix it, Quinn." Her eyes were welling now, and a tear fell, "I need you to know I didn't just give up. I even offered you an architectural firm in Spain. You wouldn't even hear me out." She burst into tears, crying now.

Birdie could see she wasn't acting. She looked raw.

"I know." Quinn said, "We both messed up, Sofía," He hugged her, "I am sorry, too."

"I cheated and left for fame, but I felt you left me long before that. I cannot apologize for that anymore. Please do not keep bringing it up to hurt me. I own it. I will never make that mistake again. Not to our kids, not to my partner." Birdie tried to leave, this was too intimate a conversation for her to listen to, but Quinn grabbed her hand. His intentions were clear. They were a couple. She was to stay.

"I get so stressed out and filled with anxiety when I need to see you all. I know what I am going to hear. You get so angry around me, saying harsh things... You look like the hero, and I look like a failure. I react. I am not proud of it, but I hear it enough in my own mind. You keep saying it-" She took a deep breath, "I want to not be scared to see the kids. I own I shouldn't have hit you. I promised the last time and I broke that promise. I am so sorry for that. I have much work to do on myself."

He nodded, "As we all do. Had that reporter not almost made me drop Lucy, this might have been very different. But to be honest, I do not think we would have worked out, regardless." He said softly.

She nodded, "You always loved Birdie. I knew it."

Birdie looked shocked. Sofía actually smiled at her through her tears.

"He told me about his first crush; Kiera used to tease him, too. Then he would watch specials or news with you. I knew even then. I was jealous."

Quinn blushed, but Birdie squeezed his hand.

"From this moment on, I want us to be friends. Alright? All of us. I will try my hardest to work on my anger. But let's face it, I come from fiery blood. I will be a work in progress." Sofía tried to laugh, wiping her eyes.

"Friends and co-parents, my rules still stand: Never talk badly about the other. I have kept my word," Quinn pointed out.

"I have not, with Jazmín only, though. So I need to fix that. She resents me because of it. I love you, Quinn, like family, but it is still love. You have raised my kids wonderfully."

"OUR kids." He laughed.

"Yes, of course, ours." She laughed, wiping her tears.

Then they heard, "But I want Mami to come and see." Clearly, Jazmín was holding the kids off right outside the door.

Quinn shook his head, "Everyone, please come in. We need to tell you something." He sighed. Today was a day of truths.

When Tommy heard, his face lit up! Lucy looked unsure, worried about her mother.

"Daddy and I are the best of friends. We made the best kids. I have Jorge now, he wants to meet you all. Daddy has Birdie and Sailor now. We will be one big extended family. I am happy for Daddy, and he is happy for me. Alright?" She lifted Lucy, and Lucy smiled.

Then Tommy smiled, "Jazmín, you guessed it right!"

"And I really promise this time, to be around more. Maybe I can pay you to keep the Miami place and you visit there as much as I visit wherever you finally buy a place. Ok? I am not acting anymore. I am actually thinking of writing a book, or doing a podcast, something that I can get up and go whenever. Jorge is a bit older; he wants to work less, maybe travel too."

Birdie could see that she really put thought into this. Birdie actually believed Sofía made a big change. She faced her demons. She looked less wound up after the talk with Quinn.

"I am sorry, kids, that I was not around enough." She took Tommy's hand. "I messed up. I was always afraid I would be forgotten if I stepped away from acting. I didn't realize that I stepped away from the wrong thing. I never meant to do that. Do not fire me as your Mami, ok? Please." She said to Tommy.

He nodded. Lucy threw her hands around her neck. "We love you, Mami." Sofía cried a bit, then put Lucy down to hug Tommy, too.

Then she looked at Jazmín, "I messed up with you the most. I treated you like a friend and confidant, not as a daughter. I talked badly about Papi to you when I got mad or hurt. For that, I am sorry."

Jazmín's eyes welled, "I don't like it when you do that, Mami. He's the only Dad who ever wanted me. Even if he isn't my real one."

"Actually, what if I was? Maybe I could adopt her? Just so I am her legal father. So the three kids are OUR kids." Quinn said.

Jazmín burst into real tears, and Sofía smiled, eyes welled again, and said, "Yes. You are the only one she ever had. Thank you, Papi. I will get the lawyers to do that."

"Good. We will be patient with each other and figure out the next steps. We are here for a year give or take. You and Jorge can come to visit. The kids will visit you around school. I may keep the Miami home."

"I'll pay-"

"It's paid for Sofía. And I did it on my own, without your money. I wanted you to see that. Every penny you sent went into bank accounts for the kids." Quinn said proudly.

"Taking a step backward, Quinn." Birdie pointed out, shaking her head, annoyed. Sofía looked at Birdie thankfully. She smiled at Birdie.

"Sorry." He sighed.

"I am proud of you, Quinn. I told you that you were talented. I still have clippings of you being in the paper." Sofía admitted. Now, it was Quinn's turn to be surprised. He sighed, "We will both do better. For the kids, for our friendship." Quinn said.

SAILOR WREN

Sailor was nervously holding her mother's hand in the school office. She would have been twice as scared had she not found out that she and Tommy would be put in the same class due to how close he was to turning eight and Sailor never having attended a traditional school so they thought the transition would be easier.

Quinn rushed in and took Lucy's and Tommy's hand, "Thank you for staying with them while I took Jazi next door to the high school."

"Of course." Her mom smiled.

Lupe smiled at Sailor, "I will miss you today." Sailor could see her eyes welling up. Sailor hugged her tightly.

Then, the principal and the assistant principal introduced themselves. Both were so sweet. They spoke a bit until Sailor and Lucy looked a bit more comfortable. Then, the principal took Sailor and Tommy to their class, while the assistant principal took Lucy to her class. Sailor was so excited she just took in everything.

QUINN RYAN

Quinn took Birdie's hand and led them out.

"Everyone at this school is super nice." He assured both Birdie and Lupe.

They nodded. Both looked like a mixture of emotions. Sad for themselves, but super proud Sailor went happily. Having Tommy in her class helped Sailor's confidence.

"I'm taking Lupe to radiation. Nancy said she would still do Saturdays. See you back at home." Birdie told Quinn. He nodded. They kissed and went back to their cars.

BIRDIE BLUE

Lupe was resting in her room. Birdie hadn't realized how fast the radiation treatment was. Lupe seemed fine walking out, too, which calmed Birdie a lot.

When home, Birdie climbed up the stairs of the scaffolding to paint the ballroom ceiling. She started it two days ago; it was slow going, but she was grateful for the distraction. It took her mind off of panicking about whether she should get Sailor. Quinn came up to bring her a sandwich at noon, but they ended up making love right there on the scaffolding before eating together. Then he snuck out, praying no one caught them.

At quarter to three, her alarm went off on her watch. She closed the paint cans, took care of her brushes, and climbed down. After washing up, she all but ran to the gate.

She saw Lupe looking out from her seat on the second-floor porch, too. Then Quinn came up to her, "You survived." Quinn teased Birdie.

"I only called you once since lunch." Birdie laughed.

"Twice before lunch. I could tell you started to panic again." Quinn laughed.

Birdie punched his arm, "This is new to me."

"It's Lucy's first day of kindergarten, too; I'm just as anxious to see how she did. Jazi looked scared, but she texted me at lunch. Kids are being overly nice to her." He sighed, relieved.

"Can't they all have phones? So that I can check in?"

Quinn laughed. Then he saw that Birdie had been serious.

"No, Birdie. Not allowed. She is fine, and Tommy is with her. They are buddies."

Birdie nodded, thankful for that.

"Are we going to wait here for ten minutes?" He asked, smiling.

"Yes."

He laughed and pulled her into a kiss. A deep kiss.

"Didn't I satisfy you before?" Birdie laughed into his lips.

"Never enough." He grinned. Birdie laughed.

When the bus came, Birdie ran over. Jazmín held Lucy's hand to help her down, and Sailor and Tommy followed. All had wide grins on their faces. Birdie was so relieved.

They spent the next hour together having a snack and hearing about their day at school. Even Nancy and Cora were seated, hanging onto every word. Birdie loved every minute of it.

QUINN RYAN
AGE 15

Quinn had searched every bit of Haven House. His father told them there were five secret entrances, yet he only ever found three: the bar in the office, the wall leading up to Sir Oliver's room, and the one in the kitchen leading to the fuse box below. The beadboard was so precise in the kitchen that the door was completely invisible. But Quinn needed to know where the two others were. He had quietly touched every painting, statue, wall, sconce, and trim he could. He meticulously did floor by floor. He even set off the art hallway alarm once.

After two weeks of intently searching, he found one.

He noticed that the grandfather clock barely touched the floor. How could such a large and heavy-looking clock not touch the floor in a spot? He looked at the clock for a long time until he saw a worn spot to the left of the bottom half of the tall clock. He pressed, pulled, shoved, yet nothing. Finally, in total frustration, he told his dad he found another secret door. His father laughed, "Just the one? I thought you would have found both by now. I have seen you eyeing the walls." His father laughed.

Quinn blushed. He thought he had been so discreet and secretive about it, yet he had been found out after all. He even had gotten away with the alarm being triggered, he thought, though Cora did eye him suspiciously.

"Cora told me the same thing. She thinks you pulled the trim off of the library wall. Did you?"

Quinn's face went red, but he nodded, "Sorry, Dad. I tried to fix it."

"Next time, tell me, please. I fixed it after you did." His father shook his head with a smile. "Next time, wood glue, not Elmer's glue. Alright, let's get you some answers."

"Thanks, Dad; I just find these so cool," Quinn said eagerly.

"So, which did you find?" His father asked, not angry.

"The grandfather clock."

His father smiled, "I'm surprised you entered it."

"Uh, I can't open it."

"Come. We need the next generation to know this house as well as Sir Oliver and I do." His father led him to the split stairs ending to the right. To the right of the landing stood the clock, backed up against the triangle-shaped wall leading up.

His father lifted a piece of trim behind the worn spot, then pushed the worn spot, and it clicked open. The clock was on wheels! The entire clock opened like a door. But it looked dark inside. No wonder his father said he was surprised he entered it.

"We haven't gotten motion sensor lights yet." His father felt inside and flipped a switch. Suddenly, a set of stairs went down.

"Shall we?" His father asked.

Quinn nodded excitedly.

They climbed down two flights of stairs. This tunnel had to be below the basement. Then Quinn's father switched on another light. It was the longest tunnel, with only light sconces. The tunnel was narrow, the walls looked like any other hallway, and the floor was hard tile. It was chilly down there as they continued along the corridor. It went on for a while. As they reached the end, they turned on another set of lights and made a right for about fifty feet, then another left. Then he saw stairs leading up.

Quinn was mystified as he ascended. Where did this lead to? What was so far on this property? Did it take them off the property, like an escape route? He was rich, after all. Maybe this was to get to safety. If anyone tried to rob him, Quinn thought.

Then he opened a door, and there stood two black limousines, a two-seater convertible, and an old Lincoln Town Car. Quinn looked at his father, amazed. "The garage?" he asked.

His father laughed, "Yes. If it rained or he wanted to take a drive without a driver, he wanted a covered path, but the gardens were in the way, and he did not want to ruin them."

They shut all the lights and walked back. Quinn's father showed him how to open and close the grandfather clock properly. Quinn tried it and was excited he could do it alone.

"Dad? Can you tell me the last one?"

"I won't let you in the last one; even I haven't been in it, as it is his vault. But come to the Parlor."

Quinn was confused. He touched every single thing on every wall of the Parlor, but nothing had moved. His father only pointed to the credenza. "Sir Oliver showed me where it was. I believe it is password-protected or maybe a vault door. I am not exactly sure. I just know you move the credenza, lift the carpet and there is a hatch. I have never been inside it before. You better not ever try either. That is personal," his father warned firmly.

"I won't, Dad; I just needed to solve the mystery. I have been looking ever since you told me there are five."

"I am surprised you hadn't asked sooner. I thought you forgot months ago." His father chuckled. "Quinn, I mean it about entering this one."

"I would never, Dad."

His father nodded, "You were always a good kid, Quinn. Had you not been, I would have never told you."

Quinn smiled.

BIRDIE BLUE

Birdie's phone rang, "Hello."

It was Frank, and he was checking up on her again, mainly her arm, as Lupe told Frank she had been pushing herself these last five weeks doing the ballroom ceiling. It was going way slower than she imagined. Maybe she should have done what Michelangelo did and lie down, she mused. Though, wasn't that an urban legend? He was probably just as sore as she felt these days.

"Yes, I am resting my arm. Decided to go for a walk in the gardens." She placated, not telling him that, in fact, her arm was in agony. Constantly looking up, stepping back, and holding her arm and head up at that angle all but crippled her. Her neck, too.

"Yes, I am keeping to the schedule of forced days off." She worked on it on Mondays and Tuesdays, took a break on Wednesdays to be with Lupe, and then was back at it on Thursdays and Fridays. Saturdays and Sundays were strictly her time with Sailor, Lupe, Quinn, and all the kids. However, she needed a bigger break now until the throbbing stopped, so Birdie was resting today.

"Yes, she is doing great. She loves going with the other kids." Birdie thought of how much Sailor loved school and how much bolder she had become now. She came home with scraped knees, and a dirty face and never looked happier. The school even asked to advance her to the next grade, but Birdie said 'no.' Though academically she was advanced, socially she was not. Tommy guided her a lot. He had become quite the protector of Sailor. It was sweet to see them together, just like she and Quinn when younger.

"How are you guys? I am reading a ton in the society papers about the Art Gallery. People are adoring your latest find. He is going to take off."

Frank laughed in her ear, telling her they just knew he represented Birdie, and for that alone, any new person he associates himself with suddenly gets press.

"Oh, stop. He is good. I like his work, too. I want to buy the pink one with neon on it."

He laughed. She wanted his favorite piece. "Keep it there. Just mark it as sold. Yes, yes, that is fine. Bill me,"

He told her the price, "Frank, make your normal commission. This is business." She rolled her eyes.

"Alright, fine, fifteen percent off is good. Fifty is too much. Just bill me, and when he leaves, I will tell you where to send it. It's for Sailor's room."

"Yes, I will see the chiropractor, DAD." Birdie then laughed at his comment about not raising her right after that.

"Love ya. I am good. Just admiring the view, not painting at all. Promise."

She hung up, still smiling.

Birdie walked the gardens, one of her favorite things to do. She was thinking of how much her visit to Haven House had changed her, yet again, like it did the first time. She roamed the gardens, looking at the flowers, butterflies, and birds. It was so relaxing out here, no wonder Eloise loved it so much, Birdie thought. She used the gardens to think things out, pray, or plan the next steps in her mind. She would miss these gardens so much when they had to go. It also was a way to run into Quinn if she were lucky. Not today, though. Apparently, the gardeners found a hole under the gate, far behind the garage. He finally told Birdie of three prior thefts of Sir Oliver's possessions over the last year and they are assuming the hole was how they got onto the property. Quinn was so mad when he found it that he wanted to put a trap in the hole and cover it with leaves. But when Cora heard his idea she went off on him like he was a five-year-old, making Birdie and the kids giggle as he quickly agreed he would never do such a thing. So he was adding cement there now and they plan to upgrade security by adding cameras by the garage area and double security rounds.

Birdie decided to walk to the back of the property to see Quinn. The kids were at school anyway, and she had time. The walk was pretty long, even if she cut through the gardens. As she walked she happily thought about her and Quinn being a real couple now. How happy both seemed to be that they had taken to each other's kids. She knew he was especially happy about Birdie and Jazmín's close relationship. Birdie could tell Jazmín needed extra female attention, and he seemed relieved to have someone there to guide him on teenage females. So, the blending of their families was working out way easier than they had hoped. Sailor adored him and was comfortable just sitting on his lap, next to Lucy, of course, when he read stories to them. Tommy, always making sure Lucy gave Sailor enough room as he sat next to them, Birdie smiled.

Birdie exited the gardens and walked towards the pond. The new deck at one end now held six Adirondack Chairs and a matching two-cushion swing. The pond wasn't terribly big, but sitting out there and relaxing on summer nights was nice.

As she passed the pond, she thought of Sofía and how she was mostly keeping her promise, too. She and Jorge stayed at Haven House for two separate weekends, and they were all super polite and patient with each other. It was weird to see Sofía calm. Jorge had this very soothing quality about him that could de-escalate her if she started up. She also was doing therapy independently and started a family therapy session every other Saturday morning with the three kids. Seeing their relationship start to change was remarkable. Birdie thought having Quinn adopt Jazmín was the catalyst for all the new changes in both Quinn and Sofía. It showed trust on both sides. It was great to see them co-parenting and keeping to new promises.

And then there was Lupe, Birdie thought sadly as she walked along, seeing the garage from a distance. Lupe and Birdie spent Wednesdays together alone, first radiation, then lunch, before being at the gate for Sailor to return. Lupe was showing more side effects to her tumor, like using the wrong names, dropping things a lot more, and forgetting thoughts mid-sentence. Her left hand was becoming more and more useless as well. It scared Birdie a lot, but Quinn had been so great when she needed to cry away from Lupe.

Lupe slept a lot after radiation and on non-radiation days. Birdie talked Lupe, per the doctor's request, into physical and occupational therapy, too, which further tired Lupe. This forced Birdie to take over all of Lupe's tasks for Sailor completely. Birdie was happy to finally feel like an everyday mother. She was gaining her confidence, too. Also, if she was busy, she had people like Cora, Molly, or Quinn who could help out if she was working. It was actually better than she had hoped.

Birdie was coming to terms with the fact that Lupe would not be with them for the full two years. She was not improving with the radiation this last month and a half. The tumor was still growing. Birdie sometimes felt cried out but was mentally preparing herself that Lupe could leave them any time. Maybe knowing she had Quinn, Sailor, and the other kids helped, Birdie thought. Also, Cora was starting to mother her, too, fussing over Birdie like she did Kiera and Quinn. So she knew when the time came, she would have support. She was so grateful for that. How scary would this have been had she not come to Haven House and reunited with them all? She literally would have been alone with Sailor, only with no emotional support at all. She couldn't even imagine how that would have played out.

It touched Birdie to see Quinn treating Sailor like another one of his kids, too. He even talked of adopting Sailor once they married. Not that they were engaged yet, but they spoke of it often.

As she got closer to the garage, she thought of Sofía and Jorge getting married last weekend at their house in a private ceremony that included all of them. It was sweet to see that both exes were invited, too, showing a ton of respect to their children by that gesture. Jorge flew them all in and flew them home the next day on his jet. He was a nice guy who said he learned a lot from all his past mistakes in his first marriage and swore to do better from then on. That Jorge and Quinn actually liked the other helped. Both were 'family first' guys, and they respected each other. Sofía now happily lives on Star Island in Miami, Florida. She is often recognized by the Latino community when at restaurants, but when home, she feels safe in the ultra-exclusive gated community. Also, there are many wealthy or famous people there so she has the best of all worlds now outside of Spain.

Jorge Morales

Birdie even had Jorge's ex-wife, Tatum, and son, Christopher, come for a day visit while Sofía and Jorge were there for the weekend as he looked at law schools in South Carolina. Cora thought it odd how they all just got along until she heard Jorge say, "We all love our kids more than our pride." All eyes welled at that because it was true.

Birdie could see Quinn and a helper pouring cement into a hole. Wow, the hole was bigger than she thought. She stayed where she was to avoid disturbing them as she took in the scene. The hole was a good three hundred feet from the back of the garage. It looked like no one went to this area. Quinn mentioned talking to the gardeners about fixing it up instead of leaving it wild as it always was to show that people frequented the area.

As she watched, she thought of Nancy's daughter, Molly, deciding to do her master's online and assist in driving the kids to after-school activities and babysitting as needed. Since Nancy and Molly's house was only a mile away, she was always nearby and on call. It was nice to have a date night knowing the kids were being watched by both Cora for Sailor and Molly in the Carriage House for Quinn's three.

Quinn looked up at her and waved, "Need me?"

She shook her head, "Just watching."

He smiled and went back to work.

Birdie could not believe how much had changed in such a short time. All because of Sir Oliver inheriting this house, wanting his ballroom painted. Because of Sir Oliver, they now had each other; she had a relationship, and they were becoming a family in such a short time.

Birdie's phone beeped. A text from Jazmín. 'Talk Dad into me going to the Taylor Swift concert with my friends, please.' Birdie laughed. Jazmín was a whole lot. No way would Quinn allow a thirteen-year-old to go to the concert with friends alone.

'Who is going? How much are the tickets?' Birdie asked back, already considering whether she should order them.

'Kate, Emma, Stacy, and me; I'll ask Jorge to get them for us.'

Birdie rolled her eyes. She was already playing her new stepfather. Yep, not everything was perfect. Jazmín still occasionally acted up, but Quinn usually corrected it quickly when he saw it. Birdie suspected she did it on purpose just to see his reaction because she was never upset when he did. Unless she went too far and Quinn took her phone away.

'Deleting this text, do the same, or Dad won't be happy. He will expect a grown-up to go.'

'I know just the one' with a winking emoji. Jazmín was referring to her, Birdie sighed.

'Not me. I won't leave Lupe. I did it for a day and a half for your mother's wedding, and she almost fell down the stairs.' Which was true. She now had a male nurse to help her up and down each day. If only she could buy Haven House and install an elevator.

'Birdie pleeeeeeeeeeease'

'Ask your father and mother, please. Maybe she will want to go with you all.'

'Oh! Good idea. Mother/daughter bonding!' Another winking emoji.

Birdie sighed, not how she meant it.

'That is not what I said. Ask your parents if you can go first.'

'Yea, yea... teacher said to put my phone away. She's such an annoying Bruja! Bye'

Luckily for Birdie, she thought, shaking her head, Jazmín adored her. They had art in common. Birdie even made a sewing room in an empty room next to the theater on the third floor and brought in a fashion teacher every Friday evening. She had bolts and bolts of fabric, threads, accessories, and her own sewing machine—gifts from Jorge and Birdie. Quinn had been overruled when Birdie argued with him saying it was the same as buying art stuff for Sailor or cleats and travel soccer for Tommy. Birdie told him that when she sees a passion in a kid, they should give it all the tools necessary to embrace it. He conceded once she said that. And, of course, he knew he had to compromise. Jazmín did show natural talent and the very first smock dress she made was for Sailor, 'her first customer,' which touched all. Well, except Lucy, she cried until Jazmín promised to make her the matching one in pink the following week. Jazmín could be really sweet, too.

It was nice that they all really got along as if they all wanted the missing pieces in their lives as badly as she and Sailor had. The pond deck was completed earlier that week, so Quinn's list was finished minus the daily groundskeeper work, which worked out as he was working on his business more. Kiera and Quinn decided to get an established partner for Miami instead and keep the South Carolina work just for them. Birdie also convinced Quinn and Kiera to keep both houses in Miami as the kids would be spending time at their mother's home in Miami, and they would have somewhere to stay for business.

So Birdie was happy. Next week or so, she would start painting the children's room if her neck and arm felt better, and she could finish the little bit of detail she wanted to do on the ceiling before the scaffolding was disassembled and taken out. But secretly, she did not want to rush it. Her tasks were the last on the Sir Oliver to-do list before the will was revealed, and they would need to leave and she really loved living at Haven House. Whoever got to keep this house would be the luckiest person in the world.

When Quinn was done, he came over and kissed her. "Do you need a hug?" His term for, 'Are you upset and ready to cry?'

"I'm ok. I think I need to go to the chiropractor, though."

"Birdie, I keep telling you not to keep pushing yourself. You said a year. You are rushing through it at a crazy pace." He shook his head. Birdie smiled. It was nice to have a male partner who cared about her.

"My normal pace. The only issue is I never did a ceiling and am using muscles I never used before."

"Want me to take you?" Quinn asked, rubbing her arm and shoulder as Birdie felt herself melt. Having a guy dote on her was going to take some getting used to, but it was so nice, Birdie thought.

She shook her head but turned and kissed him again. "I should be back by three p.m... If not, you'll wait for them?"

"Yes."

"Thanks." Birdie walked back to the house.

QUINN RYAN

"Absolutely not, in Dallas?!" Did she not hear the thousands of talks on safety for rich kids? Kids of famous people?

Jazmín started to cry, "Jorge said he would fly us and Mami and Jorge will go with us. They will have a team of bodyguards."

"And the three other girl's parents are OK with this?"

"Yeah." but Quinn could tell she did not sound exactly sure.

"Let's call each one."

"...Call them? Now?" Jazmín looked panicked.

"Yep, start with Emma's mom," Quinn said.

She hesitated. "Um, let me just text-" she went to reach for her phone.

"Jazmín, do the parents know?" He asked firmly.

She looked down. "They know they want to go, and Jorge can probably get us tickets."

"Do they know about flying on Jorge's plane?"

She shrugged.

"Do they know it is in Dallas?"

She shrugged.

"Mom did not call me. We agreed to discuss this first."

"Only if you said 'no'. You haven't yet."

"Does she think I already agreed?"

"I told her I would talk to you, Dad; you can ask. I did." Jazmín pouted.

"The answer is no unless we call all three parents and they say yes. No texts first."

"It's not fair!" Jazmín shouted, annoyed.

He pointed to her room, "We discussed how to talk when angry."

She started stomping away, but he stopped her, took the phone, and let her go. She started to cry for real but rushed off to her room.

He sighed.

He then went outside to talk to Sofía. It took everything in his power not to call angrily.

However, Sofía was under the impression he said 'yes' if they could find a way to go there safely, and of course, Jorge offered to fly them and have his driver and security watch over all the kids.

"Punish her, Quinn!" In English, so she must be using it more.

"I did. Sofía, with big things like this, can we please talk to each other first and then give her an answer?" he begged.

"Of course. Every time I think she is getting better, she does another spunt."

"Stunt. But yes," he said, wanting to smile now. She had far to go with English, but she was trying, so he was proud of her. This conversation was working exactly as they promised each other—calm, making rules they agreed on.

"Tell her no tickets and no plane for lying. In fact, let me call her," Sofía said, mad.

"I took her phone."

"Put yours on speakerphone, please. I need to start being her parent, too, and she needs to know I am upset she tricked me." Quinn was super proud that time. This was all he wanted all along, even from a distance. Two of them in sync, disciplining when needed but being on the same page and holding firm.

He went to Jazmín, and she turned away angrily, wiping at her eyes. "Speak Sofía." The verbal dressing down in Spanish lasted a full three minutes before Jazmín actually looked ashamed.

"Jazmín." Quinn nodded to the phone.

"Sorry, Mami. Tell Jorge sorry too. I thought we could all go together."

"You little sneak." Quinn said, "Don't you dare guilt your Mom by playing on her emotions."

Jazmín looked down, "Sorry. But it would be fun to do something with Mami and my friends one day." she whispered and she said it truthfully.

Sofía sighed, "I would love to do that, but not this, not now. You lied. We will pick something else. I keep telling you I want to spend time with you. Meet your friends." "Taylor Swift is coming to Florida this summer!" Jazmín beamed.

"Something local, your friends may not be allowed to travel," Quinn suggested.

"Can we ask them together? Maybe Emma's mom can stay with us at the Miami house?"

"If Mom is alright, we can do that. But each parent must attend and watch over their own child and pay for their own ticket-"

"Jorge will fly them all together," Sofía said, interjecting.

"Taylor Swift tickets. I assume you will treat the girls." Quinn said knowingly.

"Of course. First, we ask all parents. Then I get a waiver to be signed by each. Then we get tickets. Jazmín? No more lying." Sofía said firmly.

"Yes, Mami," she was all but jumping up and down.

"Papi, her phone is gone for the weekend for tricking and manipulating us. That is from me." Sofía said, "And whatever else Papi said."

Jazmín huffed and sat down on her bed in a mad pout. But again, Quinn was super proud of both. Sofía's first real punishment to Jazmín was actually stated with a calm explanation, and Jazmín was actually abiding by it. Progress.

BIRDIE BLUE

Quinn was flying to Miami with Kiera to sign contracts that day on the Miami office partnership. Lupe was asleep, and Sailor was in bed. Birdie was bored, so she went down to Sir Oliver's office. She randomly picked out another journal, volume VIII, and turned on the light by the settee. She again asked out loud if she could read it.

Friday - September 24th

Eloise just does not seem right. I cannot figure out what it is. We have taken her for tests twice now. They think there may be a blockage. I pray to God that we figure this out. She thinks I am being too much of a worry-wart, but I can tell something is not right.

Birdie switched books; she took out Volume XIII, one of his last ones.

Wednesday - April 10th

I met the most extraordinary young lady today. It was Dalton Blythe's daughter.

Birdie could not believe he had written about her, and more shocking was that she had found it. Was she meant to read this? She looked up silently, asking for a sign out loud. The clock struck nine-thirty at that moment. She continued.

She is almost the same age as Sarah, and her full name is Birdie Blue Blythe. When I heard her name, it all but surprised me. She is quite the pip, too. She is so intelligent. She said she loved to paint on walls. Can you imagine any parent allowing that? Well, maybe an artist. Oh, how inquisitive she was. I haven't smiled like that in years. She was like a little ray of sunshine.

When she told me she painted, I immediately asked her to paint something for me. Who knows what I will get back? Whatever it is, I shall display it proudly.

Birdie flipped through pages of her father's work, talk of a tunnel, and other little projects around the house. Then she saw the entry she was looking for. The day she gave him the painting.

Saturday - May 11th

I am at a loss for words. Seriously, I am in utter shock. The little pip just presented me with the most fabulous piece of art. She is only eight years old! And the piece fits perfectly where I needed artwork. I mentioned my library was dull, and Birdie analyzed it and incorporated such minute details that I was surprised she remembered. She made three fairies sitting in my library. The wall detail, the library desk detail, the faces on the fairies... how is it that God gave such talent to such a young, untrained child?

I even insulted her and Dalton by asking if he had created it. Shameful of me, I know, but the artwork is fantastic, and I had to ask. So I asked her to come the next time her father came to do an actual mural. I shall have them stay for a week, or however long it takes. I must see this child paint with my own eyes. If she did this herself, she may be even more talented than her father. I made her sign the painting, it was that brilliant.

Again, Birdie flipped through some entries about kitchen upgrades, Cora and Nancy coddling him, and John's family. She stopped and read that; it was interesting to see how sweetly Sir Oliver spoke of John's 'extremely behaved' children.

Thursday - June 6th

Birdie is back, and I am stunned by how she went straight to work. She wanted to know my theme. I showed her a photograph of the gardens out back. First, she sketched in pencil on my office wall, then she went about getting paint, putting down a drop cloth, and eyeing the wall texture for a good minute or two. Her seriousness about painting shocked me.

I let her be so as not to distract her. I went up to rest but came down several times by the secret passage and peaked. She was painting it alone. There was no input from her father or checking up on her, though her nanny was sitting in the room, reading a book.

Sunday - June 9th

She finished. I am awestruck. There are no words. Birdie Blue Blythe. I shall follow her career until my dying breath.

Birdie put the journal down. Wow. She always believed he thought she was a cute little girl with some talent. But Sir Oliver studied art; he was a collector of real art and knew art. He honestly thought highly of her talent. Saying it to her was one thing out of politeness, but honestly, privately believing it was a whole other thing. Reading that passage had to be the best compliment she had ever received. She took a picture of both entries on her phone. She put the book back, said, 'Thank you, Sir Oliver,' and went to bed.

QUINN RYAN

Kiera and Quinn signed everything. Then she helped him shop for an engagement ring. He planned to propose before Christmas. He found a gorgeous 2.5-carat oval ring with twelve mini solitaire diamonds around it. The platinum setting was beautiful.

"No fair, it's bigger than mine." Kiera teased.

"Maybe she wants a five-carat ring or larger." Quinn worried.

"This will be too big for her. Look at her; she does not wear jewelry at all."

"Oh... will she like this then?" Quinn worried. "An engagement ring, after you both talk about it weekly? Yes, Dufus." Kiera laughed.

He smiled; he was panicking needlessly. Birdie wanted to get married. She was okay with him adopting Sailor. She even planned to counter whoever the new owner of Haven House was and try to buy it from them, even if she had to pay double its worth.

Quinn's portion of the Sir Oliver to-do list was completed, so he just did the Caretaker's job around business as they were just waiting on Birdie now. She needed to complete the children's room and Solarium floors. Birdie said it should not take longer than a month. She picked a different Monet artwork to paint each Solarium floor. It came out better than Quinn imagined. Birdie showed him the original artwork she copied, he was amazed by the likeness. It still awed Quinn that she could paint like that and so fast too.

The attorneys were to set a date for the will reading once Birdie sent photos of her portion complete.

Nancy made a celebration dinner once everything was completed, though it ended up being more somber than expected. All knew the days at Haven House were coming to an end. Cora told Birdie and Lupe about Sir Oliver's cousin's son. And how he has tried to visit some ten times the first year Sir Oliver died. Constantly calling Cora to be allowed to inventory the house. The attorneys had a cease and desist order created and inventoried everything themselves. He randomly called them, asking if the work was complete so the will could finally be settled. Apparently, the attorneys said all the stakeholders would be contacted. They all focused on the word 'all.' Quinn wondered who they were. He had assumed there was only Sir Oliver's one known relative. Cora seemed to think that Sir Oliver was not a fan of him. If not only him, then who else?

Quinn and Birdie hoped whoever it was wanted to stay in England and would be willing to sell Haven House. But they had to wait and see. If not Haven House, they decided to find a home in Eastover, so the kids stayed in the same schools. It was nice for both of them to plan a life together. She never had a partner; he had an absent one, so it was new to both of them.

SAILOR WREN

Sailor was so excited. She and the kids were helping decorate Haven House for Christmas, even though it was before Thanksgiving. Quinn had told her it took a long time to do it all at Haven House. Nancy, Molly, Lupe, and the kids were decorating the huge tree in the Parlor while Cora, Quinn, and her mom were doing the one in the living room. TWO trees!! They split up because Cora said the ones in the living room were antique ornaments, and the kids could not touch those. No one used the living room anyway, Sailor thought. Everyone used the Parlor, though, so she was happy to be working on that one.

Sailor is happy that Lupe looked rested today. Lupe was sitting on the couch handing out an ornament to each child from a box. The kids put on the hooks, as Lupe's left hand did not like to move anymore and added them to the tree per Nancy's direction. Sailor wanted to remember this happy day because she knew that Lupe had decided to stop radiation last week. She said it was not helping slow the tumor, so she planned to just have fun with the kids until Jesus wanted her. At first, Sailor was scared; didn't all medicine work? But Lupe has talked to her about it a lot since then. She explained she wanted to spend every minute with them. She didn't want to be sleeping all the time. She said it wasn't fun and Sailor agreed she was having more fun now. She smiled a lot now, too, Sailor thought. That made her happy to see Lupe smiling again. She looked... calm or peaceful. Sailor wasn't sure of the right word. If only her mother understood better, she heard her mom fighting with Lupe about stopping radiation. Her mom even yelled at Lupe. Then she ran out of Haven House crying. Sailor panicked at how scared her mom seemed. Sailor ran to the window and watched her mom rush into Quinn's arms as he was weeding the garden. Then Sailor watched them speak as he was hugging her and rubbing her back soothingly. Sailor was glad that Quinn was good at getting her mother to stop crying. Sailor felt like crying, too, watching this. She could see her mom wanted Lupe to try everything until they found a cure, but Lupe was getting skinnier and skinnier. Her head and a part of her forehead were always red and swollen. Lupe looked like she struggled to get up and was in bed for most of the day. So Sailor understood. Lupe making a decision to be happy, meant her mom was upset that she stopped trying. Sailor knew her mom was scared to lose Lupe. She told Sailor why she had acted so badly after she had come up crying, apologizing to Lupe and telling her to do whatever she wanted, that 'she would support all of her decisions' even if her mother looked heartbroken when she said it. Her mother had spoken to Sailor alone, too, to explain it in a way she understood, and Sailor decided to do the same. She, too, wanted Lupe to do whatever she wanted while here with them.

BIRDIE BLUE

Birdie walked into the Parlor looking for everyone and stopped in shock. Quinn stood before a large lit-up 'Will you marry me?' sign in front of the Parlor Christmas tree. He was on one knee, the four kids jumping up and down around him. Jazmín had tears running down her eyes, smiling brightly.

"Birdie Blue Blythe, I have loved you since I was twelve years old. Will you marry me?"

She stood there, looked at each hopeful kid, and then looked at Lupe, who was seated on the settee covered with a blanket, eyes welling too. Then she felt two more people behind her, Cora and Nancy, openly bawling. She turned back to Quinn, still patiently waiting on his knee. She ran to him, "Yes! Yes, with all my heart." Then they kissed for a full minute before they heard the laughter.

They all hugged each other, and Birdie could not stop crying.

"Mami said I can call you 'Mom' once you get married." Jazmín said, hugging her tightly, "OK?"

Birdie nodded, looking at Quinn happily.

The next day was Thanksgiving. They all had dinner together; Nancy's kids were there, too. Kiera, Jason, and Amanda came for dessert after being at Jason's parents' house. Afterward, Quinn went to Birdie's room after ten p.m. They made love, and then he rushed back to the Carriage House. She couldn't wait until they all lived together in one house.

SAILOR WREN

Sailor was in bed with Lupe. They spent a bit of time together every day after school, as Sailor told Lupe about the day's events. It was always after snack and homework, so Sailor wasn't rushing her time with Lupe. Today, Sailor was telling her about the school lunch.

"It did not look yummy, Lupe. It was a turkey burger and cut-up stinky broccoli." Sailor made a face. "Lucky for you, Nancy makes you all lunch." Lupe smiled, weakly. Sailor noticed she was talking very quietly today.

Sailor nodded, "I have to do a read/response by next week. Have I ever done that before?" Sailor asked her.

"Yes."

Sailor thought, "Oh! Guess what? Mrs. Lambert told me that I may paint next month's bulletin board. I am so excited.

Mommy mentioned I painted a lot when she offered to paint the front desk wall for them. I have been enjoying painting just as much as pastels lately."

Lupe looked confused, "I did not know your mother offered to paint for them."

"She did when they called her in to discuss moving me to another grade. I told Mommy 'no,' and she agreed. Fourth graders look scary," Sailor said, and Lupe smiled.

"It's not scary, just new. I know you want to stay with Tommy," Lupe said softly, almost a whisper.

Sailor smiled broadly, "He's my best friend, even though he will be my brother soon. But Quinn said Kiera was his best friend growing up, so brothers and sisters could be best friends."

Lupe smiled tiredly, "I am so happy for you, Mamita. Quinn will be a great Dad to you. You will have siblings. God is good." She said so softly, closing her eyes. Sailor barely heard her that time. Sailor knew that meant she was tired. She kissed Lupe and shut her door quietly. Sailor went to her room and thought out several ideas to paint. She will show them to Mrs. Lambert tomorrow.

An hour later, Sailor heard the scariest sound. A loud, strangled wail. She ran out of her room and saw her mother crumpled on Lupe's floor sobbing as Cora ran up the stairs, past Sailor pulling up her mom into a hug. Sailor felt sad her mom was so upset. Did they fight again, she wondered. She couldn't understand why Cora was holding her up on her feet. It was as if her mother couldn't stand alone, without assistance. Then Cora told Sailor to rush and get Quinn.

Sailor did, her heart pounding. Now she was scared something happened to her mom's legs. Once she told him, crying herself, she saw him rush into the house. She followed worriedly.

Suddenly, everyone was outside of Lupe's room. Sailor heard Jazmín whisper to Tommy that Lupe died. "She died? Lupe died?" And suddenly, everything went black.

BIRDIE BLUE

"Oh my God! Sailor! Dad, come quick, Sailor fell!" Jazmín screamed. It was the only thing that got Birdie to her feet in an instant as she ran out of Lupe's room. Nothing else could have pulled her away from Lupe at that moment. Only Sailor. Quinn was carrying her and gently laid her on her bed. Jazmín was busy fanning her with Sailor's sketchbook, and Birdie was lightly rubbing her face to come to. "Sailor please, wake up." Quinn was saying gently over and over. Her eyes started to flutter, looking confused.

"What - why am I in bed?" Sailor asked, and Birdie sobbed relieved. Birdie pulled her into a tight hug, "You fainted, my girl." Birdie cried into her hair.

"Lupe..." Sailor said as if remembering.

"She went to be with Grandpa and Grandma, Sailor." Her mother said, but her voice sounded so hoarse. "Let me call an ambulance-" Quinn started to say.

"I already did," Cora said, coming in. "I opened the gates. Kids stay in this room. Let's shut the door, please. Little eyes do not need to see anything. Quinn." Cora gave him a clear look. He was to watch Birdie and keep everyone in that room. He nodded.

Birdie was torn. She wanted to go to Lupe but needed to be with Sailor. Quinn pulled them into a hug, "The Medical Examiner will be called. It will take some time. Please let the paramedics confirm the situation." He said softly. Birdie nodded. She lay in bed with Sailor and told the other kids, "Climb in. We will miss Lupe, but at least we can comfort each other."

Jazmín looked sad, "I liked her Birdie, a lot."

"Me too. She was always nice to me," Tommy said sadly, leaning on Birdie's legs as Quinn put Lucy next to Birdie, making sure all could fit.

"Let's tell her to come in bed here too, then," Lucy said, clearly not understanding.

"She can't honey. She died." Quinn said as gently as possible, sitting next to her as Birdie looked at Quinn. This was probably the first person to die in his kid's lives. Lucy burst into tears, "What?!" Quinn picked her up onto his lap.

"She was sick." Birdie started to say, but Quinn finished her sentence.

"Not sick like we get colds and fevers, a serious sickness where she had a boo-boo inside her head. None of you can get this. You can't catch it." He assured all. Then he looked at Birdie, "Kiera hadn't understood when my mom died as a child; I hope you don't mind me over-explaining."

"Of course not."

"Should I call Molly and ask her to watch the kids upstairs?" Birdie shook her head, "No, thank you. I want to be together."

He nodded, sitting next to her until he heard the gate beep. He looked at Birdie. She nodded for him to go on. He left them.

Quinn gently woke her up, it seemed that all of them except Jazmín fell asleep on Sailor's bed. Jazmín had been on her phone, still carrying Lucy on her lap as she slept. "The Medical Examiner took her. You and I are needed at the funeral home tomorrow at ten a.m. Can you do it?"

Birdie, eyes welling again, nodded.

"Let me move Tommy over. Jazmín said she would sleep with him tonight. Molly will spend the night up there, too, and stay tomorrow. Cora and I will go with you."

Birdie nodded. Numb, she felt numb. Thankfully, Quinn was taking the lead on all of this.

"Want me to sleep with you tonight? We are engaged now, and everyone will understand." But he looked at Jazmín, and she smiled sadly.

Birdie nodded.

"I am running out for pizza. I already ordered it. Nancy was too upset to cook. They had become good friends. Come down and be with Cora."

She shook her head.

"I do not want to leave you alone. I will ask Cora to come up then-"

"No, Quinn, please. I need quiet. I need to think." She begged. He nodded, "Cora is stubborn. She may come up even if I tell her not to." Birdie actually smiled. He was right. He quickly left.

Birdie went to Lupe's room after laying Lucy next to Sailor, where she had been. Jazmín followed, "I am not leaving you alone. I won't say a word, but I am staying. Ok?"

Birdie nodded. Jazmín sat in an overstuffed chair in the corner. Birdie sat on the bed, silently crying, not wanting to scare Jazmín further. She picked up Lupe's pillow and could still smell her. She hugged it tight. The tears just poured out of her into the pillow. She felt Jazmín come over and hug her without saying a word as Birdie continued sobbing.

She lost the only mother figure she had known, as she had no memories of her real mother at all. Lupe taught her how to read, write, tie her shoes, and take her own showers, to name a few of the many skills she would use in life. She had also taught her manners, to be respectful, thankful, and a ton of other qualities. She had taught the same to Sailor too. This day came too fast. She hadn't been ready, Birdie sobbed. Just that morning Lupe and Birdie spoke about how excited she was to make wedding plans. That Quinn and Birdie needed to rush to make sure Lupe was there. Lupe had patted her hand, 'I will be there, Mi hija, I will be there'. And now she wouldn't be. Not in the way Birdie had wanted her to be.

Then, a thought popped up: she needed to call Lupe's family in Mexico. When she went to get up, Jazmín was still hugging her tightly.

"Thank you, Jaz. I need to call her family." Jazmín let go but stayed, determined not to leave her alone. Birdie went to Lupe's pocketbook. Her phone was not in there.

"What are you looking for?"

"Her cell phone."

"It's by the desk," Jazmín said, pointing. Birdie went to it; it was dead. She didn't even know the password anyway, if she had one. So she went into her drawers and found a personal phone book with an envelope over it. It had one word on it: 'Birdie,' and Birdie had a bad case of deja vu.

Mi hija,

I know this is not a good day for you, but for me, I am finally free of this burdensome tumor. I am home with Dios, happy. Trust Mi hija. As I know you already know, raising you was the highlight of my life. Without you, I would never have experienced motherhood. Sailor, my little doll, made me a grandmother. What a gift she was. You have each other now. You have Quinn and his kids now, too. Nancy and Cora made promises to me, so you let them mother you all they want. Alright, mi niña?

You are strong, smart, and capable. You have become the most amazing and loving mother, not just to Sailor but also to the other three. They adore you. Treat them all the same, Mi hija, and let Quinn be Sailor's father.

Fathers sometimes say 'no' more than mothers do, so let him. Sailor needs two loving parents.

I tried to make it to your wedding, really I did.

Birdie broke down into more sobs, then catching her breath and wiping her eyes, she tried to read on. Jazmín came over nervously.

"I am ok. She mentioned the wedding." Birdie sniffed.

Jazmín rushed and brought her a tissue box, her own eyes tearing herself now.

"I wanted her there," Birdie said, taking one, her voice breaking. Another round of tears; Jazmín was now crying into her chest, too.

"She loved you, Birdie, so much," Jazmín said tearfully.

"I know." Birdie agreed, wiping her eyes and blowing her nose. She threw the tissue out, took another, and wiped Jazmín's eyes, too. Jazmín smiled up at her, "I love you, Birdie." Jazmín said, hugging her. Birdie was surprised, though she had said it to the kids. Jazmín always smiled happily but never said it back, as if she was scared to. "I am sorry this happened to you."

Birdie hugged her and took a deep breath. "I need to read the rest," Jazmín nodded.

I tried to make it to your wedding, really I did. I guess I will just have to watch it from up above with your parents. So please do not be sad that day. I want you smiling the whole day, promise me. Quinn is a good man, and I couldn't have asked for a better partner for you. You now have a big family, enjoy it.

Please tell my brother-in-law NOT to tell my sister. There is no need to distress her further. I do not want anyone coming to my service from Mexico. Please just arrange for the service to be viewed from there through the computer so they can at least see the service. I DO NOT want an open casket. I will not scare my Sailor. I want to be cremated and my urn to be put into the ground. Wherever you make a home, please put me near there in a cemetery - NOT Mexico - my life was here. Then, I want you only to keep the good memories and forget everything else. Life goes on. And I want you to enjoy it. When you think of me, look up and wave with a smile. For I will always be smiling down on you all. Please give my savings to Pablo for the care of my sister.

I am so happy to have met you, my brilliant, talented, spunky child. Always pray. Always see the positive in every situation. Know your priorities: God, you, your kids, Quinn, art, in that order, and you will never be alone. And if you decide that you are tired of painting, take a break: a month, a year, a decade, or forever. Life is short, Mi hija. You are one of the few who can sit back if you want to as you have money to allow this luxury many do not have. And if painting helps you cope, as it always has before, then do it. The choice will always be yours.

I know you never got to see what a good married couple looked like, so here is the secret that I have learned watching other couples - Communication. Be patient, hear out what the other is feeling, be clear on what you're feeling and be mindful of each other. Never say words you cannot take back.

As for being a mother, you have all the skills already. Just do not spoil them with things. Gifts, toys, etc. are nice, but spoil them more with your time and doing things together as a family. Those are the memories that they will take with them in life.

Mi hija, I love you so very much, and we will be together one day soon. Until then, look up and smile.

Besos,

Lupe tu otra Madre

Birdie's throat felt raw. She folded the letter and pulled out the address book. Two numbers were highlighted. A post-it note on top said:

Call Pablo and then Clarita. They will tell all.

So Birdie went to call, but Jazmín stopped her. "Do you know what time it is there?"

Birdie shook her head.

"Dad said to always check time zones before calling other countries."

Birdie nodded. She looked up their address. Checked the time zone. It was earlier, so she could call. Pablo kept saying, 'Oh no, oh no' over and over again. She told him that all of Lupe's money was going to him to care for his wife, and he broke down crying, 'No, no, no.' Birdie told him she would Western Union it next week and then called Clarita, her younger cousin's daughter. Birdie had quite a time telling her Lupe's wishes that no one comes but to listen to the live service. At one point, Birdie was about to send her airline tickets, but then Clarita said she cared for her mother, who had MS, and it was probably best. Birdie knew she was matching Lupe's savings and sending it to Clarita, saying it was from Lupe. Clearly, Lupe used her money to help her family back home. Birdie was just hanging up when Quinn came in. "Thank you, Jazi, for staying with Birdie. Go eat. I woke the kids." Jazmín saw he wanted to talk to Birdie alone and left, but not before Quinn kissed the top of Jazmín's head.

"Are you alright?" Quinn asked Birdie once alone. She nodded and handed him Lupe's final letter. He looked at her and said, "Are you sure you want me to read it?"

Birdie nodded. Communication is all she thought to herself. Quinn was her partner now. He read it and then hugged her.

Quinn tried to get Birdie to eat, but she couldn't.

The next few days had been super hard, but she fulfilled Lupe's wishes. Sailor seemed to be ok, with the help of Tommy, who had not left her side since the news of Lupe's passing.

Cora fussed over Birdie nonstop until she started eating again. Quinn had been the best support system she could have asked for. They decided to bury her urn in Eastover Cemetery, where Eloise and Sir Oliver's large headstones were. They were across from each other, so she would visit them all together when the headstone came.

Then Birdie got to work. She needed it to get over Lupe's death. Arm pain or not, Birdie had already completed all the tasks on Sir Oliver's list but decided to do a portrait of Sir Oliver and Eloise. She found a photo of them by the Gardens in his office. She decided it belonged in the Parlor, so she got to painting.

They had yet to hear any news regarding the will. Birdie thought it possible that the attorney had already contacted the will's recipients.

"Should I leave?" Birdie asked Cora when the painting was done and she had nothing left to do.

"Absolutely not, I called the attorneys. Letters are going out today."

"Oh." Suddenly, the thought of her leaving Haven House was overwhelming.

Birdie went to the Parlor in thought. Maybe she should start looking at some houses nearby. She needed to talk to Quinn, but he was back in Miami for two days finishing a huge project.

Cora hired the landscapers full-time so Quinn could get the offices ready. Short of emergency fixes, Quinn has been doing more of his architectural work, only doing odds and ends and overseeing the new gardener's work. Quinn and Kiera's local office was opening in three weeks. They already hired an office manager who would also initially do billing and had resumes for additional architects if it took off. A lot of the homes around here were old. Some homes were even historical, which required both Quinn and Kiera to research local zoning laws and changes that could be prohibited. Though many owners of historical homes initially loved the original details, many needed better kitchens, great rooms, etc. So, there was a local need for architects. Birdie told Quinn he had to expect a slow start for at least three years, and he understood. It wasn't as if they needed the money, as Miami was still bringing in a lot of money, and Birdie could support them if needed.

"Birdie, Lucy took my toy again. Tell her to give it back." Tommy pouted, leaning on her mushily. It wasn't like Tommy to tattle, let alone lean on her like that. She noticed his face was flushed. She felt his forehead. He was hot.

"Are you sick, sweetie?" Tommy shrugged, hugging her lazily.

"Come." She took his hand and went up to Sailor's bathroom. She took out the thermometer. 101.2. He had a fever. She called Quinn.

"Can you tell Cora? She will give him Tylenol and stay with him-"

"I will give him Tylenol and stay with him."

"Oh, uh, sure. I can't be back until tomorrow evening at the earliest."

"I know."

"He may need to see the pediatrician."

"Why I called. I need a name. I need one for Sailor locally anyway."

"You'll take him? Thank you. Let me call Cora-"

"Quinn Ryan Callahan, I can handle this," Birdie said, mad. Did he doubt her abilities to mother his kids? Did he think she was a bad parent?

"Birdie, I meant to watch the girls as you take him." He said patiently.

"Oh... I just thought you didn't think I could handle it." She said softly.

"I trust you, Birdie. Stop overthinking. I hate to be away from the kids when they are sick. I just cannot leave today unless there is an emergency. Please call me from the doctor's office."

"I will. Sorry, Quinn, for assuming. I know I am still learning myself," Birdie said, her eyes welling.

"As am I and every other parent. Call me, I need to go. Love you." He hung up.

Birdie smiled. He was right; all parents were figuring it out as they went.

She took him to the doctor's office; he had an ear infection. The doctor prescribed Amoxicillin, and they picked it up. Then Birdie tucked him in the upstairs guest bedroom bed. Lucy had been sleeping with Sailor for these two days, and Jazmín was right next door to him. Molly had the third bedroom on the upper floor, too, so they weren't alone at night until Quinn returned. Thank God for all the extra bedrooms, Birdie thought.

Cora must have been up there because the side table had juice, snacks, comic books, and tissues. Birdie called Cora, "I will stay here until Molly returns. Can you send the girls up to the theater or children's room? So I can constantly check on Tommy?"

"Nancy has them making Tommy's favorite banana muffins. When done, I will send them up."

"OK, thank you."

So Birdie stayed in bed with him, putting on a movie for him. He fell asleep after twenty minutes, and she lay there looking at him. He looked so much like Quinn that it was almost eerie. Though Quinn probably felt that way about Sailor, she thought, smiling. And that out of four kids, the two closest were Tommy and Sailor, as Quinn and Birdie had been, was pretty amazing, too, when she thought about it.

Her phone rang, and she answered quickly so he didn't wake. It was Quinn via FaceTime.

"Sorry, I was in a client meeting before."

"He's asleep." She turned the camera to face Tommy.

"Awe. Fever down?"

"Yes. 99.7 last I checked."

"You do not need to stay in bed with him." Quinn chuckled.

"Until the girls come up, they are baking muffins for Tommy with Nancy."

He smiled, "Thank you for mothering him."

Birdie smiled.

"Seriously, he doesn't get it much."

"Well, I am here, and it was sweet to see him so mushy with me."

Quinn laughed, "He gets needy when sick, like all men."

"I wouldn't know. I, too, am learning every day." Birdie laughed.

He laughed again. "Should I come back?"

"Cora, Nancy, Molly, and I can handle it, really, Quinn."

"Alright, just feeling guilty."

"Under control."

"Thank you. I will call later to say 'goodnight'."

"Alright. I love you."

"Love you more."

Birdie smiled, so this was what a relationship was like. She never imagined herself in one and wished she had tried it sooner. Though, without Quinn in the equation, would she have even been interested?

QUINN RYAN

The gate rang, "Hello?"

"Yes, messenger for Quinn Callahan, Birdie Blythe, Nancy Finnigan, and Cora Casey. I need signatures, please."

His phone rang, and it was Kiera, but he ignored it. "Coming now."

Signatures, Quinn wondered? Were the new owners evicting them? Quinn suddenly felt sick. He felt his childhood home being pulled away from him and there was nothing he could do about it.

As he walked the driveway towards the gate, he called Cora and told her to get Birdie and Nancy.

They all met up and signed, taking the fat envelopes.

He received another call from Kiera, but he couldn't talk at the moment. He texted her, 'Call you back.'

Cora, Birdie, Nancy and Quinn all looked at each other, worried looks on their faces. All wondered the same thing, could it be Notices of Eviction? Cora took her letter, "Let's go into the Parlor." All the kids were at school, so it was quiet, and they could read in peace.

"Oh, I have food cooking; I will open it in the kitchen. Go on." Nancy took off.

The rest all opened at once.

Cora said, "I don't understand; I told him 'no.'" Cora said, confused.

Quinn looked at his letter, shocked. The letter stated that he was listed in Sir Oliver's will and that the attorney would be coming that Saturday at noon to do a formal reading. His attendance was required. He looked up at Birdie, and she, too, looked confused, like Cora. "I'm in the will. Maybe he is giving me back my artwork." Birdie said, guessing.

Quinn came over and checked out both letters; they were identical. His phone rang again: "CALL ME!!!!!!" from Kiera. Instantly, he suspected she got one, too. After he called her, it was confirmed that all five had received the same letter.

"I wonder how many other ones went out?" Birdie asked.

All looked at each other, curious themselves.

BIRDIE BLUE

It was Saturday, and Kiera and Jason were there. At noon, Molly was coming to watch the kids upstairs, with strict rules NOT to come down until called. Lunch, movies, snacks, diapers, pack-n-play, etc., were already set up for Molly, who was being paid double if everyone stayed out of the way. Jazmín was also offered fifty dollars, too, if she assisted.

Jason Summers

The gate rang. Expecting it to be the attorney, Quinn's face looked shocked. Birdie looked at him, concerned. Quinn buzzed the person in.

"What Quinn? Tell us."

"An English gentleman who was told to attend today's meeting." Quinn looked crushed. Their worst fear had just come true. At least one relative came, and maybe a few more were coming too. They all looked at each other concerned.

"Just how many people were sent a letter?" Kiera asked. Quinn shrugged.

Nancy came into the Parlor from the kitchen. Quinn was baffled by two large security personnel entering the house with the English gentleman. Finally, Mrs. Davis, the attorney, arrived.

"All are here, I see. Thank you, Lord Astor, for attending," Mrs. Davis said, looking at the sixty-ish-year-old thin and lanky man in a tweed sports coat. A Lord, thought Birdie?!

"Hoping transport was to your satisfaction?" Ms. Davis asked Lord Astor. He gave a slight nod.

Then Mrs. Davis looked at both security men standing behind Lord Astor. Why were they needed, she wondered. Lord Astor must have hired them if they were to be escorted off the property immediately, though no one would be surprised if that happened. If truth be told, they all expected it. She hoped he would give them the day to pack.

"So, I see all the items were completed. Thank you for sending pictures, Ms. Blythe. I am sure Sir Oliver would have loved everything you did." Mrs. Davis smiled and looked all around. "Everything stated here today is as Sir Oliver requested it. Every person in attendance is per Sir Oliver's request. The details I am about to convey are also by Sir Oliver. First, there will be a reading, followed by a video message from Sir Oliver himself."

All looked at each other nervously.

"All decisions made here are legally binding both here and in England. There are stipulations that state anyone who argues the Last Will and Testament of Sir Oliver James Astor will be excluded from inheriting even a penny. I am to have you each sign the documents stating you understand the terms of his will." She then proceeded to give everyone a letter and pen.

"Yes, yes, take it. Signed as requested. Please proceed. I took the red-eye and am tired." Lord Astor said rudely. Everyone looked at him, shocked by his arrogance. Mrs. Davis, however, took her time comparing every signature. She then put the letters in her briefcase and locked it.

"May I ask who everyone is? Are there no manners in America?" Lord Astor added, looking down his nose at everyone in the room.

Introductions were made by Mrs. Davis, and Lord Astor looked baffled. "The help? And the help's children?"

"Lord Astor, really!" Mrs. Davis said, standing up, and security stood at attention. Ready to protect Lord Astor, no doubt, Birdie thought.

Cora suddenly laughed, "You must be Cecil."

"Lord Astor, to you," he said distinctly. Birdie had to grab Quinn's hand fast to hold him back. She gave him a look. They wanted to buy the house from him, so Quinn had to stay civil with him. Cora kept chuckling to herself. This confused most of them, except for an irritated Lord Astor.

Mrs. Davis looked at Cora, "Please, Mrs. Casey."

Cora got a hold of herself, "Excuse me. Please go on."

"The will is broken into several pieces. No one person shall-" "What?! I am the only family here!!!" Lord Astor stood up angrily, all but spitting as he spoke.

"Yes, if you will allow me to read this. Please have a seat."

"No, thank you. My ears work just fine standing." Lord Astor said indignantly.

"Then I shall not read further." Mrs. Davis said, putting the document away and locking it in her briefcase.

All color drained from Lord Astor's face, "Fine." He sat.

Birdie and Quinn peeked at each other, trying not to laugh at Mrs. Davis' tough stance. Who knew she could be so tough?

"As I said," Mrs. Davis unlocked the briefcase, pulled out the will, and locked it again.

"Sir Oliver very thoughtfully laid out the will and how it would be presented. His estate is broken into many parts. Sir Oliver's art collection, valued at 15.4 million dollars, is bestowed to Birdie Blue Blythe-"

"WHAT?!" Lord Astor stood up, face red, eyes wild. "That was all I wanted!"

"Are we done for today, shall we reconvene another day? Say next week?" Mrs. Davis asked Lord Astor sharply.

Birdie was in utter shock; Sir Oliver left her his most prized possession, his art collection. Quinn looked at Birdie dumb founded.

"Eloise Astor's jewelry collection is to be split as follows: The Pearl necklace, bracelet, ring, and earrings valued at two-hundred and seventy-five thousand dollars will be given to Cora Casey for years of service. Here is a picture of the pieces bequeathed." Mrs. Davis gave the picture to Cora, and her mouth dropped open. The pearl bracelet and necklace were four strands thick, with diamonds between them.

"Thank you," Cora muttered, shocked, staring at the picture.

"The emerald choker and earrings valued at one hundred and seventy-five thousand dollars are for Nancy Finnley. Here is your picture." Nancy stood up to take the picture, her mouth opened in amazement.

Birdie was shocked. Sir Oliver was being super generous to non-family members.

"He knows that he bought you a house, Mrs. Casey, and paid off your house payments, Mrs. Finnley, but he wanted to leave you both a token for years of service." Mrs. Davis said. Nancy and Cora looked at each other tearfully.

"The rest of Eloise's jewelry, valued around five-hundred and eighty-seven thousand dollars, will be given to Kiera Callahan Summers." Kiera and Jason looked at each other. Kiera was speechless.

Each name read made Lord Astor's face turn redder. "Some of these are family heirlooms," he said, seething.

Mrs. Davis ignored him. "Haven House, minus the art collection and jewelry, will go to Quinn Callahan, along with five million dollars to maintain the grounds." Quinn looked like he would pass out. Birdie felt her eyes well. Sir Oliver was too generous. Haven House was all they ever wanted.

"But..." Lord Astor was at a loss for words. Face draining of color.

"This includes vehicles, the Carriage House, shed, garages, and all his land in South Carolina." Mrs Davis said.

"Jesus, Mary, and Joseph," Nancy gasped, beyond shocked. Cora slapped her arm but looked just as stunned.

Mrs. Davis gave the five of them their copies of the will. Then she looked at Lord Astor and said, "There is a message to be viewed before I go further."

Lord Astor's face was now getting redder and angrier by the moment.

She opened a laptop, and there stood an elderly but very alert Sir Oliver.

"Oh, how I wish I were there to communicate this in person to you all." He started with a chuckle. He had a twinkle in his eye when he said it. Birdie missed him so much.

"It is with great love for you that I bestow what you have been told. For I know you all will appreciate what is given to you. Please note: I am fine with you all selling anything I gifted if you financially need to do so one day. No pressure to keep it just for me. My hope is that it will alleviate any stressors in life. But do wear the jewelry at least once and have a party!" Sir Oliver laughed with a wink, making everyone tear up and chuckle simultaneously.

"Cecil, you are probably wondering what is left to endow you. The answer is that you will not be told until you hand over the following ten family heirlooms that you sold from the family estate. You have exactly thirty days from this date to produce all ten items. Mrs. Davis will give you the document with pictures and descriptions. If, after thirty days, you fail to produce all ten, you will be cut out of the will entirely. Your share will be added to charities I have pre-selected."

Lord Astor's face lost all color. Birdie and Quinn looked at each other quickly, then back to Lord Astor. Sir Oliver's tone was not sweet like they were used to.

"I hope that by the time you see this message, you will have stopped gambling, drinking, womanizing, and whatever other useless verb there is. You were given everything in life-"

Lord Astor stood up angrily.

"...and you never appreciated any of it. You are a disgrace to the Astor name. You got your title, but without money, it is useless, as I am sure you have found out. Ten items, thirty days, Cecil. Please have security escort him off the grounds. Please make sure he has the document with the required items."

The video was stopped.

Suddenly, the security guards had a hand under each arm as he argued and shouted. He was put into the limousine he had come in and driven out of there.

All stood stunned. When Mrs. Davis came back, she said, "Shall we listen to the rest?" Numbly, all nodded.

"Please only play for those I bequeathed items to." Sir Oliver's voice paused for a good minute.

"Good! Now, my dearest Cora, Nancy, Kiera, Quinn, and Birdie. When I lost Eloise, I thought life was over. I did not have a reason to go on. There was nothing to look forward to anymore. But then children came into my life. Their sweet innocence filled my heart. I so looked forward to Birdie's letters, Quinn's talk of all his future plans, and Kiera's chatter, always redesigning each room. Oh, how you gave me life back. Cora and Nancy, you kept me alive and fretted over me more than anyone could ever properly understand. For that, I am forever grateful. So enjoy it. The vault code is to be given to Cora. She is to hand out the jewelry right now. Also, there are some good old-fashioned American dollars in there. Split it five ways. If you ever have children of your own, make college accounts for each. Travel. May I suggest the Louvre in Paris, Birdie? Add to the collection as you see fit. The system that protects the art can be installed at its new location. The attorneys should have already changed the ownership name to you. Please give Birdie all the necessary information, as she will need to change the name on the insurance. Also, all passwords shall be given to you when you call the alarm company. Enjoy them, Birdie. I can't wait to see what you have painted during your stay in Haven House. Especially the Solariums. I will have the best view from above." Sir Oliver laughed.

Then he went on, "The attorneys have already been gifted their bonus and been paid in full. To whomever executed my wishes, thank you. I know a lot of thought went into this. Enjoy life, everyone, because of you all, I did whilst I was living. God Bless."

The screen went dark. All had tears in their eyes.

Mrs Davis said, "The art collection will need to be moved discreetly-"

"No need." Birdie smiled, "We are engaged and plan to live here now that Quinn is the new owner."

Mrs. Davis looked at the ring, surprised.

"We are already family. Everyone here will share this home every holiday, whenever anyone wants to stay over." Quinn said, looking at Cora and Nancy specifically.

"Splendid." Mrs. Davis smiled.

"The security that came with Lord Astor? They did not belong to him?" Cora asked, confused.

Mrs. Davis smiled, "No. He is financially destitute. He has been asking us about the will since Sir Oliver died. Called us every few weeks. His list of things to do was a way to teach him a lesson, per Sir Oliver. He knew full well none of these items would be found, nor did he have the money to buy it back." Mrs. Davis said, "Though don't feel too bad for him. Rich people want titles. He will find a wealthy girl wanting a title, trust me. I have seen it before."

"And if he gets the ten items?" Nancy asked worriedly.

"They go to Haven House, so they will belong to Quinn. But he won't. They are expensive items."

"But if he does?" Nancy insisted.

"Then he will get his inheritance—a nice three hundred and thirty-five dollars that is left in the bank account. The rest is in cash in the vault—some two million." Mrs. Davis laughed. Sir Oliver might have been old and not always healthy, but his brain was smarter than most in their prime."

Quinn's eyes widened as everyone nervously laughed. Had they been in the same house as two million dollars all this time?

"The thefts? Were they not Lord Astor, as you guessed? The shadow was shorter." Cora said, probably referring to images they caught on the security cameras.

"He must have hired someone. I doubt he did it himself. But he had to be the one giving information to the thief. He must have known what items to get and how to get in and out quickly." Quinn said, "Assuming the person used the tunnel from the garages into the house, it's an easy way in and never seen. We added cameras to the tunnels and silent alerts to all phones."

Mrs. Davis nodded, "Maybe you could add a locked gate or two, as well."

Quinn nodded, "Good idea. We never use it."

That night, after Mrs. Davis left, everyone could not stop talking. Kiera was gifted with almost thirty pieces of jewelry.

Quinn asked that the kids not find out about the vault or the money, and all agreed. They had too much as it was between Sofía and Birdie.

Birdie kissed Quinn, "Move in today, please." She said, making Quinn chuckle.

EPILOGUE

The wedding ceremony was held in Haven House's gardens. The guests all sat in white caned chairs. Each chair had a fan with one of Sailor's colorful paintings on it, signed of course. The guests all quietly talked to themselves until the music started. Quinn, with Jason as best man, stood alongside him up on the altar. First Lucy came out, then Sailor, both super excited to be junior bridesmaids. Then Tommy came out, ring bearer, he was carrying the pillow with their rings proudly. Then Jazmín came out, she was a bridesmaid proudly wearing a dress she sketched and Bridie had made by a seamstress in the same fabric as the others. She looked stunning. Kiera then came out all smiles, eyes welled, happy her brother finally found a life partner. Kiera waited at the front of the aisle as Amanda was let out as the flower girl. The awes were contagious as she meticulously dropped one petal with every step. Kiera called her to hurry up from the front as everyone laughed. After a full minute, she finally got to the front, and Kiera's mother-in-law had her sit with them.

"We practiced that a lot, people. I just did not know I had to work on speed." Kiera grinned as the crowd laughed, too. Then the quartet played the 'Here Comes the Bride' song as all stood.

Birdie could not believe it as Frank stood next to her, "Are you ready?" He asked. Birdie nodded, the smile so big she could not contain it. She was about to marry Quinn! Her dress was perfect. She felt beautiful. The dress, hair, and makeup, so unlike how she normally dressed, looked amazing. She wore her mother's diamond earrings, her father's diamond pin on the breast of her dress, and Lupe's blue sapphire ring to ensure all her family were with her.

"We can still back out, and you can go back to work. My dogs are losing weight." Frank teased.

Birdie laughed, "The art gallery is now a full-time gig, and your dogs are becoming fat." She teased back. He laughed, "I'm going to miss you, kid." He kissed her cheek.

"Then visit. Get me to my groom already." She laughed excitedly. They walked to the door leading out to the gardens. Then Birdie stopped. She saw all the people, she saw the kids, and then the giant smile on Quinn's face. She took in a breath and then walked down the aisle to Quinn, eyes never leaving his.

The sun shone, the birds were chirping, and an occasional butterfly fluttered by them. It was the perfect April day. As the priest had them repeat their vows, they made an additional promise to each other. The words were Lupe's, but both took them very much to heart, "The key to a successful marriage is communication. So remember to be patient with your partner, hear out what the other is feeling, be clear to communicate what you are feeling and be mindful of each other at all times. Never say words you cannot take back. Do you both promise to do this?" The priest read.

"I do," Quinn said.

"I do," Birdie smiled, her eyes welling. It was very important to Birdie to have Lupe part of the ceremony, and this was how she wanted her honored. Her words were there for all to hear.

"I now pronounce you husband and wife. You may kiss your bride." The kiss went on and on as all cheered.

The reception was held in the ballroom with seventy-five close friends and family, including Sofía, Jorge, Tatum, and Christopher. Everyone kept talking about the beautifully painted ceiling. Frank updated everyone that Birdie had just done it. Then he pointed to one corner; it was a bunch of clouds.

Tatum Morales

"Squint, and an image will be shown." They all did. It faintly showed three people. It was Sir Oliver, Eloise, and Sarah in the clouds, smiling down on all. Birdie had quite the time finding pictures of Sarah but finally found albums in the library. Birdie told no one her plan in case she could not pull it off. And she thought she failed until the scaffolding was removed. From a distance, you could see it much better than Birdie had hoped. And those who knew Sir Oliver felt him smiling down on them. Birdie felt Lupe, her father, and most likely her mother, too. She could feel all of them there.

Birdie used one of her father's artworks as the dance floor image, the same one she used as a background on their invitations. She wanted it as cohesive as possible. During the cocktail hour, all were sent on a tour of the house, in and out, each floor having different hors d'oeuvres as they took family photos in the gardens. Once that was over, they danced to an amazing band, ate delicious food that was brought in, and enjoyed their friends and families. It was the perfect day they had hoped for.

"Can I call you 'Mommy' now?" Lucy asked, in Quinn's arms as the three danced together.

"Mami said it was ok." Birdie nodded, smiling.

No one was more shocked by how much Birdie and Sofía befriended each other and talked now. Any issue with the kids was discussed via phone and decided on together. Birdie may be the everyday mother, but the kids had a real mother who loved them, even from afar. They spoke more than Quinn and Sofía did lately, and it worked. The respect they were making sure to give the other showed to the kids, too. Jazmín no longer tried to play parents against each other because it no longer worked. It was nice to co-parent like this.

"Yay! Except Tommy said he is not calling you 'Mommy,' he told me." Lucy said, making Quinn frown. "He said he is big now and is going to call you 'Mom,'" Lucy said. Birdie burst out laughing at Quinn's relieved face. Birdie kissed Lucy's cheek.

"I will answer to both. Sailor has been calling him 'Daddy' for two weeks now. She couldn't wait." Birdie smiled, and Quinn beamed.

Molly

At around ten p.m., Molly put Lucy, Sailor, and Tommy to bed. Jazmín came over to Birdie and said, "He's cute, right? Too bad he's my stepbrother now." Jazmín's mischievous face teased.

Birdie laughed. Jazmín loved to say outlandish things to Birdie, knowing it wouldn't go any further.

"He's seven years older than you, AND he is your stepbrother. Not a good choice."

"Maybe I like older men- ow!" Sofía came over and swatted her daughter's arm.

"Behave. Go dance, Papi said, until eleven p.m. only." Jazmín made a face, nodded, and took off as Birdie and Sofía looked at each other laughing.

"Jorge realized right away." Sofía laughed, "She likes two of his friends, too."

"She likes all boys." Birdie laughed.

"It's the age. Are you sure you don't want us to take the kids tonight?"

"We don't leave for another two days. We will fly to Miami with them, drop them off as planned, and then go straight to the airport. We have tickets to France. Are you sure Sailor will be okay to stay for both weeks?"

"Yes, of course, you met our nanny many times. You both said you approved." Sofía said, concerned.

Birdie smiled, "We do. I just wanted to double-check: four kids is a lot." She met the nanny. She was excellent with the kids. She reminded Birdie of Lupe so much in so many ways. The kids noticed it, too. Sailor especially loved her the few times she stayed with them.

"Two weeks with a ton of things planned, security at everything. It will be nothing. You have four kids daily." Sofía laughed. "And I have a nanny. She watched Christopher for years and has been with Jorge's family forever. She is happy to be back at his house when needed."

"Thank you, Sofía."

"You are very welcome. I just came over to tell you that you look beautiful." Sofía smiled sincerely. "Because of your makeup artist and hairdresser," Birdie laughed. She had no idea how to do either herself. Shawna brought over ten wedding dresses, and they struggled to pick one, as Shawna knew the perfect choices for her body shape. Sailor and Jazmín especially loved the one they ended up with, so they all agreed on that one.

"A small gift. I am happy you are with Quinn. Enjoy the rest of your evening." With a kiss on Birdie's cheek, Sofía returned to Jorge, who was twirling Jazmín around the dance floor happily.

Quinn returned for a slow song, and they danced, only having eyes for the other. "I love you, Mrs. Callahan."

"I love you, Mr. Callahan."

Both kissed.

"Thank you for not correcting me. I know you are keeping your last name." Quinn chuckled, "I just wanted to call you that once."

"I am only keeping Blythe professionally. I want my new name to be just for our family. Mrs. Callahan will be on all my documents once I change them over." Making Quinn smile, shocked.

"I have no idea how the paparazzi did not hear of it yet." Quinn said, baffled.

"I told them in the interview last month that I was no longer painting at locations until the kids were all grown up and in college. That I was making an art studio at my house. The word 'kids' confused all, and now the rumor mill is going nuts that I am pregnant again. Not one person even asked who the father was." Birdie laughed, knowing that Quinn's name had not yet gotten out to the press. They planned to be discreet as long as possible.

Quinn smiled, "That's tomorrow's headache. Today, we dance." They danced and kissed.

At the end of the night, the guests all left. They checked on the kids in bed and then stole off to the Carriage House, where they planned to spend the night. They might as well use it before turning it into an art studio for Birdie.

"I cannot believe this all happened. It's like a fairy tale come true."

"Same. We actually own Haven House, as we hoped. He always said I knew it best next to him and my father. He said it proudly. I think he knew I loved it." Quinn said, amazed.

"It shows." Birdie kissed him.

"We owe Sir Oliver so much." Quinn said, "We met because he hired your father to paint his ballroom. Then we got together again for you to paint all those other rooms, and then Sir Oliver gave us this home. He orchestrated all of it unknowingly. He always said Haven House needed to be a lived-in home filled with children, and now it is." Birdie nodded. Haven House was finally the family home Sir Oliver always meant for it to be.

"Yes, it is. And we have one more reason to thank him." Birdie smiled. Holding this in for the last four days had been all but impossible. Faking drinking champagne, while having Jazmín sneak her ginger ale in the fluted glass when no one was looking because she was the only one who knew by accident. Jazmín came looking for Birdie to have her sign something for school when she saw the pregnancy test on the counter. She all but screamed until Birdie covered her mouth, and they waited together to see the result. Jazmín was crying just as much as Birdie was when the word 'pregnant' showed up on the test. Then she swore her to secrecy.

"Why?" Quinn asked.

"The house is about to be even fuller," Birdie said, eyes welling.

It took Quinn a quick second to realize what she meant. He swiftly lifted her and swung her around, "This day just keeps getting better and better. We wanted this so badly." He kissed her.

"Yes, we did." She kissed him back.

This time, she had no fear of being pregnant. She knew she had a partner who would go through all of it with her.

Together, they could face anything.

ABOUT THE AUTHOR

Christina Creado is an emerging author who was raised in New York. She has worked in the software, gaming, and print mail industries. Christina works part-time at the local Elementary School, volunteers, and cares for her family. She is married and has three children and two dogs. Her love of creating characters and stories that show real-life trials and tribulations is evident in her writing. Her debut novel, Haven House, is a contemporary romance but mainly a love story between many people.